IT'S NOT OVER

KAYLEE RYAN

LACEY BLACK

Copyright © 2019 Kaylee Ryan

Copyright © 2019 Lacey Black

All Rights Reserved.

This book may not be reproduced in any manner whatsoever without the written permission of Kaylee Ryan, or Lacey Black, except for the use of brief quotations in articles and or reviews.

This book is a work of fiction. Names, characters, events, locations, businesses and plot are products of the author's imagination and meant to be used in a fictitious manner. Any resemblance to actual persons, living or dead, or actual events throughout the story are purely coincidental. The author acknowledges trademark owners and trademarked status of various products referenced in this work of fiction, which have been used without permission. The publication and use of these trademarks are not authorized, sponsored or associated by or with the trademark owners.

The following story contains sexual situations and strong language. It is intended for adult readers.

Cover Design: Sommer Stein, Perfect Pear Creative Covers
Cover Photography: Sara Eirew
Models: Alex and Karina Boivin
Editing: Hot Tree Editing
Proofreading: Deaton Author Services &
Kara Hildebrand

Created with Vellum

CHAPTER 1

Harrison

I left the office early today. I couldn't focus. Not that it did me any good. I didn't want to go home either. Not to an empty, lifeless apartment. I have a queen-sized bed, a dresser, and a recliner. Pathetic I know, but when I leased the place, I didn't think it would be permanent. When my wife said we needed a break, I thought I would be there for a week or two, and then I would be moving home. I thought I was doing the right thing by giving her the space she asked for. Little did I know that day changed the course of our future. Here we are almost nine months later, and not only am I not living in the house we bought together, but I'm also less than twenty-four hours from the court hearing that will separate us in the eyes of the law.

I'm hours away from divorcing the love of my life.

How did we get here?

I wish I knew.

I wish that there was a defining moment in our marriage that got us to this point. Unfortunately, I don't have the answers. We've talked about it, been to marriage counseling. We tried. We fought for our love, for the vows that we shared, but in the end, we couldn't make it work. It seemed like nothing I did those last few years made her happy. Everything I did, hell everything I do, it's with her in mind.

For our future.

The one that no longer exists.

So, yeah, I didn't want to go home to a lonely, empty apartment. Instead, I came here, to the local pub on Main, Twist of Lime. It's a small hole-in-the-wall joint. Winnie, that's my wife or soon-to-be ex-wife—that's going to take some getting used to—anyway, Winnie and I used to come here when we first got married. We had date nights. She'd dress up, and I would bring her here. Maybe that's why our marriage failed. I want to blame it on that, but I know better. Winnie loved this place. It's very low-key, and their wings are the best in town.

Sure, being here is like taking a knife to the chest, but so is that reminder on my calendar for tomorrow. The one that reminds me I'm going home alone tonight and every night moving forward. I just can't picture myself with anyone but her.

"Can I get you another, Harrison?" Cliff, the bartender, asks me.

"No." I raise my half-empty glass. "Still working on this one."

"You've been here for over two hours, and that's still your first. Let me get you a fresh one." Before I can tell him not to bother, he whisks my mug away and replaces it with a new frosty one.

"Thanks," I mumble. I really am torturing myself by being here, I wasn't exaggerating, but I can't seem to make myself get off this stool and go home. Maybe that's the problem. It's not home.

Home is with my wife.

My soon-to-be ex-wife.

"Thought I might find you here."

I don't bother to turn my head to see who it is. I would recognize that voice anywhere. My best friend, Chase. We met in college, around the same time Winnie and I met. He works for me now. I should have known that when he couldn't find me at the office, he would come looking for me.

"You found me," I say, taking a large swig of my new ice-cold beer.

"Why are you doing this to yourself, Harrison?" he asks, holding up his finger to get the bartender's attention. "Bottle of water," he orders.

"You're going to let me drink alone?"

"Someone has to drag your drunk ass home," he counters.

"I've been here two hours and haven't managed to finish one beer." He raises his eyebrows and looks at the fresh frosty mug in front of me. "Cliff felt sorry for me drinking warm beer," I explain.

"Here you go. He's right, you know. Barely drank any of the first. He's obviously got a lot on his mind and drinking piss-warm beer is not going to help." Cliff taps the counter twice and heads to the other end of the bar to wait on another customer.

"Look, man, you gave it all you had, and it just didn't work. These things happen. You have to stand up, dust yourself off, and move on," Chase rambles in my ear.

See, my best friend likes to play the field. I've never seen him with the same woman twice. That's just not his style.

"I told you not to marry her," he smarts.

Turning in my stool, I give him a menacing look. The same one I gave him in college when he told me that exact thing. "Fuck you," I seethe. "You have no right to talk about my wife like that."

"Your ex-wife," he challenges.

"One of these days, my man, you are going to fall ass over elbows and I'm going to sit back and enjoy the show."

"Not happening. You think I want to be here?" He points to where I sit on the barstool, drowning my sorrows in draft beer. "No thanks. I'd rather have new pussy as often as I want than to be miserably tied to one."

"That's just it. We weren't always miserable." It's true. Winnie and I were inseparable from our first date. After college, getting married was what we both wanted. It's after we said "I do," that things start to get foggy. I can't pinpoint what it was, a particular day or argument that led us here. What I do know is that tomorrow she's no longer my Winnie, and fuck me, but I'm not okay with that.

"No," he agrees. "Not in the beginning, but people change. They grow apart. It's done, Harrison, you can't change it. Even if you were contesting, which I know you're not, the judge can still grant the divorce. It's over, buddy. The sooner you accept that, the sooner you can move on with your life."

"Yeah." I know he's right, but I hate it. I hate that this is what we've come to. That the woman I love, with everything I am—we're talking deep in my soul, can never love another—is no longer going to be mine. There's a chance she'll even change her name back, and fuck, that's going to wreck me.

I've been through our marriage time and time again.

What did I do wrong?

What did she do wrong?

Where did we go wrong?

I let work take over my life. I let my focus drift to building for our future, for the family we one day hoped to have. Working six and seven days a week, ten- and fourteen-hour days to make it work. One day I came home, and we just... weren't the same. I got caught up in work and let the love of my life feel as though she was anything but.

I tried to fix it, but the business was still there, still needing my attention and in the end, it wasn't enough.

I wasn't enough.

I tried to cut back on my hours, but we were opening a second location, and I'm the owner. I had to be there. Even when I wasn't, my phone was blowing up and our time, the time we were using to find our way back to one another, was interrupted. She told me we needed space.

I did it for us, for the family we dreamed of, but I couldn't make her see that. Looking back, I didn't try hard enough. I heard what she was telling me, but I didn't listen, if that makes any sense. I half-assed the attention I gave her. I failed her, and this is my punishment.

Losing her.

"I'm heading out." I pull some cash out of my wallet and drop it on the bar. Cliff nods that he sees me.

"You want some company?" Chase asks.

"Nah, I'm good."

"I'll call you," he adds.

I lift my hand to wave, not bothering to turn around, and walk out of the bar. Climbing behind the wheel of my truck, I fight back against the vise that seems to be gripping my chest. On impulse, I pull my phone out of my pocket and dial her number. It rings three times before she finally answers.

"Harrison." Her sweet voice washes over me.

"Winnie." *Fuck me.* I want to beg her to stop this. To change her mind. I want to go back nine months before I moved out, giving her the space she asked for. I should have stayed and fought for her. I should have fought harder for us.

"You there?"

"Yeah, I uh, just wanted to check on you. Hear your voice."

"Harrison." She sighs. "We can't keep doing this to each other."

"I love you."

"I love you too," she says softly.

"We can fix this, Win, I know we can."

"We've tried. We gave it our all and couldn't make it work."

"We can try harder," I growl, my anger at losing her getting the best of me.

"I should go," she says, shutting down.

"I'm sorry, but fuck, Gwendolyn, you're my fucking heart. I don't know what to do without you."

I hear her sniffle; I've gone and upset her. "Please," she cries. "We have to stop doing this to each other. It's over, Harrison." The line goes dead. Balling my hand into a fist, I pound at the center of my chest to try and mask the pain. Swallowing back my emotions, I put my truck in drive and head to my empty, lonely apartment.

I slept like shit, barely falling into a slumber before my alarm was going off, reminding me that today is the day. The day the love of my life is no longer my wife. Rushing through a shower, I throw on a suit—something I have not done since our wedding day, ironically enough—and head to the courthouse.

I arrive a few minutes early, meeting my lawyer, Greg, in the lobby.

"Good morning." He holds his hand out in greeting.

I take it. "Morning."

"So, since neither of you are contesting, this is going to be a quick process. Just you and me, Gwendolyn, and her lawyer, the judge, and bailiff. We should be in and out in no time."

"Yeah." I follow him into a small room, which is not what I was expecting. Winnie and her lawyer are sitting on the opposite side of the table. "Hey," I say, my eyes taking her in. She really is the most beautiful woman I've ever laid eyes on. Today, her long black hair is pulled back in a ponytail exposing her slender neck. The same neck I've spent hours kissing. Worshiping really.

"Hey, Harrison," she replies. Sadness fills her green eyes.

I take the seat next to my lawyer and we wait for the judge. Awkward silence surrounds us, and I hate it. This isn't us. We used to talk about everything and nothing at all. A few minutes pass, and finally, the judge enters the room taking her seat at the head of the table. She begins sifting through the papers and then finally looks up.

"Everything is in order. The alimony amount has been signed by both parties, assets have been divided."

What she should say is that Winnie gets it all. I told her I didn't want anything. Well, except for pictures, which she already made me copies of. Other than my clothes, I didn't want anything to remind me of the failure I was at our marriage.

"Do we have any objections from either party?" she asks.

"No, your honor," we reply at the same time.

"All right, looks like the only information I'm missing is from you, Gwendolyn. Do you plan on keeping your married name? If not, now is the time to change that."

My eyes snap to Winnie. She's biting down on her bottom lip and tears well in her eyes. I have to grip the edge of the table to keep from rushing to her. I always hated to see her upset.

When she looks up, she gives me a soft, sad smile. "I'd like to remain Gwendolyn Drake, your honor," she says, never taking her eyes off me.

Fuck! I've never wanted to pull her into my arms and kiss the hell out of her more than I do this minute.

"Very well," the judge says. She signs her name on the papers, the same ones we signed a few weeks ago. "As of today, your divorce is final. Best of luck to both of you." She stands and leaves the room as if we were discussing the weather.

"It's been a pleasure." Greg holds his hand out for me to shake. On autopilot, I take it. He turns and walks out of the room, but I stay back. Waiting on her. I hear her lawyer ask if she wants her to stay and she tells her to go on.

"Hey," I say when it's finally just the two of us.

"Hey."

We walk toward the door, and I rest my hand on the small of her back. I miss her so fucking much. "You going to work today?"

"No. You probably need to get going though." She looks at her watch checking the time.

"I'm not going either," I tell her, and I can see the shock on her face. "I'd be useless anyway."

She nods. "I have some of your things. I was cleaning and found a few shirts, a pair of shorts. You can stop and pick them up if you want."

It's been two months, give or take a few days, since I've been there. The house we bought with big plans of making it our home, of raising our kids there. "Yeah, I can follow you if that's okay."

"Sure." She hesitates. "I guess I'll see you soon."

"See you soon." I open the door of her SUV and wait for her to climb in before closing it. I jog back to my truck and follow her home.

To *her* home.

It's no longer mine.

I park beside her on the driveway just like I used to, and climb out. She's waiting for me on the front porch. I watch as her hand shakes when she tries to unlock the door.

"Let me," I say gently, snaking my arms around her, and placing my hands over hers. A sob breaks free from her chest and that loud crack you hear, that's my heart. I didn't think it was possible for it to be any more broken.

I was wrong.

Instead of pulling the key from her hand and unlocking the door, I turn her in my arms and hold her tightly against my chest. I'm battling with my own emotions, not only from seeing her like this, but from losing her. I don't know how much time passes while we hold each other. It's when a car honks as they drive by that I decide it's time for us to move inside.

"Let's get you into the house," I whisper. Stepping back, she hands me the key, but I snake my arm around her waist and hold her close to me. This might be my last chance to hold her, and you can bet your ass I'm taking it. Quickly, I unlock the door and usher her inside. I drop the keys on the hall table and kick the door shut with my foot. Stepping in front of her, I cup her face in my hands. "You okay?"

She shakes her head. "I will be," she says.

"You kept my name," I whisper, leaning in a little closer.

"Yeah, I just—" She looks down for three heartbeats. I know because I counted them before she gives me her sad eyes. "I wanted to keep a piece of you, a piece of us."

"Winnie," I whisper as my lips collide with hers. She's hesitant at first, but eventually throws caution to the wind and kisses me back. Placing my hands on the back of her thighs, I lift her, and she immediately wraps her legs around my waist. We've done this song and dance so many times. We move in sync with one another, something that comes from years of intimacy. My tongue slides against hers, exploring her, tasting her again after all these months. When she grinds her hips against my hard cock, I moan, resting my forehead against hers.

"Winnie," I pant.

"Just this once," she murmurs.

That's all I need to hear and my feet are moving. She places her mouth over mine and we barely make it down the hall and to our room—

—*her* room, before we're ripping each other's clothes off.

CHAPTER 2

Winnie

Familiarity wraps around me like a warm blanket as my husband's hands grip my ass, the hard muscles of his arms pressing into my body and caging me in.

No, not my husband.

My *ex*-husband.

Just the thought steals my breath.

Ignoring the pain that shoots through my body, ricocheting off my bruised and battered heart, I give in to the comfort of his lips, his tongue, his taste. For so long he was my everything. But now... now he's here. With his arms wrapped around me and the hard length of his erection pressed firmly between my legs, I can't stop the groan that slips through my lips.

"Winnie," he whispers, gently tracing his lips along my jaw until he finds my ear. I instantly shudder. He knows that one little touch drives me absolutely wild.

"Just tonight," I say aloud, more as a reminder to myself than to him. If there's one thing I need to keep in mind, it's that *this* is just temporary.

To be honest, *this* won't help any. Not one bit. Falling into bed with my now ex-husband ranks right up there with bungee jumping over a pool of sharks as one of the worst things I could possibly do. But as he draws my earlobe into his warm mouth, I give up the ability to care.

Because it's him.

Harrison.

It's always been him. From the first moment I saw him in the library our sophomore year at State, we were inseparable. We weren't in the same study group—not even in the same part of the library—but the moment my green eyes connected with his chocolate brown ones, I knew I was forever gone. I felt it immediately and started to fall even faster. He was headed to the restroom and bumped into my chair, knocking my notebook onto the floor. He bent to pick it up, our eyes and hands connecting at the same time. It was in that exact moment that I knew my life would never be the same. He was there with a small group, a few guys and one girl who kept throwing daggers at me, but I paid her no attention. Not when Harrison was there. He has this way of commanding a room wherever he goes. It's what makes him the most sought-after trainer in town.

We both worked hard through school—me in early education and him in kinesiology. Our classes were completely different, but that didn't matter. We always found time to be together, even if it was for a late-night study session. There was always plenty of kissing, too. He learned quickly that the fastest way to get my motor running was to gently trace his lips along my jaw and to nibble on my earlobes.

Just. Like. Now.

"Harrison," I gasp, blood swooshing through my veins and igniting my body.

"Fuck, I've missed the way you say my name."

I don't bring up the fact that this is just temporary. A one-time thing. Two old flames doing something wild and crazy, something they definitely shouldn't be doing. But when have I ever listened when it comes to Harrison Drake? I've always been the woman at his side, the one who would follow him to the end of the earth and not bat an eye at it.

But then it changed.

Everything changed.

Pushing those thoughts out of my head, I concentrate on the way he gently lays me down as if I were made of glass on top of our bed. *My* bed. The one that I had to immediately buy new bedding for because I couldn't stand the thought of sleeping on those same sheets without him. He swipes at the throw pillows, the ones I added after he left. He always hated them, you know. Didn't understand why you'd need to make your bed with fancy little pillows just to mess it up again at night. Anyway, those fancy little pillows he despises so much fly across the room and land in a heap on my bedroom floor.

My shirt quickly follows. With the quickness of a jungle cat and the expertise of a professional clothes-remover, my button-down shirt is practically ripped from my body, tiny buttons raining down on the bedspread. He slowly helps me out of the sleeves, never rushing or risking hurting me. No, Harrison would rather cut off his own arm than see anything cause me pain. He's always been my biggest protector, my biggest supporter, and if there's ever a tear in my eye, he'd make sure whoever caused it knew true pain.

At least he was. A long time ago.

But even though Harrison is big, muscular, and maybe even a tad intimidating, I've only ever known the gentle teddy bear side of him. The side that loves fiercely and protects viciously, and for so long, *I* was that sole focus. Now, he turns it on once more, but this time I know it's only temporary. It has to be.

He pulls back and gazes down at my exposed midsection. "You've lost weight," he says in a disapproving tone.

"That's not for you to worry about," I remind him, my words coming out in short little pants.

"Angel, I will always worry about you." He bends down and runs his nose along my neck. "Always."

A shiver sweeps through my body and my hands dive into his dark hair. Not wanting to think about the tenderness and meaning behind his words, I pull his face back to mine and swipe my tongue along the seam of his lips. It has the exact response it always has. His eyes dilate and his nostrils flare. He's moments away from losing all control.

And I know just how to push him over the edge.

Wrapping my legs around his hips once more, I gyrate against his incredibly hard, exceptionally large erection. The man is hung, and the moment I grind my pubis against him, he growls, flexing his hips and rubbing in the place I need him most.

I grab at his shirt, anxious to see the incredible physique I've missed for nine long months. Harrison grips the back of the neck and pulls it over his head in one swift motion. His pecs flex, his abs dance, and his corded arms twitch as I drink my fill of his impressive body. Young Harrison was amazing, but adult Harrison is unbelievable. His time training and working out shows on every square inch of his body.

My hands immediately move to his chest. They glide effortlessly over the smooth skin and tangle in the light dusting of dark hair. A sense of familiarity comforts me. This is Harrison. *My* Harrison.

But he's not anymore.

As if he can sense where my thoughts are leading, he bends down and takes my lips with his once more. The kiss lets me know there's no room for thought, especially those of the past. He unsnaps my black dress slacks and slowly pulls them over my hips, without breaking the kiss. Cool midafternoon air caresses my bare legs as I shimmy out of the pants, flipping off my no-frills flats as I go. I tense the moment his hands glide down my waist and reach for my panties.

"You okay?" he whispers, concern filling those deep brown eyes.

"Yes, I... I'm just different than before."

His eyes soften. "Different how?"

I close my eyes, fighting the embarrassment that tries to sweep in. "I just... God, why is this so hard?"

"What's wrong, Winnie?" His eyes hold a pain that I'm not prepared for.

I steel my back and just spit out the words. "I started taking care of myself differently. Down there."

I follow his eyes as they drop to the tiny scrap of panties I'm wearing. They're way more risqué than the ones I used to don while married. Back then, I found comfort in low-cut bikinis or boy-cut shorts. They drove Harrison wild. But now? Now, I'm wearing the smallest lace thong I own, and there's not a hair in sight. After the separation, I had to do *something* to make me feel like a woman. To make me feel wanted. Desired. No, that was never the problem between my husband and me, but it helped tremendously with my self-confidence.

His large hands slowly start to remove the little scrap of material, revealing smooth, bare skin. He hisses in response, his eyes wild with lust and teetering on the edge of dangerous. "The fuck?" he whispers, almost to himself.

"I just needed a change. For me."

"For you?" he asks, his words laced with jealousy. He couldn't possibly be thinking I'd do this for someone else, could he?

"Yes, for me. I needed to feel alive."

His eyes turn molten. "Baby, I'm going to show you just how alive you are."

My panties slide down my legs and are tossed somewhere in the room. Before I can even take a breath, his mouth descends on my core. My entire body sparks to life with the first swipe of his tongue. He devours my flesh, licking and sucking, and bringing me right to the edge of an orgasm. I'm a livewire, energy and desire coursing through me recklessly. He slides his tongue into my wetness and gently rolls my clit, causing me to detonate immediately. My thighs clamp around his head as I ride wave after wave of pleasure.

Barely given any time to recoup from my orgasm, Harrison stands up and removes the rest of his clothes. He never takes his eyes off me as I lie boneless and panting from my first release. Anticipation slides through me because if there's one thing I know for certain, it's that more will follow. Harrison never gives them out in anything less than multiples. He's crazy talented in the orgasm-giving department.

The moment he's completely naked, he slides back in bed, climbing on top of me. His touch is gentle as he caresses my jaw, running his hand down my neck. When he gets to my heart, he pauses. I know what he's looking at. Pain ricochets through my body as the memories come flooding back. The simple H tattoo that I had inked over my heart on our honeymoon. It matches the one he had put on his hand. While I wanted to keep mine private, something just for him or me to see, he chose to put his right in the soft skin between his thumb and first finger. Somewhere he could always see it.

His eyes flash to mine, a mixture of angst and fury. Not at me, I know. He has never directed any of his anger my way. At the situation. Our situation. I open my mouth to speak, but nothing comes out. Those dark eyes soften and hold mine as he slowly bends down and places his lips on my chest. Right over my heart. Right over the letter that stands for him. I have to fight the tears that burn my eyes. I will not cry. Not anymore.

It's over.

As if to gently remind me that it's anything but, his chiseled features take on a determination I haven't seen in a while. His hands move to my thighs as he repositions himself between them. Something's different, but I don't know what. I can't figure it out. My mind won't even begin to wrap around this weird sense of purpose that settles in. It's as if *this* isn't just sex, as if something greater is about to happen.

I should stop this. I should. But I don't.

I can't.

I need him too much.

Want him more than I ever have.

We're about to do something we can never go back from, but I can't seem to find an ounce of care. I'll deal with the consequences later, and something tells me there'll be plenty of those. Right now, I just need him. I need the old Harrison. I need to forget the hurt and the nights alone. I just want to... remember.

"Please," I beg, my voice husky and needy.

Harrison reaches down and positions himself between my legs. I can feel the tip of his cock slide against my clit, jolts of pleasure rippling through my body. "You're sure?" he asks, his eyes burning with intensity and desire.

"Yes."

When that one word falls from my lips, he thrusts, filling me so completely that it steals the very air I breathe. I gasp his name, my body tight with the need to come once more. He's so big, bigger than I remember, but it feels like something else, something more. Home. I fight the tears, willing them away. I refuse to be the weak woman, the one who caves and takes him back. We didn't work. We proved that. But this? Sex, intimacy, it always worked.

"Fuck," he mumbles, holding completely still and letting me adjust to his size. "I gotta move, baby." It comes out a pant, a plea.

"Yes, move. Move, Harrison."

And he does. He pulls almost completely out and pivots his hips once more. From the beginning, he sets a hard pace. The bed slams into the wall, the painting above our heads shakes, but I don't care. This. This is all I care about, at least for now. The feel of his body pressing me into the mattress, the feel of his skin sliding against mine.

His hand goes to my jaw, cradling me as he so often would. His eyes burn into me with an honesty I don't want to see, don't want to feel. But I do. I feel everything. His hips slam into my inner thighs and my muscles start to burn, a subtle reminder that I haven't used them in quite a while. Harrison pounds into me with force, a man already past the point of losing control. I've always loved the way he lets go, orchestrating my body perfectly and taking me places no one before him ever could. He knows me, knows my needs, my desires.

And he never disappoints.

At least when it comes to sex.

The flex of his hips causes his cock to rub against my G-spot. Stars burst behind my eyes. Everything else just floats away until I'm left teetering on the edge, so very close to ultimate euphoria. He knows I'm close and chooses that moment to slow down. I don't even realize I'm groaning in protest until his chuckle fills the room. "Patience, love. I'll get you there."

He will.

He always does.

Harrison adjusts our position, spinning us around until I'm straddling him. He knows. He remembers. This has always been my favorite position. He thrusts his hips upward, robbing me of any ability to think or speak. "Work with me, Winnie. Take control," he whispers, gripping my hips in his big hands and hanging on tight.

I start to move, up and down, rocking my body and taking all of him. He's so deep, so big, so... yeah. My movements become more frantic. He holds on firmly, no doubt going to leave fingermarks on my pasty skin. I'll wear them as a badge of honor, though. I always have.

Before too long, my desire takes complete control. I'm there, ready to detonate like a bomb, and I can tell by the tightness around his mouth and the way his Adam's apple bobs that he's there too. The need to come is too great, and I'm not strong enough to deny it anymore. My hips gyrate as I slam back down on his cock, my body jolting as the release starts.

"Winnie," he grunts, watching as I implode around him. I think I say his name, but I can't be sure. I'm not sure of anything right now except the way he makes me feel.

Familiar.

Harrison's fingers grip and dig into my flesh as he holds on, thrusting his hips upward and finding his own release. Our gazes never falter as we both come, the sounds of our orgasms filling the room in song. I memorize everything about this moment because when it's all said and done, and he leaves as planned, I want to think back and recall just how explosive, how magical we were.

When I'm boneless and gasping for air, my body falls forward. His arms instantly wrap around me, holding me firmly against his broad chest. The afternoon sunlight filters through the open blinds, and I'm not really sure what to say. Maybe there's no need for words. What more could possibly be said that hasn't been hashed out over recent months?

I instantly relax, listening to his heartbeat and his breathing evening out. Something that feels like regret creeps in. This was definitely a bad idea. The waters have been muddy between Harrison and me for a while—months, even, before the separation—but the one thing that has always been right has been this.

This.

So, for now, I ignore the tinge of regret that's waiting in the wings and allow myself to find refuge in his arms. As I lie here, it's that comfort that lulls me to sleep.

CHAPTER 3

Harrison

It's been two weeks since I made the biggest mistake of my life. Two weeks of wishing things were different. Two weeks of wondering how to change it, how to go back. As I sit here at my desk staring at the piles of paperwork I need to sift through, I can't seem to find it in me to do it. I love this gym. All Fit is my passion. I never dreamed when I started working here right after college, that I would someday be the owner. I've busted my ass to make it a success, and I've done that. I'm in the process of opening two more new locations, and all my hard work has paid off. Except for one small detail.

I lost my wife.

Biggest mistake of my life.

Some might say the mistake is sleeping with said ex-wife on the day of your divorce, but any amount of time with Winnie is never a regret. Before that day, it had been months since I'd touched her soft skin, tasted her sweet lips. Sadly, it had been even longer since I'd been inside her. It's not something a man ever forgets, but the memory of making love to her is nothing like the real thing.

We're still explosive together. I guess you have that with years of familiarity under your belt. Although not everything was familiar, such as her bare pussy. Rage had hit me when I thought she'd done that for someone else. It's the same exact rage racing through me just from the thought that another man gets to touch her. Could be touching her. "Fuck," I mumble, shifting in my chair to adjust my hard cock. That's something else that will never change, not when it comes to Winnie. Just thinking of her has me hard as steel. It's been that way since the day I first laid eyes on her, and I imagine it will be that way until the day I die. She is my Winnie, after all.

She used to be mine.

Balling my hands into fists, my eyes focus in on the W tattoo, a constant reminder of the failure I am. I couldn't keep her happy, and this job was the reason. I didn't put her first, but in my mind, I was doing just that. I was securing us financially for the future, for the family we never got to have. I let myself get zoned into giving her the world, yet lost her in the process.

I miss my wife.

I miss her with an ache deep in my soul. I fucked up, and I don't know how to fix it. I've tried to call her a couple of times since D-day, with no answer. I've sent text messages that have gone unread. I've done everything but show up on our— I mean, *her* doorstep. Picking up my phone, I pull up my calendar to see what day it is. They've all become one big blur these past two weeks. My chest literally hurts when I see the reminder for today.

Three weeks until Winnie's birthday.

I was so busy last year that I didn't remember her birthday until the day before. I rushed out to buy her a gift, ended up with a necklace, a heart-shaped pendant that apparently, she already had. In my defense, I never pay much attention to those kinds of things. Not when I can stare into those green eyes of hers, or run my fingers through her soft silky hair, grip her ass... You see where I'm going with this. I should have paid more attention. So I added a reminder starting today to alert me once per week until the day is here. Never again did I want to fail her like that.

My finger hovers over the reminder. I should delete it. I'm just torturing myself by leaving it on my calendar, but I can't do it. I can't bring myself to remove it, delete her from my life.

"What did that phone ever do to you?" Chase asks from the doorway of my office.

Closing my calendar, I set my phone on my desk. "What do you want, Chase?"

"Aww, you're still in a shitty moody," he coos.

"Fuck off. Do you have a reason for interrupting me? I'm trying to get some work done."

"Right," he says with a laugh, drawing out the word. "You looked more like you were trying to plot ways to blow up your phone."

"Again, did you need something?" I ask, my irritation rising.

"Yeah, I need the linen contract for the West location."

As I mentioned, All Fit is expanding. Just locally, we are currently in the easternmost part of the state, making the original location also the east location. We have two new sites in progress; one in the west and one in the south. I'm searching for properties for the north location too. It's not like I want to be worldwide, but I'm making strides here in my home state, and I'm proud of that. I just wish Winnie was here to share it all.

"Harrison," Chase prompts.

"Sorry, I don't think I've run across that one yet." I sift through the piles of paperwork and folders that litter my desk. I've gotten shit done these past couple of weeks.

"Careful, we might lose you to all that paper," Chase jokes.

"Very funny, jackass. I've had a lot going on."

"Listen, man. I know you're torn up about the divorce, but you need to start moving on. You can't live your life pining after her. She's gone."

"She's not gone," I bite back.

"Yeah, Harrison, she is. She divorced your ass. You've got to move on."

"I don't fucking want to move on!" I shout, way too loud for this time of day. I have a gym full of customers out there. "I don't want to," I say, softer this time. "It was a mistake, a huge mistake, and fuck me if I know how to fix it."

"Let's go out tonight. We can have a few beers at Twist of Lime. You need to put yourself back out there."

"Jesus, Chase. Do you hear yourself right now? The ink is barely dry on the divorce papers, and you're already pushing me to find someone else." Not that I'm surprised. Chase and Winnie got along, but he never could understand how I could tie myself to one woman. He's a self-proclaimed bachelor and owns it like a boss. You would think that I would have envied him, but it was the exact opposite. I felt sorry for him, and I still do. I may be divorced, but I know what it's like to come home to the love of your life. To fall asleep with her tucked tight against your chest and wake up the same way. I know what it's like to have her wake me up in the middle of the night to make love, and me her. Chase kicks them out before the condom hits the trash can. I know what it's like to always have her in my corner, always. Sure, we lost our way, but in no way could I ever regret the time we had together.

"What do you think she's doing, Harrison? Do you think she's sitting at home pining away for you? She wanted this, dude. The papers are signed, you have to accept it."

"I don't know how I'm going to do that," I say honestly.

"I don't know, man. What I do know is that you can't keep going like this. You've busted your ass—" He hesitates. "—you lost her from all the work you were putting in, at least that's your version. Are you just going to let all this slip away?"

Frustration tears through me. I want them both. I want this franchise to be successful, and I want my wife. Finding the folder he needs, I quickly sign off on the linen contract for the West location and hand it to him. "I did it for her," I tell him. "All of it, for her, for us and now that she's... now that we're divorced, I don't see the point."

"You need to get your shit together, man. This is your livelihood. With or without Gwendolyn, this is who you are. Unless you plan to pull the plug and lose the money and time you have invested, I suggest you pull your head out of your ass." He points to the stacks on my desk. "You've got shit to do. Don't get so far inside your own head, inside your pain and forget that. You have to keep going." He turns and walks to the door. Stopping just at the threshold, he turns to face me. "If you did it for her, make it worth it. Make it the best it can be, the best I know you can make it. If you want to fight for her, fine, but don't throw away your career. Hire more people, delegate whatever the fuck you need to do to make this happen."

I drop my pen on my desk and sit back in my chair, running my hands through my hair. "What do I do then?"

"You meet me tonight at seven at Twist of Lime. We'll eat greasy food, have a few beers, and shoot the shit. Other than that, you want your wife back... you fight for her." With that, he leaves my office.

Fight for her.

How in the hell do I fight for her when she won't even talk to me or return my calls? Grabbing my phone, I dial her number. It rings six times and then goes to voice mail. I didn't count the rings. I didn't have to. I've already counted them. Countless times while holding my breath, waiting for her to answer. "Hey, Win, it's me. I was uh... just calling to see how you're doing. I miss you. I know I'm not supposed to say that, but it's true. I miss you. I miss us and... just call me. Please."

Tossing my phone back onto my desk, I think about what Chase said. I agree it's time I pull my head out of my ass before I lose everything I have left. I'm not going to hire someone to do the work I'm fully capable of doing. Besides, it will be a good distraction, at least I hope it will be. I need to throw myself into work and let it consume me. I can't make her call me, or return my text messages, no matter how badly I want to. How do you fight for someone who doesn't want you to? How do I convince her that we made a mistake?

Shaking out of my thoughts, forcing them to the back of my mind, I grab the first folder and get to work. I need to focus on what's here and now. Maybe she just needs some time, perhaps if I give her that, her heart will ache like mine and one day when I call she'll pick up. That's my new plan. I'll continue to call and text and engross myself in work. I am waiting for the day she reaches out. It doesn't matter how long it takes her. I'll wait forever.

I always assumed there would be time. I thought that we would figure it out. Days led to weeks, and weeks led to months. The next thing I knew I was being served with divorce papers. I can't say why I didn't fight then. I guess maybe I thought we wouldn't go through with it. Regardless, I never should have let it get that far. I never should have signed those papers.

I want my wife back.

I push through pile after pile, signing invoices and contracts. I lost myself in the job, something that I'm apparently, extremely good at. It's not until my phone alerts me to a message that I break my concentration.

Chase: 30 minutes

Shit. Looking at the clock, I see it's six thirty. Shutting down my laptop, I grab the items that need to be mailed so I can drop them off on my way to the bar. Lucky for me, I pull into the lot just behind Chase.

"Didn't think you'd show." He smirks when we're both out of our trucks.

"A man's gotta eat, right?"

"See? That's the spirit." He slaps me on the shoulder and pushes open the door.

This place is familiarity and sadness. It makes me think of my wife, and if I can't be with her, this is the next best thing. Not bothering where Chase is headed, I set my eyes on the booth in the back corner, the one we always used to sit at. It's torture but I sit there anyway. I slide into the booth and grab a menu even though I don't need it. They've served the same things since we started coming here all those years ago. Chase eventually catches on to where I went and slides in across from me.

"What are you feeling?" Chase asks.

Really? Since when is he all about feelings? "I thought we came here to eat and drink?"

He gives me a confused look. "We are. What are you feeling?" He points to the menu.

Well, fuck. "Bacon cheeseburger, and fries," I say, placing the menu back in its holder.

"Ah," he says, sitting back in the booth and crossing his arms over his chest. "You thought I was getting all soft on you."

"It's been one of those days."

The waitress comes to take our order before he replies. "You decide what you're going to do?"

"Can we not do this again?"

He holds his hands up in surrender. "Hey, I'm just trying to help my buddy out."

"Okay, what exactly do you suggest?"

"Considering finding a new pu... companion," he corrects himself, "is out of the question, your only options are to be a miserable fuck or fight for her."

"Tell me, ole wise one, how do I fight for her when she won't return my calls?"

He shrugs. "Go see her."

"Stalk her, that's your answer? Terrific. I'm doomed." The waitress drops off our food, and we both dive in.

"I don't know, Harrison. What I do know is that you need to figure your shit out. Work is suffering, you're suffering." He gives me a pointed look. "Man up and make a decision. Commit to a plan and make it happen."

The waitress brings us fresh beers, which is a good time to change the subject. "You find a truck yet?" I ask. He's been looking to buy a new truck for a few weeks now but can't seem to find what he wants.

"Nah, just been looking. I'm going tomorrow to drive a couple. You want to come?"

"Sure." It will do me some good to get out of my apartment and not be at the office either.

"Hey, there," a sultry voice greets us. Looking up, I see a blonde bombshell. She's stacked, curves for days, and she's on the prowl.

"You guys want to join us for a game of pool?" her redheaded friend asks. She too is a looker.

Chase looks across the booth at me and raises his eyebrows, challenging me. "Sure, just let us finish up here." I grab my beer and down it. "Let me pay the tab, and we'll be right there."

"I'll be waiting." The blonde rakes her fingernail, which is bright red and pointy, down my arm. Nothing like Winnie's rounded and white-tipped nails. Talk about sexy as fuck. Nothing hotter.

"That's what I'm talking about." Chase holds his fist out for me to bump as soon as the ladies are out of earshot.

"It's just a game of pool," I remind him.

"It starts with a game of pool. Next thing you know Harrison's got his groove back." He wags his eyebrows.

"Fuck off." I slide out of the booth and go to the bar to pay our check. I order Chase another beer, but I switch over to water. No way do I want to make the mistake of taking one of them home with me or me going home with them. That's not what I want.

I want my wife.

"Water?" Chase laughs. "You going soft on me, Drake?" he asks.

"You're on my team." The blonde pushes her double Ds out for me to get a better look. It's so predictable it's comical. Winnie and I used to people watch on the nights we were here. She would have a field day with blondie.

By the end of the first game, I'm over it. Blondie keeps rubbing her tits on my arm, my back when I'm leaning over the table. Her voice is like nails on a chalkboard, and I've had all I can take.

"I'm heading out. Thanks for the game." I walk my cue stick over to the rack and put it away.

"No," she whines. Yes, she whines as if she's two. "I thought maybe we could go back to my place," she says in her baby voice while sticking her lip out, pouting.

Newsflash, ladies: guys don't like the idea of fucking a baby. It's not sexy, so don't do it. It's a sure-fire way to kill any hard-on he has going. As for me, she doesn't do it for me. Her hair's the wrong color, her eyes too. Her tits are too big, and those nails... She's not Winnie, that's for damn sure.

"Sorry, I have an early day tomorrow." I grab her hands that are clutching my shirt and remove them.

"I thought you were going car shopping with me?" Chase asks.

Fucker. "Yeah, I need to go into the gym beforehand. There are a few things I need to do before Monday."

"Oh, I love a man who works out."

"He actually—"

I hold up my hand, stopping him. "Sorry, I really need to go. Chase, call me when you're ready." I turn on my heel and walk as fast as I can out of the bar. I hear Blondie yell in her whiny voice for me to come back, but I don't bother to stop and address her. I need out of here. I don't know why I let Chase talk me into this. I'm not ready, and I'm not sure I ever will be.

CHAPTER 4

Winnie
> *Three weeks later*

I glance down at the phone in my hand, reading the text message for a third time.

Harrison: I miss you. Hope you have a wonderful day.

I don't respond to this one, like I've opted not to for all the previous ones. Dropping the phone back on my desk, I run my hands across my tired face. That message makes nearly three-weeks straight of similar messages. Sometimes they arrive in the morning before I wake, some hit my phone sporadically throughout the day, and a handful reach me just before I go to sleep. The man knows my routine, probably better than I know it.

He's also persistent as hell.

When the man sets his sights on something, he refuses to give in until he's accomplished his task. At one time, it was one of the many things I loved about him. Now, I wonder why that determination stopped. When I was ready to leave, he didn't stop me. Sure, he may have said he didn't want to go—didn't want to divorce—but his actions lacked the gumption I know he had. It was like, deep down, he wanted the separation. The divorce. Even though I really didn't. I wanted him to fight. I wanted him to fight for me as much as I wanted to fight for him. I started off slipping on the proverbial boxing gloves and getting ready to duke it out to the finish, but when those nights remained as empty as our bed, I just... gave up the fight.

The bell rings, letting me know I'm about to be hit with fourteen preschoolers, all anxious to tell me their weekend plans. My plans? I'm hoping to fall asleep tonight and wake Sunday morning. Tomorrow is a day filled with dread, though not for the reason you may think. The calendar lets me know it's my thirtieth birthday, a day that most people celebrate and hate just the same, but it's more than that. It's a reminder of my failures. The life I had planned but didn't have the ability to follow through. Our plan.

The plan that will never come to be.

I push all thoughts of Harrison and our marriage out of my mind and stand to greet my students. As soon as I do, the nausea sweeps in, and I feel a little lightheaded. I sit quickly, setting a shaky hand over my stomach. This flu bug is going to be the death of me. I've been feeling crummy for several days, though I've never spiked a fever. My stomach protests just about everything I put in my mouth, and I can't seem to shake the bone-deep fatigue that accompanies whatever strand of sickness I have.

As a preschool teacher, I'm accustomed to sickness. I live it, practically daily. I've been puked on more times since school started this year than I care to even admit aloud. Young kids are still learning the signs of trouble looming, and often, by the time I'm made aware, it's too late. The vomit is flying.

They forget to tell you that part when you're in college and student teaching.

I meet them at the doorway, anxiously pushing aside the nausea. Pulling a mint from my pocket, I stick it in my mouth before the first student comes down the hallway. "Good morning, Allie," I say brightly to the cute little brunette.

"Hi, Mrs. Drake," she replies eagerly.

I wave her inside, ready to greet the rest of the class and ignoring the pang of longing I get every time someone says my name. Mrs. Drake. Technically, it's Ms. Drake now, but little kids don't seem to understand the difference, and I'm not really in any position to teach them that variance. Sure, I could have taken my maiden name back, but when the judge asked—and I knew she was going to—I just couldn't do it. I couldn't go back. It was like I was erasing Harrison completely, eradicating every aspect of him from my life. He may not have been there physically, but by keeping his last name, I was able to hang on to a tiny sliver of what we used to be.

The rest of the students make their way down the hallway toward our classroom. Two boys push at each other, knocking into a quiet little redhead with long pigtails. She doesn't say anything to them—she rarely says anything at all—so it's my job to make sure the boys understand that horsing around isn't permitted inside the school and remind them to apologize to little Emily. Her father passed away last year, and the little one hasn't been the same since. I've spent many moments on the phone with her mother or visiting with her in person to assure that we're doing everything we can to help Emily learn and grow as a person, and hopefully, come out of her shell soon. It'll take time, and only the child knows the schedule.

"Good morning, Emily," I say sweetly and quietly as she gets ready to pass through the door.

"Hi." That's all I get. That's all I ever get for a greeting.

Closing my eyes, I get ready for my day. I push aside the looming sickness, the sadness I feel when I think about my ex-husband, and the despair that engulfs me for little Emily. That one right there is what makes my heart race in overtime. It's part of the reason I pushed Harrison away when I did. We had a plan, and that plan was to transpire by my thirtieth birthday.

Tomorrow.

And it's a reminder that we failed.

I slip inside my classroom and meet the students at the hooks in the back. I watch as they go through their routine of hanging their jackets and book bags from their designated hooks, place their empty folders in the take-home folder bin, and gather around the brightly colored reading rug. As soon as everyone's set, I join them, sitting cross-legged in their circle. "Good morning, friends. Are you ready to begin?" I ask, watching as they all nod. "Well, it's Friday, so we're going to go around the circle and you can tell your classmates what you're excited about for this weekend. Allie, you're the room leader today, so you go first."

We go around the room, each student eagerly sharing their weekend plans or something they're looking forward to. When it's Emily's turn, she tucks her chin and whispers, "I'm going to my grandma's house."

My heart pitter-patters a heavy beat in my chest. Emily's mom had confided in me that Emily often spends the weekend with her grandma so she could work at a local diner, where she's a waitress. The weekend shifts bring in more money, which has been scarce ever since her husband passed away. They've managed to stay in their family home, as well as seek a few additional services from a counselor for Emily, but I know money is very tight for them.

"That sounds like fun. I'm sure you and your grandma are going to have a wonderful weekend together," I tell her with a soft smile. She doesn't return it. "You know, you're very lucky, Emily. My grandparents passed away either before I was born or when I was very young. The fact that you get to spend time with your grandma is wonderful." Again, I offer a reassuring, friendly smile to the little girl who has already experienced so much heartache and hurt in her short four years.

"My grandpa watches *The Price is Right* all day! He smokes cigars and calls his neighbor a jerk," Carson says proudly, making the other students giggle.

"We don't say jerk," I state.

"My papa smells like fish!" Helena proclaims, again sending another round of laughter through my room.

I smile, listening to them all share their stories, not even worrying a second that we've reached the end of our time on the rug. But coloring and working on word association for the letter P can wait a few more minutes. The train wreck that is my life can wait. Spending the morning with these precious little beings is my top priority, and their laughter does wonders for my soul.

Today, they're just what I needed.

"Happy Birthday to Gwen, Happy Birthday to you!" the crowd sings, bringing a smile to my face. I bend forward and blow the two candles. A three and a zero. In that exact order.

"Happy Birthday, sweetheart," my mom says, wrapping her arms around me and pulling me into her petite frame.

"Thanks, Mom. So glad you guys could be here," I tell her, glancing around at the familiar walls of Twist of Lime, my favorite local hangout. Well, it used to be my favorite. Now, it seems to hold too many memories of my past. I haven't been here in nearly a year, and when my sister informed me we were headed here, I tried to back out. I didn't want to come.

Not without Harrison.

"Look! Aunt Tina is here! Let's go say hello," Mom says to Dad, grabbing him by the arm and pulling him toward the front door.

"Here," my little sister, Gabriella, or Gabby as I call her, says as she thrusts a plate of chocolate cake in my hand. "I can't believe my big sister is finally thirty."

"Me either," I reply, shoveling a bite of the rich chocolaty cake into my mouth before I say too much.

"Stop being so damn gloomy, Gwen. It's a celebration," she argues, firmly planting her hands on her hips.

"You look like Mom when you have that face," I inform her, my mouth full of dessert.

She gasps. "Do not!"

I can't help but laugh. "Do too. You're gonna be just like her," I tease.

"Not me," Gabby says. "*You're* just like her."

The thought stops my fork and causes my heart to stutter. I used to think just that; that I was just like her. Married at twenty-two to the love of her life. Maybe a baby on the way not too long after. Of course, my dream turned out much different than my mom's. My dream was a cute little dark-haired, dark-eyed son or daughter running around who was the spitting image of his or her father. Actually, that was *both* our dreams. Though, he'd argue the baby would look just like me.

Twenty-five.

That's when we thought it would happen.

But life stepped in.

Harrison became the most sought-after trainer at the gym. Even though, as the boss, he had control of his hours, he was busy, his schedule packed. Then the owner approached with the offer: Buy the gym and keep it local. A large corporation wanted it, but the man who built it from his blood, sweat, and tears didn't want that to happen. Together, we made the decision that forever altered our lives. All Fit became his—ours, technically. Even though my name is on the business, I've never had anything to do with it. Even now, after the divorce, he insisted I stay on as co-owner. A silent partner, if you will, that could receive a small check of the profits each year.

With that one life-altering change, everything else became modified as well. Our dream of becoming parents at twenty-five was pushed to twenty-seven. Then twenty-eight. He started working six and seven days a week, more hours than any one person should. It was for the business, I know. The gym took off, and in a way, so did my husband. That one single gym will branch into two, and eventually three. In the last few years, All Fit has become a household name, including fitness videos, vitamin supplements, and other tools to improve the mind, as well as the body. The business is growing in leaps and bounds, and by the end of the year, there should be two additional All Fit locations joining the flagship location.

I've always been proud of him and probably always will be. His dream wasn't to own a gym and watch it grow like weeds in a flowerbed, but it did. His life changed with that one decision and forever changed the course of our path together. We hit the fork in the road. He went one way, and I went the other.

Sadness sweeps in and my stomach rolls. The once-delicious cake now tastes like sawdust in my mouth. "Stop it," Gabby chastises.

"Stop what?" I ask, though I know exactly what she's talking about.

"You know what. Push him out of your mind, Gwen," she says, and my eyes inadvertently sweep to the front door one more time. He's not coming tonight, I know, but I can't stop looking for him. It's like he's embedded in my brain somehow. "He probably would have missed tonight anyway," she adds with annoyance.

Gabby loved Harrison. Being two years younger than me, she was that bratty little sister who followed me everywhere. When I met Harrison in college, her senior year of high school, Gabby instantly took a liking to him, and he her. In a way, he became the older brother neither of us ever had and often treated her as such. He was overprotective and overbearing where she was concerned, but that never bothered her. She thrived off it.

Now, after the divorce, she's not exactly his biggest fan. Even though I've told her many times that he wasn't the only factor in the demise of our marriage, she refuses to see him as anything but the sole reason for our separation. She's angry at him because he left her too, and my heart breaks a little every time I see the devastation reflecting in her eyes. Divorce has a way of taking a toll on everyone, not just the husband and wife.

"He wouldn't have," I quickly defend. Harrison wasn't always there when I needed him, but I know in my heart, this was an event he wouldn't have missed for anything.

Gabby rolls her eyes and stares at the door. "He would have insisted on more decorations," she says softly, the hint of a smile playing on her lips.

I glance around at the single banner taped to the wall announcing my thirtieth birthday, and at the handful of helium balloons on the tables. Harrison would have gone all out, for sure. My mind quickly flips back to my twenty-fifth birthday, where he had streamers falling from the ceiling and more balloons than a party supply store. The cake had two tiers and the spread of food catered from my favorite Mexican restaurant. We celebrated my birthday hard that night, rocking it until the wee hours of the morning, before he took me home and made love to me in our bed. Everything changed a week later when he met with his boss. Nothing has been the same since.

My stomach lurches again, and I quickly deposit my plate down on the nearest table.

"Are you okay? You're looking a little... green," Gabby says, worry filling her eyes.

"Yeah, it's this stupid flu bug. One of my students shared it with me, and I can't seem to kick it."

My head starts to heat and my hands become clammy. I know what's about to happen. I take off for the bathroom, throwing open the door, and barely making it to the toilet before my body purges what little food I ate earlier in the day.

"Geez, Gwenny!" my sister bellows as she enters the bathroom and pushes on the stall door. She rushes over to the sink and grabs a paper towel to wet. The dry heaves subside and a mixture of relief and fatigue rushes through my body. "If I didn't know any better, I'd say you're knocked up."

I know she's joking, but her words strike me like a lightning bolt straight to the heart. Gasping for air, memories flood my mind—memories of Harrison and me. Together.

"...and that can't be because you'd have to have sex in order to get pregnant, and we both know that's not happening," she continues with a laugh.

Sex.

Oh, God!

We had sex!

Unprotected sex!

Gabby returns to the stall and sets the wet paper cloth over my forehead. My mind is still reeling with realization and shock as she continues to talk about the different flu strands going around her office, but I already know.

I don't have the flu.

When I begin to lose feeling in my legs from crouching beside the toilet, I start to stand. Gabby's right there to help me. "You should go home," she says, placing her hand on my forehead. "You don't have a fever, but I don't think you should stay and risk getting everyone sick."

"You're right," I mumble, my mind swimming with uncertainty as she wraps her arm around my shoulder and guides me to the bathroom door.

"I'll make regrets for you to everyone, and when I get them cleared out, I'll come over," she says.

"No, don't do that. I'm just going to head home and rest. You don't need to come over just to watch me sleep." Lie. I'm not headed home, at least not yet. I'll be making a trip to the drug store first to buy a pregnancy test.

Then what?

What if it's actually positive?

Harrison flashes through my mind.

Oh, God, I'm going to have to tell him, and say what? *Hey, Harrison, remember me, your ex-wife? The one you slept with mere minutes after our divorce was final? Well, good news, I'm pregnant.*

My stomach recoils, but I don't think it's pregnancy-related sickness. It's stress from having to tell my ex-husband that I'm pregnant with his baby. How did this happen? Well, I know *how* this happened, but *how* did this become my life? I'm like a walking episode of *The Young and the Restless*. What are my preschool parents going to think of me?

Gabby guides me down the hallway and to the table where we've stashed my purse. As if on autopilot, I smile politely while retrieving my belongings and make my way to the exit.

"Honey, are you all right?" Mom asks, coming up behind us with a look of worry on her face.

"Yeah, just a touch of the flu," I answer, the lie rolling too easily off my tongue.

"Oh, no. Well, feel better. If you're not well tomorrow, text me, and I'll bring you some soup," she replies, pulling me into her arms and giving me a warm hug.

"I will. Please give my regards to everyone. I really appreciate you all throwing me this party," I add.

"It was nothing," Mom says with the flick of her hand before setting it on my forehead. "It's not every day your oldest turns thirty."

"No, I guess not."

"Do you want Dad to drive you home?" she offers, glancing over at Gabby.

"No, that's okay. I can drive. My stomach isn't too bad now, so I think I can make it home."

She continues to look on with that motherly watchful eye, and I almost crack under the pressure. She knows I'm lying, but, if I am pregnant, I don't want to tell them first. Harrison deserves to know before my family, which is why I continue the flu charade for just a little longer. "Well, if you're sure... I'll stop by tomorrow and check on you."

"Thanks, Mom," I reply, giving her another hug, before being ushered out of the bar and escorted to my car.

"I'll text you in the morning," Gabby says, full of concern.

"I'll be fine, but thank you," I reply quickly before climbing into my car. As I crank over the engine, I throw her a wave, plaster on a fake smile, and back out of my parking spot.

My mind is a mess of nerves and excitement as I drive toward the nearest drug store. Could I really be pregnant? The symptoms match up. Nausea, tired, and tender boobs. Plus, I missed my period this month, but I just chalked that up to the stress. It's not like my monthly cycle has been normal since the separation. In fact, since I stopped taking my birth control several months back, my period has been all over the place. It's not like I had a reason to stay on the pill, anyway.

I pull up to a stoplight, my hands trembling with nerves. I release the steering wheel and try to shake them out a little, my fingers feeling a bit cold. The light changes to green, and I slowly start to pull into the intersection. I see the flash of light only moments before the horn sounds. There's nothing I can do, not even brace for impact. My vehicle jars hard as the other car makes impact, the seat belt pulling against my body and holding me in place. The airbag deploys with a loud bang as everything around me starts to fade away. It's like I'm floating, all the sounds of crunching metal, shattering glass, and horns honking vanishing. There's no sound. Even as I glance over and see a face full of fear in my driver's side window. His mouth is moving, but there's no sound.

My eyelids become heavy and the desire to sleep takes over.

The baby.

My hands drop to my still-flat stomach, and I send up a silent plea to God, his angels, and anyone else up there who'll listen. Please don't take away my baby. Please keep her safe.

And then my mind drifts to Harrison.

To the man I love.

To the one who's going to be a father and doesn't even know it yet.

My world fades to black.

My eyes open just as I'm rushed through sliding doors. A man stands on one side and a woman on the other as I'm guided into what appears to be the emergency room. "What have we got?" I hear a man ask just before his face comes into focus.

I listen as the paramedic reports to the doctor about the car accident, my vitals, which are strong, and a slight bump on the side of my head. The doctor orders a CT scan to check for bleeding on the brain, and that's when the panic sets in. "I'm pregnant," I state, causing everyone around me to stop and glance down.

The doctor gives me a smile. "Okay. How far along are you?"

"Just a few weeks. Well, I *think* I'm pregnant. I was on my way to the store to get a test."

"Well, start with a pregnancy test then," he says with another polite smile. "Just hang tight, okay?" he adds, grabbing my hand and giving it a squeeze. That small gesture goes a long way to help settle my fears, even though I'm terrified right now.

Everything after that happens quickly. I'm taken to a room and stripped down to a gown, where my blood is drawn and a few small wounds are tended to. The nurse is very pleasant as she applies an ointment to the burn on my arm caused by the airbag and puts on bandages.

"Well, Mrs. Drake, you're very lucky. They say your car was impacted at the driver's side front tire and not the door. You have a few superficial burns and lacerations from the airbag, and a mild concussion from the bump to the head, but no other signs or symptoms of anything more severe," he says, reading from my chart. "Oh, and your blood test came back positive. Congratulations, you're pregnant."

You're pregnant.

Those two words have the biggest impact on me, changing the course of my future forever. A baby. I'm having a baby.

"We do want to take a look at the baby, however. You have a bit of spotting, but that can be completely normal. There's an ultrasound technician outside, who'll come in and take a look at the baby. Hang tight, and she'll be right in. Once that's complete, we'll take you to a room for observation. Between the bump to the head and the spotting, I'd like to keep you for the night and make sure everything is okay," he says, turning to leave.

"Thank you," I reply in disbelief and fear.

"Oh, and the nurse called the emergency contact in your phone. He's on his way."

He.

Apparently, I say the word aloud.

The ER doctor gives me another smile. "Yes, your husband. It's good that you have someone listed in there for emergency situations. Not many think to include one for times like these," he says before turning and walking out the door.

Harrison.

He's coming.

And there's nothing I can do to stop it.

CHAPTER 5

Harrison

A lonely Saturday night at home. Not just any Saturday night, today is Winnie's birthday. The big three-oh and I'm not there to celebrate it with her. I sent her a text earlier, but it's still radio silence on her end. That's okay because at least she knows that I'm thinking about her. That I'm always thinking about her. I've called or sent her a text every day since the divorce was final. I guess you could say I'm having a hard time accepting it. My phone rings in my hand, and I silence the call. This is the second time Chase has called, and I've ignored him. I don't want to go out tonight.

Not without Winnie.

It rings again, and I know that persistent fucker won't stop. He's like a gnat that keeps swarming around your head you keep swatting at, but it never goes away. Don't get me wrong, he's a great guy, my best friend since college, but he's really starting to grate on my nerves with all this, go out and find someone new bullshit. Snatching my phone from the couch cushion beside me, I swipe the screen. "What?" I ask, annoyed.

He laughs. "I knew I would wear you down eventually. Let's go grab some drinks."

"Nah, not feeling it."

"Here we go again." He sighs heavily into the phone. "Harrison, come on. You can't mope. I refuse to let you."

"I'm not moping," I lie. "It's been one hell of a week, and I just want to stay in. I'm not good company tonight. Trust me on this." That part is not a complete lie. I buried myself in work this week to fill the ache, to fill this void that knowing we're divorced brings me.

"So, you're saying you're not up for being my wingman?" I can hear the humor in his voice. He knows damn good and well I'm not up for it. Not tonight or any night in the future. "I need backup."

"Afraid not, you're flying solo on this one."

"Fine," he grumbles. "I can tell by your tone that I'm not going to get you out of that apartment."

He's right. Nothing is going to get me from this recliner, my only piece of furniture in the living room, well, unless you count the TV and the TV tray I bought to eat my takeout on. I can't seem to find it in me, to try and make this place home. It's not home and will never be. It's a constant reminder that I fucked up and lost my wife. Maybe I should look into moving to a new place, one that I pick out with plans of long-term? Yeah, not ready for that either. I always thought when we moved into a bigger place, it would be because we were growing our family.

"You take the ring off yet?" he asks.

"Don't," I warn.

"Jesus, Harrison."

"Don't," I say again, not wanting to hear anything he has to say about it. I know it makes me a pussy. I get that. I know that it's over, that the ink has long since dried on our divorce papers, but damn it, I can't seem to make myself accept it. Taking off my wedding band is a part of that. My eyes dart to my left hand, where my ring still sits on the fourth digit. Then there's the W tattoo. Both reminders of what I've lost. I'm going to take it off, but I was hoping that I would run into her and she would notice. This town isn't that big, yet we've managed to avoid the awkward run-in.

"So what, you're just going to sit around and do nothing?"

"There's a John Wayne marathon on," I tell him.

"Hold me back," he jokes. "Seriously, this is the last time, man. I'm not going to let you sit and mope your life away. What happened to fighting for her?"

"She won't reply to me," I grumble, already over this conversation.

"Make her."

"Right, and how do you suppose I do that?"

"Go to her, make her listen, do something. Staying holed up in your apartment all the time is not the answer."

Again, he's right, not that I'm going to tell him that. "Drinks next weekend. None of this wingman shit, got it? Drinks, but I'm not ready for all that other shit." I don't know if I ever will be.

"Fine," he concedes. "Call me if you change your mind."

"Sure," I say, ending the call. I have no plans to change my mind. He can try all he wants, but I'm not leaving this apartment until Monday morning. I need some time to get my head together, figure out a plan. I'm going to fight for her, and I just need to decide how I'm going to do it.

I debate on whether I should drive over there. Just to see if she's home, but then I remember it's her birthday and if she's there, so is her entire family. I'm not going to show up and make a scene and make this day hard for her. We lost our way, and let things get too far out of hand. She might have signed those divorce papers, but she still loves me.

I know she does.

I can feel it.

Starting tomorrow, I'm upping my game. I'm going to fight for her with everything I have, with everything inside me. I'll do whatever it takes to prove to her she's more important than the gym. Hell, than anything. She is all that matters. I knew it the day I met her, then again the day I married her, and I sure as fuck knew it the day I divorced her. We got lost. Now it's time to find our way back. I just wish there was some kind of sign, or even a reply from her to let me know where I stand. This silence is killing me.

Grabbing the remote, I'm just about to turn the volume up on the television when my phone rings again. This time it's a number I don't recognize, so I let it ring until the voice mail picks up. Immediately it rings again, the same number. I'm ready to let it go to voice mail again, but something in my gut tells me I need to answer it. After the fifth ring, I swipe the screen and place the phone next to my ear. "Hello."

"Hi, is this Mr. Drake?"

"Yes. Who's this?" I ask skeptically. I wouldn't put it past Chase to have a random woman calling me trying to persuade me to come out with them.

"My name is Lori. I'm an Emergency Room nurse at County General. Your wife was brought in about twenty minutes ago."

My heart stops, then stutters to life with a rapid beat pounding in my chest. My grip on the remote is so tight I can feel the plastic start to give. Dropping it to the floor, I sit up in my chair. "What? What happened?" There is a heavy thump, thump, thump ringing in my ears. My mind races with all the possibilities—why is she there? Is she okay? *Please let her be okay.*

"She was in an car accident."

Shit. "How is she? Is she all right?" I ask over the lump that's already formed in the back of my throat. Where was she going? Was she alone on her birthday? Questions I don't have time to get the answers to flash in my mind.

"She's doing okay. She's very lucky. We found your information under the emergency contact in her cell phone. The doctor is going in to see her now."

"She's okay?" I ask for clarification. I think I heard her right, but this is Winnie we're talking about. I need to be certain.

"Yes. She's going to be just fine," the nurse whose name I can't remember assures me.

I'm already up and grabbing my keys. "I'm on my way. Can you please," I fight back the emotion clogging my throat, "tell her I'm on my way?"

"Absolutely, Mr. Drake. Drive safe," she says, ending the call. After slamming my apartment door, I bypass taking the elevator and opt for the stairs. I take them as fast as I can, bursting through the lobby door, and sprinting out to my truck. Tossing my phone in the cup holder, I shakily place the keys in the ignition and peel out of the lot. I break more traffic laws than I care to admit on my way, but that's the least of my worries. They can give me a ticket, but I'm not stopping this truck.

Not until I get to her.

Luck happens to be on my side. As I squeal—tires turning—into the ER parking lot, no cops are in sight. Taking the first spot I see, I jerk the keys out of the ignition, grab my phone, and jog inside. I don't stop until I reach the reception desk. "My wife, Wi-Gwendolyn Drake, they called me, a nurse, she called me and said that she was brought here," I ramble as I suck in a deep breath. I won't do either of us any good if I'm a hyperventilating mess.

"Yes, Mr. Drake." She types something on her computer then looks up at me. "The doctor just finished up. Would you like to speak to him?"

"Yes, and I want to see her."

"Of course." She gives me a kind smile. "Let me get the doctor for you, and then we can take you on back. Just have a seat down the hall." She points at where she wants me to go. "Third door on the left is consultation room three. I'll let him know you're waiting."

"Can we not do this in her room? Can I see her first?" My voice is pleading.

"I'm sorry, the doctor should fill you in on her condition. He'll be right in," she says, dismissing me. I stand here for a few heartbeats while she places the phone next to her ear and tells the doctor I'm here. "He's on his way," she says again with a kind smile. I don't offer her one of my own. I can't. Not yet. Not until I see Winnie and know that she's okay.

Making my way down the hall, I peer into every room to see if I can spot her, but without any luck. Pushing the door open on consultation room three, I barely have my ass in the seat when the door opens, and an older gentleman in a white coat walks in.

"Mr. Drake?" he asks.

"Yes, Harrison." I reach out and take his hand. "How's my wife?" I have no intention of telling him we're divorced. Not until they let me see her. It's just a piece of paper anyway, a minor technicality in the grand scheme of things.

"I'm Doctor Frazier, Gwendolyn is very lucky. She was involved in an car accident earlier this evening." He looks down at the tablet in his hands and begins swiping the screen. "Some bumps, bruises, and scrapes. Some minor burns from the airbag, but otherwise, your wife and baby are just fine."

Slumping back in my chair, relief washes over me as his words play on repeat in my head. *"Your wife and baby are just fine."* What? I grip the edge of the chair as I open my mouth, but no words come out. Trying again, I swallow hard then speak. "D-Did you, did you say baby?" I ask, my voice disbelieving.

"You didn't know?" From the look on his face, he's worried he might have spoiled the surprise.

"N-No." I didn't know, and suddenly, I'm angry. Pissed off that she's already moved on, how could she forget what we had so fast? Then there's the thought of her and another man, his hands on her, the two of them... I shake my head, not wanting to go there. I need to keep my cool. I need to see her.

"You okay?" He averts his eyes to my tight grip on the chair.

Looking down, I see the W tattoo and my wedding ring. A million things are flowing through my mind, but one stands out among the others. The day of our divorce. The last time I made love to her, just a few short weeks ago.

"H-How far?" I clear my throat. "How far along is she? I mean, the baby." I stammer over my words. I would have known that day, right? I would have been able to see the difference in her body? It would have felt... different if she were pregnant then, right?

He looks down at the tablet and swipes the screen. "A few weeks, according to her bloodwork." He keeps swiping at the screen, unaware of my mental breakdown.

A few weeks.

It's mine. This baby is mine. How could I have ever jumped to the conclusion that it wouldn't be? That's not my Winnie, divorce or not. That's not who she is, and I love her even more for it. Thank fuck I had time to process this before seeing her.

I'm going to be a father.

"Can I see her?"

"Of course." He stands from the chair. "We're going to move her to a room and keep her overnight just as a precaution with the pregnancy. The ultrasound tech should be in there with her now." He glances at his watch. "If we hurry, you might be able to catch the end of it." He turns and opens the door, and I'm hot on his heels.

I follow him down a busy hallway, with curtains pulled giving what privacy they can to the patients behind them. "There." He points to the last curtain at the end of the hall. "Go on in. I'm going to work on getting her moved to an inpatient room." With that, he turns and walks away. Closing my eyes, I take a deep breath preparing myself for what's going to be behind this curtain. *She's okay*, I mentally remind myself.

I hear a female voice that's not my wife. Carefully, I pull back the curtain and stand just inside the threshold, taking in the sight before me. Winnie has her legs in stirrups while the ultrasound tech has her hand between her legs. Their eyes are riveted to the small screen on a rolling cart. I take advantage of being unnoticed and look her over. Her arms are bandaged, she has a butterfly over one eyebrow. Other than that, I can't see much from where I'm standing. Regardless of her injuries, she's still the most beautiful woman I've ever seen, and it's been too damn long since I've set my eyes on her.

"Winnie." My voice cracks. Slowly, she turns her head to look at me. Tears fill her eyes. "Hey." My feet carry me to her. I don't stop until I'm beside her bed. On instinct, I bend down and place a kiss on her forehead. "You okay?" I know she is, but I need her to tell me.

"Yeah." She sniffs.

"Dad, I assume?" the ultrasound tech asks politely.

"Yes," I say before Winnie can answer her. "How are they?" I ask, reaching out and lacing my fingers through hers, careful not to bump her forearm where she's taped up, from I assume the burns.

"Mom and baby are both doing well. We were just finishing up." She points to the screen. "As I was telling your wife, this"—she points again—"is your baby."

Winnie squeezes my hand. Looking down, I find that her eyes are trained on me and not the screen. "I love you," I tell her. My voice is clear, and there is zero hesitation. She gives me a watery smile.

"I printed some pictures," the tech says, already cleaning up her machine; we missed that in our stare down. "They'll do another ultrasound in the morning, just as a precaution, but everything with the baby is perfect. Congratulations, you two," she says before disappearing behind the curtain, leaving us alone.

"Harrison—"

My lips pressing against hers stops her. "I love you," I tell her again, pulling away. My eyes bore into hers. "We're going to be okay," I tell her. "We've got this." I rest my hand that's not holding hers over her flat belly. "This is what we said we wanted. It's a few years later, but it's happening. This baby..." I swallow hard. "This baby is fate, Winnie. It's fate telling us that we belong together. I had already decided that I was going to fight for you, for us, and now—" I lean down and kiss her again. "—now I just have to fight harder. For you, for our baby, for our family."

She loses her battle with her tears as they begin to slide down her cheeks. Releasing her hand, I wipe them away with my thumbs. "We're divorced," she cries.

"It's a piece of paper." I try to console her.

"This is not how it was supposed to happen," she cries harder.

"I know, baby. But we're going to get through this. You and me and Peanut." Leaning in, I kiss her forehead. Seeing her upset like this, lying in a hospital bed, is wreaking havoc on my emotions as well. I've never been able to stand seeing her cry. It was my biggest weakness and why I left when she told me we needed space. I was willing to do whatever I needed to stop her tears. Looking back, I know I was wrong. I should have said fuck the tears and fought for us. I'm a man who learns from his mistakes, and I can guarantee I won't be making this one twice.

"Everything is so messed up." She weeps with her words. "We had this plan, you know, and now, now it's ruined, and I'm a single mother. I don't want to be a single mother." I place my hands over hers, trying to comfort her. She runs her thumb over the W tattoo. "What are we going to do?" she asks softly.

I don't hesitate when I drop to my knees right here in the emergency room. Carefully, I hold her hand between mine and look her in the eye. "Marry me, Gwendolyn Drake. I don't want to live a minute longer without you by my side. I'm miserable without you. Marry me, and give me a house full of babies." I grin wide, unable to hide my excitement that I'm going to be a father.

We did have a plan, but it kept getting pushed back. It never seemed like the right time with the gym expanding, but now that it's here, and it's our reality, I couldn't be more thrilled. We made a baby together after our divorce was final. I've been lost without her. This is all a sign that we belong together. I don't care what I have to do, or what I have to give up to prove it to her. Winnie and this baby are all that matters to me.

"Harrison." She's shaking her head, but her eyes tell me a different story. Her look is pleading, as if she's begging me to make this better.

I stand up and sit on the edge of her bed, taking her hand in mine. "You tell me when. First thing Monday morning we can be at the courthouse, or we can go to Vegas, or maybe a destination wedding this time. You tell me what you want, and it's yours."

"It doesn't work like that, Harrison," she murmurs.

"This is our story, baby. We can write it however we want. I want to raise this baby with you."

"Of course you will. You're the father," she scoffs.

"With you and me in the same house, sleeping in the same bed, working on siblings for Peanut. That's what I want. I want the life we planned but pushed to the side."

"How do we do that? How do we get that back? Can we get it back?" she asks.

"We can," I say adamantly.

"We signed the papers," she reminds me.

"I know that. We also signed our marriage license, something that can easily be repeated," I say, looking into her eyes.

She drops her head and traces my tattoo when suddenly her fingers stop moving. "Your ring," she whispers. "You're still wearing your ring."

"I made a promise to you when you gave me that ring. We lost our way, and I'm to blame for that, but we can make it back. I never for one second stopped loving you."

"Love was never the issue," she counters.

"I know that. I let myself get carried away with work. All the while I thought it was for us. To make the gym a success, so when we decided to start a family, we would be set financially so you could stay home if you chose to do so." I pause, letting my confession sink in. "I was an idiot."

"All right," a nurse says, barging in on us. "We've got your room set up. Here are her things. You want to follow me?" the nurse asks.

"Oh, you don't—"

"Lead the way," I say, reaching out to grab the bag of personal items from her. I step back and watch as they help Winnie into a wheelchair and drape a blanket over her lap. When they start to move, so do I. The nurse gets her settled in her new room, with a promise to come back and check in on her soon.

"Where do you want this stuff?" I ask her.

She points to the cabinet. "I guess just throw it in there for now. I hope no one messes with it in there."

"I won't let them," I tell her.

"What do you mean?"

I finish placing her bag of personal items in the small cabinet and make my way back to her bedside, sitting in the chair and pulling it closer. Reaching out, I take her hand in mine. "I'm not leaving you here all alone."

"That's crazy," she says, pulling her hand from mine.

"My wife and unborn child were in a car accident, and are staying in the hospital overnight. Why is it crazy that I want to be here with you?"

"I'm not your wife."

"Not yet. But this..." I place my hand over her belly. I can't seem to stop touching her. "This little peanut is a part of both of us. It's my job to be there for both of you, and I plan to do just that."

"Harrison, you should go home, sleep in your bed, get a good night's sleep."

"Funny," I say, except I'm far from laughing. "I've not had a good night's sleep since I moved out." It's the truth, the bed is cold and empty without her.

"Don't do that." She points her finger at me. "Don't you dare try to make me feel guilty."

"Never," I assure her. "I'm just giving you the facts." Never again will I let her think she's not the most important person in my life. She and this baby mean everything to me, and I'll make damn sure they know it.

Her eyes close and she exhales. That's when I know I've won. She can act tough all she wants, but she's scared. Our situation is not ideal, and who wants to spend the night in the hospital on their own? "I need to call my family."

"I can call them for you." I start to reach for my cell phone in my pocket.

"Wait! It's late, and there's no need wake them up, making them worry. I can call them tomorrow when I'm released. I'll need a ride home."

"I can take you home."

"Harrison—"

"Gwendolyn," I counter.

"Fine," she concedes.

That was much easier than I thought it would be. I can only assume she didn't want me calling her family, because then she would have to explain to them why I'm here. "Do they know?" I ask her.

"No. We had dinner at Twist of Lime, and I've been sick. Gabby made a comment about if she didn't know any better, she would think I was pregnant. That's when it hit me. I told them I wasn't feeling well, so I could leave to buy a test. That's where I was headed when the accident happened."

Lifting her hand to my lips, I kiss her knuckles. "That had to be scary. I'm glad it turned out all right. That you and the baby are both okay."

"Yeah." She yawns.

"Get some rest. I'll be here when you wake up." She gives me a subtle nod as her eyes drift shut.

I sit here next to her bed, her hand held in mine watching her sleep. I could have lost them both. If that's not a wake-up call, I don't know what is. "I love you, both of you so much," I whisper. Resting my head next to our joined hands, I drift off to sleep.

CHAPTER 6

Winnie

My head is a little heavy as I rouse from a deep sleep. Hair hangs in my face, but when I try to lift my hand to move it aside, it's restricted. I can't lift my hand. Panic starts to set in, when the reason I'm being held down moves.

Harrison.

He's sleeping in a chair beside me, his head resting on one of his arms, while the other shifts to hold my hand tighter. He doesn't wake though, and it gives me a moment to just watch him sleep. His hair is a little longer and his five o'clock shadow more pronounced. I always loved his scruffiness, especially when it would slide along my thighs.

No. Not going there now.

His handsome face is completely relaxed, but I can see the worry lines that mar his eyes and brow. His mouth is slightly agape and his breathing is even and steady. I used to love resting my cheek on his chest and listening to his strong heartbeat and level breathing while he slept. I miss everything about sharing a bed with him.

He hasn't moved much since we both fell asleep the last time. Once I was settled in my bed and the nurses got me hooked up to their machines, I fell asleep quickly. However, every two hours, someone came in to check my vitals or replace my fluids. Each time, Harrison was wide awake, watching closely as they monitored both the baby and me. A mild cramp started overnight in my lower abdomen, which caused me to freak out a little. The nurse informed me that some cramping during pregnancy was normal, as ligaments and muscles were beginning to stretch. And since the spotting hadn't gotten any worse, she felt that was a good sign that Peanut was still safe and snug inside me.

Peanut.

From the moment the doctor informed me that I was pregnant, I fell in love. But the moment Harrison referred to our baby as Peanut? I fell even more in love with him.

My bladder takes the opportunity to remind me that I've had an IV hooked up to me all night, pushing fluids. Gently, I pull my hand from my ex-husband's and gingerly start to move. He doesn't wake but stirs a little until he gets more comfortable. The fact that he didn't wake this time is a testament to how little sleep he's actually been getting. Carefully, I slide out of bed, cautious to make sure my legs will support me, and start to shuffle toward the small bathroom, pulling the IV pole behind me as I go.

Inside the room, I quietly pull the door closed and turn on the light. I get my first glance at the damage to my face. No, not necessarily damage, but I definitely look like I've been in a car accident. There are a few scratches that are already scabbed up, and there's no missing the bruised lump on the side of my head. Part of my forehead is a light purple color, reminding me that it definitely could have been much worse.

My bladder cries for help, which has me scurrying for the toilet. Relief washes over me, not only to finally be peeing but because there's very little blood. I was terrified that I'd glance down and find more, that I was losing the baby. After finishing my business, I carefully stand and go to wash my hands. The moment I do, my stomach lurches and the cold sweats start. I know exactly what's about to happen.

I barely make it back to the toilet before I'm throwing up. I'm not even sure *what* I'm throwing up, considering I haven't eaten anything since the party last night, and I already purged that from my gut afterward. Paying no attention to anything but my miserable puking, I don't hear the door open or the man enter. I only notice he's here when I feel my hair being swept from my neck and pulled back. Harrison sets his big hand on my back and rubs gentle circles. As soon as the heaving has subsided, I find instant comfort in his touch, even if I shouldn't.

"Are you finished?" he whispers, his voice pulling me from the fog in my brain.

I take a quick moment to make sure, and nod.

Harrison helps me stand at the sink while I brush my teeth. The moment I've finished, he takes the brush from my hand and sets it on the sink. "Come on, Winnie," he gently replies, scooping me up in his arms and carrying me from the bathroom.

I hold on tight around his neck, considering he's got me with one arm and is dragging the IV behind us in the other. "Put me down, Harrison. I can walk."

"But there's no need, baby. I've got you." He places a kiss on my forehead and lowers me back to the bed.

Pushing up on my elbows, I reply, "I need to start gathering my things." Then I try to swing my legs out of bed, but his hands stop my movement.

"You can in a bit. Right now, you need to relax and get your strength back."

"I'm *fine*, Harrison. I'm pregnant, not bedridden."

My breathing stills in my throat when his eyes darken. Harrison leans forward until we're nose to nose, his hands settling on the bed at my hips. "I know you're *pregnant*, Winnie." There's a harshness to his tone that tells me something else is going on.

I go ahead and sit back on the bed, using the remote to raise the head. As soon as I do, I exhale loudly. "Say it."

He continues to watch me, his arms crossed over his broad chest. The muscles in his arms flex as he shifts his weight. "Say what?"

"Whatever it is that's on your mind." I grab my hands, wringing them on my lap and wait him out. He seems to be in an internal battle with himself, like I might not like the question he's about to ask.

Or he won't like the answer.

Finally, he walks over and sits down on the chair beside my bed. He doesn't take my hand this time, which I notice right away and miss just as quickly. His gaze holds mine as he asks, "Were you going to tell me?"

I don't have to ask what he's referring to. I know. "Yes, of course," I insist, and that's the truth. I never would have or *could have* held this from him. First off, it's his right to know he's going to be a father, and even though we're not together anymore, there's not a doubt in my mind that he would make an amazing dad. Also, it's not like we live in a big city. Fair Lakes is a small town, surrounded by other small towns, in the heart of Missouri. Unless I relocated to the other side of the state, there's no way I could avoid running into Harrison every now and again. No way our friends and families wouldn't continue to talk. No way would it not get back to him that I was pregnant.

He relaxes immediately. It's like the weight of his question was weighing him down. His shoulders sag and the relief rushes through his body. "Okay, good. Not that I thought you would have held that from me, but since you're not answering my calls or texts, I just wasn't sure. Not talking to you hasn't been easy, Winnie."

I swallow hard. "It hasn't been easy on me either," I confess.

"Then why haven't you?" he asks, the vulnerability all over his face.

"Because I knew it would be too hard. I knew that if I talked to you once, I would want to talk to you again and again. There wasn't a doubt in my mind that I would run straight back into the comfort of your arms, and I needed to prove it to myself first."

"Prove what?" he asks, clearing his throat.

"That I can be *me*. That I was strong and independent and could do this on my own," I whisper, tears burning my throat.

Harrison leans forward and takes my hand. "There is no doubt in my mind that you could and would be able to do anything on your own, Winnie. You're the strongest woman I know." His hands around mine provide so much comfort that I want to snuggle into his chest and wrap myself in his warmth.

"I'm not, though," I reply, a tear slipping down my cheek. "I mean, within an hour after the divorce, I slept with you, right?" I ask, the small smile on my lips matching his.

"Is that what you want? To do this alone?"

Immediately, I shake my head. "No, not the pregnancy. That changes everything. It's hard to describe, and I don't think I'm doing a very good job of it. I guess I just wanted to prove to myself that I could stand on my own two feet again. I wanted to show the world that I'm more than just Mrs. Harrison Drake, owner of a successful gym and most sought-after trainer in the county."

He moves, crouching down beside my bed and bringing my hand to his lips. "You are, baby. You've always been so much more. You were the glue that held us together," he says, making me roll my eyes. "It's true. Why do you think we fell apart when you stopped trying?"

His words hit me hard.

"And I don't mean that as an insult or I'm pointing fingers. I was working so hard on the gym and lost my focus. It wasn't until you asked me to leave that I realized what I had done. And the worst part was, even though I was completely miserable, I knew you'd be okay. You are strong and independent and would have gotten up, dusted yourself off, and come out stronger on the other side. You're amazing, Winnie," he whispers, kissing the hand that doesn't have the IV. "Always have been and always will be."

I sniffle and wipe my eyes. I'm sure I look even worse now that you add in tears. "So what now?"

He strokes my hand and gives me a knowing smile. "Well, I thought I wanted to remarry you," he starts, making my heart slam against my chest.

"And now you don't?" I ask, the words hurting more when they're said aloud than when I just thought them.

"Oh, hell no, baby. My end game is to remarry you," he says with a smirk. "But first, I'm going to date you."

That catches my attention. "Date me?"

"Yep," he says, that cocky swagger I fell in love with back and written all over his face. "I'm going to date you like we did in the beginning. I'm going to pick you up for dinner and steal kisses in the back of the movie theater. I'm going to hold your hand when I'm driving my truck, and hopefully, cop a feel in the library when no one's looking."

I laugh. "The only library I've been to lately is the one in my classroom, and I don't think it would be appropriate to cop a feel with preschoolers in the room."

"You're probably right. I'll have to come up with another creative way to get my hands on your amazing body," he whispers, flipping my hand over and kissing my palm. A shiver sweeps through my body.

I stare into his dark eyes, wishing with everything I have that things could have been different. Wishing the ending was different.

And maybe now it is.

In fact, something tells me this is a whole new chapter beginning.

Harrison sets our joined hands down on my abdomen. "We still have a lot to figure out. We have a lot of talking to do, something we stopped doing there at the end. That's my fault."

"That's both our faults," I assure him. I played a big part in that problem too. When he stopped talking because of work, I shut him out.

"Maybe," he says, rubbing his thumb over our baby. "I'll still always blame myself fully for what happened. I did so much wrong."

"We both did." My throat feels tight and burns a little from all the emotion rolling around in the small hospital room.

"We're going to fix this, Winnie. For you and me, but for the baby too. *Our* baby. Peanut."

There's no way to stop the tears that fall. "What if we still can't make this work? What if we try and just can't fix it? I don't think my heart could go through another breakup, Harrison."

"Then we won't, sweetheart. I'm not going to let us fail this time, and do you know why? Because you are my world and I won't let us fall again. I won't let go of us." His words are everything I've wanted to hear, yet everything I fear. Because what-if?

"Don't be afraid, Winnie. I let you down once, but I'd rather die than do it a second time. Trust me."

I take a deep breath. "I want to."

"You can. You will. Eventually, when you're ready, when I've proven it to you. I have a lot of ground to make up now, but I'm in this for the long haul. I'm going to fight for you, baby. I'm going to fight for us... our family," he says, moments before he punctuates his statement with his lips on mine. His kiss is chaste, yet urgent and full of so much emotion. "We're gonna take this slow, okay? We're going to get to know each other, trust each other again."

"We're going to date," I reply, my mind swimming with uncertainty and fear, yet buried deep down is a tiny bubble of hope.

"Exactly," he agrees, placing his lips on mine once more. "I am so gonna love dating you, Winnie."

I offer a small smile, hoping I'm not making a big mistake by considering this entire plan of his. He wants us to date, to get to know each other, and hopefully, together, work through and get past our problems. Easy peasy, right? Probably not even close to easy. I have a feeling this is going to be hard.

But I also have a choice: I could walk away. I could move forward and put my previous life behind me... but that won't work. With this tiny life growing inside me, there'll be no walking away. Harrison will always be there. Maybe not as my husband, but as my child's father. He'll be a part of my life in one way or another for the rest of my life.

Or I could take door number two.

I could date my ex-husband, the love of my life. The one that I let go, but have regretted doing so more than I thought possible. We could end up in worse shape than we are now. That's the funny thing about life: it's unpredictable as hell and just when you think you have it figured out, along comes another curveball.

"Okay."

"Okay?" His voice is hopeful, his eyes shining for the first time in I don't know how long.

"Okay. I'll date you." Deep breath.

His smile is boyish and practically splits his face in half, it's so wide. It's the smile I miss most of all, the one I love.

"We've got this, Winnie. I promise we're going to fix this."

I start to open my mouth, to reassure him that it's going to take a lot of work on both our parts, when the door opens. "Knock, knock," a lady says politely as she enters my room, pushing a cart. "I'm Courtney, and I'm going to do an ultrasound for you this morning." My heartbeat kicks up as I sit up straight in bed. The young tech wheels her machine over to my bedside and quickly gets it set up. "Do you want your company to stay?" she asks, glancing over her shoulder at Harrison, who's lingering in the corner.

"He's the father," I reply, resulting in her smile.

"Okay, good. Give me a second and we'll begin," she adds.

Harrison comes over and stands at my head, giving himself a clear view of the monitor. Courtney gets ready and rolls a condom over the wand. "Uhh, what are you doing? I don't think it's going to get her pregnant again," he says.

She smiles in return. "It's not for protection, Mr. Drake." She glances my way next. "Ready to take a peek at your baby?"

"Definitely," I answer excitedly.

I hold my breath as she inserts the wand and moves it around. It only takes a moment before the image on the screen displays a tiny peanut. *Our* peanut.

"There she is," Courtney says, pointing to the screen.

"She? You know it's a girl?" Harrison asks, kneeling beside my bed to get on my level. He reaches out and grabs hold, mindful of the IV in my hand.

"No, it's too early to know that. I just always refer to fetuses as shes," she replies with a shrug. We watch as she takes measurements, much like the tech did last night down in the ER. Then she clicks a button and a fast beat fills the room. "And that is your baby's heartbeat."

Harrison gasps. "It's so fast."

"They are," she confirms. "One hundred and forty-five beats per minute. Good and strong. I'd say your little one is doing quite well today," she adds, taking several images of the baby.

I can feel his eyes on me and am surprised to find them a little misty. They're so full of wonder, amazement, and love. "Thank you," he whispers, right before his lips find mine. The kiss could easily turn heated, but he doesn't let it. Instead, we turn and watch the rest of the ultrasound, staring in awe at the sight on the small screen.

"You're all set. I'm going to send this to the doctor, and he'll be in shortly. What OB will you be using? We'll make sure to send all our reports to their office as well," Courtney says as she shuts down the computer system and unplugs it from the wall.

"Westlakes OB," I inform her. Even though I haven't given it much thought, that's where I go for my lady appointments, so why not continue with the same doctors?

"They're wonderful there. They delivered my daughter last year," the young woman adds, giving us a wave before exiting the room.

We barely have time to think, let alone talk about what we just witnessed, when the door pushes open. The morning nurse and admitting doctor come in together. "Good morning, Mrs. Drake. How was your night?"

"Not bad," I inform him, making sure everything is covered up below the waist.

"How's the spotting?" he asks, reading over the report from the ultrasound.

"Barely any this morning when I used the restroom."

"Perfect, that's what we had hoped for. Everything is looking good, and I see no reason to keep you any longer. I would make an appointment with your OB tomorrow morning, and take it easy for a few days. If you start to see spots or have trouble focusing, come back to the ER right away, but the bump to your head isn't showing signs of any damage."

"So I can go?" I ask, suddenly wanting nothing more than to go home, shower, and put on my own clothes.

"You're free. Jackie will get your discharge papers and instructions ready, and she'll bring up the wheelchair shortly," he confirms.

"What about orders at home? Anything she should or shouldn't be doing?" Harrison asks, his focus on the doctor and his posture rigid.

"She's free to resume normal activity as she feels up to it. As I said, definitely take it easy for the next couple of days. As I mentioned earlier, if the cramping or spotting becomes worse, or you start to have trouble with dizziness or loss of vision, come to the ER right away."

"I will, thank you," I confirm, ready to get out of here.

The nurse removes the IV before I start to gather what little personal items I have. I realize I'm going to have to put on last night's clothes since I don't have an overnight bag with me. I pull the bag from the cabinet and find my top and capris, my stomach dipping just a little when I see the tinges of blood and holes from the airbag. Oh, well, it'll have to do.

"I should have run and bought you new clothes," Harrison says, noticing the state of my attire.

"It'll be fine for now. I just want to go home, take a shower, and crawl into bed."

"You need to eat," he says absently without looking my way.

"I will, but first a shower." I head to the small bathroom to change, but stop before I cross the threshold. "You can head home, you know. I can call Gabby to come get me and take me home."

His eyes fly to mine, burning with annoyance. "Not happening, sweetheart. I'm not going anywhere," he says, crossing his arms. My eyes are drawn to the corded muscles of his forearms, something I used to love staring at while we were married.

"Fine, you can take me home. I'll call you when I have the appointment lined up with the OB," I concede, stepping into the bathroom.

Before I can pull the door closed, his hand stops it. "What do you think I meant when I said I wasn't going anywhere?" Dark eyes like lasers hold my gaze and make me squirm.

"What does that mean?" I ask, steeling my back and preparing for the fight I know is coming.

"I'm. Not. Going. Anywhere."

"You're not staying with me! You don't live there anymore," I insist, my mind reeling.

"You still have the guest bedroom, right?" He doesn't wait for me to answer. "I'll stay there, but I'm not leaving you alone. Not when you were just in a car accident that required an overnight hospital stay for a potential head injury. Not when you're carrying our baby and have been spotting. Get used to it, Winnie. I'm not going anywhere."

Then he punctuates his demand with a chaste kiss, turns, and walks away, seemingly having the last word and ending the conversation.

"One night, tops, mister," I tell him before shutting the door with a little too much force.

There.

Now who has the last word?

Only with the door closed, I no doubt miss the smug smirk on his handsome face that lets me know one night isn't what he has in mind.

One night will never be enough.

Not for Harrison.

CHAPTER 7

Harrison

One night. She can't be serious. No way am I leaving her alone after what she's just been through. Hell, I don't want to leave her alone just for the fact that she's agreed to give me another chance. Sure, she could call her sister, Gabby, or her parents, but why, when I'm readily available? I am the baby's father, after all. I deserve to be there for this, every fucking minute of it. I don't want to miss a single second.

After taking the elevator to the ground floor, I head out to the parking lot to get my truck. I pull up under the canopy, by the Patient Pick-up sign and turn on my hazards. I can't help but grin when I think about her up in her room, steaming from my high-handed comments. I'll sleep in the guest room, for now. However, my end game is getting my family back and giving her all the babies she wants. The minute I heard about Peanut, I knew this was what I should be doing — loving her, making babies, making a life.

I love the gym, but it can't keep me warm at night. I've lived without her, I know what that's like, and I never want to do it again.

"Ready to go?" I ask, walking into her room. She holds her finger up telling me to wait, and that's when I see her phone next to her ear.

"I know, I'm sorry. I should have called last night, but I'm fine, and well... Harrison stayed with me." She stops to listen. "Yeah, he was still listed as my emergency contact."

Another pause. "Gabby, I'm fine. We're heading home now."

My chest tightens at her words. She could have said he's taking me home, but she didn't. That tells me all I need to know. She wants this, wants me. She's just scared. It's my job as her husband, yes husband, and I don't give a fuck what the papers say. As her husband, it's my job to show her how much I love her. To show her this time things are going to be different.

"Fine, yes, we should be there in about thirty minutes," she tells her sister. "Yeah, I'll call Mom. Love you too. Bye." She ends the call.

"All set?" There is no need to ask about the call. I know Gabby isn't my biggest fan, at least not anymore. I walk to where she's sitting on the side of the bed.

"Yes, please. I'm ready for a shower and some clean clothes." She stands, and I place my hand on the small of her back, ready to help her if she needs me.

"We'll get you home, and while you're showering, I'll get you something to eat, both of you." I place my other hand over her still flat belly.

"I feel fine."

"Good." Leaning in, I kiss her temple. "It's my job to make sure it stays that way." She grumbles and then tries to tell the nurse she's capable of walking and doesn't need a wheelchair. She loses that fight too. Once she's in my truck and has her seat belt fastened, I rush to the driver's side and climb in. Looking over at her, sitting here with me again, brings a flood of memories rushing back. This woman is my world, and I was a fool to not fight for her. Reaching over, I lace my fingers through hers and rest our hands on her thigh. With one hand, I manage to put the truck in drive and pull out of the lot.

"Looks like you've marked something off your list," she says softly.

Glancing over, I see she's staring out the window. "What's that?" I wish we were stationary so I could look at her eyes, watch her facial expressions, but I keep my eyes on the road. I have precious cargo on board. No way am I risking either of them.

"Holding my hand in your truck."

"Yeah," I agree. "Get used to this." I pull her hand to my lips and kiss her knuckles.

"Are you sure about this, Harrison? Are we doing the right thing?"

"Yes." There is zero hesitation in my answer. "We're doing... well, I'm doing what I should have done a long time ago. I should have fought, Winnie, and this time, I'm going to."

"I want that," she says softly.

"Me too, baby. Me too." The rest of the ride home is silent as we both get lost in our thoughts. For me, I'm forming a plan. A plan to prove to her that I'm worth a second chance. To prove that she and this baby are my number one. I need to make some changes at the gym, and from this day forward, nothing will come before either of them.

Nothing.

"Stay put," I tell her as soon as we pull into the driveway. I climb out of the truck and rush to her side. Stubborn as she is, she already has her belt off and the door open. Gently, I place my hands on her hips and lift her from the truck. Her feet are on the ground for mere seconds, before I'm lifting her, cradling her in my arms.

"Harrison," she squeals. "I can walk."

"I know you can," I say, my lips next to her ear. "But I can carry you. Let me take care of you, Winnie."

I know she's given in when she rests her head on my chest and loops her arms around my neck. I slow my gait, wanting to savor this time with her in my arms. It's been too damn long. When we reach the front door, I set her on her feet, but keep my hands on her waist. I'm pushing my luck, but I can't seem to help myself.

Not when it comes to her.

"Head on up to the shower," I tell her. "I'll make you something to eat. Anything sound good?"

She bites her bottom lip and nods. "Your grilled cheese. No matter how many times I've tried, I can't seem to make them like you do."

I want to puff out my chest and beat against it with my fist; my girl needs me. Instead, I slide my hand under her hair and cradle the back of her neck. Leaning in, I place a feather-soft kiss on her forehead. "I've got you," I tell her. I mean more than the grilled cheese, and by the way she's peering up at me, she gets my double meaning. Reluctantly, I drop my hand and watch her walk upstairs to the master bedroom. The one we shared, the one I hope to share with her again soon.

I'm in the kitchen gathering everything I need to make her my famous grilled cheese when her cell rings. Tracing back to the front door, I find her bag sitting on the floor, her cell sticking out of the side pocket. Grabbing it, I see Gabby, my sister-in-law's name flash on the screen. I'm sure she just wants to make sure she got home okay, and I don't want her to worry, so I answer.

"Hey, Gab," I greet.

"Harrison. Where's my sister?"

She's not exactly rude, but she's not giving me the warm and fuzzy vibe either. "In the shower. I'm making her something to eat now." Not that she needed to know that, but I do need her to know I'm capable of taking care of my wife.

"I'm on my way, and you can go."

"I'm sure she'll be happy to see you, but I'm not going anywhere." Losing her changed me. I'm not going to put anything before my family, and those who are close to us, they need to know that. The divorce hurt more than just Winnie and me. It hurt our families too.

"What does that mean exactly?" Her voice is hesitant.

"It means that my wife was in a car accident, and I'm taking care of her."

"Ex-wife," she counters.

"That's a piece of paper that never should have been filed. I'm taking care of her."

"How does my sister feel about this?"

"She's okay with it. I'm staying in the spare bedroom. For now," I add, letting her know my true intentions.

She coughs as if she's choking. "Wow, when you say you're not going anywhere you really mean it."

"Yep."

"You hurt her, Harrison."

"I know. I'm fixing it." I know that I have my work cut out for me. Not only do I have to prove myself to Winnie but to our families as well. Nothing worth fighting for comes easy.

"That remains to be seen. I'm on my way. If Gwen wants you to go, we'll call the cops if we have to."

"I'm exactly where we both want me to be."

"Don't be so sure of yourself." With that, she hangs up on me.

Sliding Winnie's phone into my back pocket, I head back to the kitchen to make lunch. I'm just placing our sandwiches on plates when she appears in the doorway of the kitchen.

"Those smell amazing."

"I made you two. I wasn't sure how hungry you were."

"Starving," she says, placing her hand over her belly. My eyes follow the motion.

"It's still hard to believe there is a piece of me, a piece of both of us, growing in there." I point to her belly.

"I feel different," she whispers. "I know that sounds crazy; I'm not even showing yet."

Setting our plates on the island, I go to her, wrapping my arms around her. "Not crazy. I feel it too. This little one is bringing us home, together where we're meant to be."

"I want to believe that, Harrison. I really do."

"You will," I say with conviction. "Here." I reach into my pocket and hand her the phone. "Gabby called. I answered, not wanting her to worry when she couldn't reach you. She's on her way over."

"Thanks."

"Knock, knock," Gabby says loudly.

Reluctantly, I release Winnie and lead her to the island, pulling out a chair for her. "Water? Milk maybe?"

"Milk, but uh, I think I want chocolate, but I can get it." She starts to stand, and I hold up my hand, stopping her.

"I've got it. You need to eat." I busy myself making her a tall glass of chocolate milk. She's not one for the powdered stuff. My girl likes milk and chocolate syrup, a lot of it.

"How are you?" Gabby asks.

Winnie looks up at me, and I nod. I want to shout it to the world that we're having a baby. There is no need for us to hide it from our families. "Good," she finally says.

"Good? That's all you've got for me? You had to stay in the hospital overnight, Gwendolyn," she says, concern lacing her voice.

"Here you go, babe." I set the glass of chocolate milk in front of her and take my seat beside her.

"About that. Turns out you were right."

"Of course I was right. Wait, right about what?"

Turning to face her sister, she spills our news. "We're pregnant."

I don't have to see her face to know she's smiling. I can hear it in her voice. And me, well, my smile is wide. We're pregnant.

"Pregnant?" Gabby asks.

"Yeah." She looks at me over her shoulder. "We're having a baby."

Not able to resist, I lean in and kiss her cheek. "Peanut," I whisper. Her answering smile is blinding.

"How did this happen? I mean, I know how it happened. But how did this happen?" Gabby asks, her face scrunched up, trying to work it out in her head.

Winnie looks back at her sister. "We had a moment of... weakness."

She's not wrong. We were both weak that day. Not from the emotions of the divorce, but the loss of connection, from our bodies being deprived of the other's touch for so long.

"It's his?" Gabby asks.

"Watch it." My voice is stern, leaving no room for argument.

"Of course it's his," Winnie replies snidely.

"Sorry." Gabby holds up her hands in defense. "This is just... not what I was expecting."

"Us either." She turns to look at me. "But we're happy about it."

"What does this mean?"

"It means that Harrison and I are having a baby."

"For the two of you?" Gabby corrects.

I open my mouth to reply, but Winnie beats me to it. "It means we're working it out. Regardless of where we end up in our relationship, one thing will hold true for the rest of our lives. We share this baby." She places her hand over her belly.

"Just like that? He knocks you up, so you're just going to take him back, just like that?"

Again, I start to speak to defend us, but my girl beats me to the punch. "The demise of our marriage is not all on Harrison. We were both equal partners in our marriage, and we both did things—" She stops. "Regardless of what you think you know, you don't. Love was never the issue for us. I'm confident we both will love this child unconditionally."

"Hey," I say, my voice gruff. Winnie turns to look at me. I cup her face in my hands. "I love you." Leaning in, I place a kiss on the corner of her mouth. Her eyes are glassy as her tears threaten to bubble over.

"Have you told Mom and Dad?" Gabby asks, oblivious to the moment we're having.

"Not yet. We haven't really discussed when to tell our parents or anyone for that matter," Winnie answers her, but never takes her eyes off mine.

"I want to shout it from the rooftops. You tell me when you're ready, and I'll make it happen."

"That easy?" Gabby crosses her arms over her chest. "Where were you a year ago, Harrison? Why now after all this time?" Her eyes are boring into mine. I can see the hurt and the worry for her sister.

I debate on whether or not to answer her. I want to tell her it's none of her damn business. However, the reality is that Winnie is close to Gabby. And as much as I hate the need to explain or defend myself, winning over Gabby isn't a hardship. She's like a little sister to me too. I understand where she's coming from, but that doesn't mean I like it. "I didn't fight for us like I should have. I put the gym before Winnie, but not because I didn't love her. I was trying to build it into something that would secure our future, and the future of our family."

Gabby scoffs, and I clamp my mouth shut, refusing to react.

"I didn't fight either," Winnie tells her. "We both are to blame for how things ended, and equally so for this little miracle." She once again places her hands over her belly. "It will be our decision on how we move forward. I love you, Gab, but this is our choice. As my sister, you have to respect whatever decisions we decide to make."

"So, he's living here again?" Gabby asks. She's fighting against this, but I can see through her tough-girl act. She was hurt when we divorced. She needs some time to catch up to where we are. She'll come around.

"I'm staying with her to take care of her, of both of them." I take a calming breath. I know Gabby means well, she's hurt, and I have to remind myself of that before I continue on. "I know what it's like to live without her. I know what it's like to want to tell her something from my day and not be able to. I know what it's like to go to bed without her and wake up just as alone. None of that is enticing to me. I know what I had, what I lost, and I know that this is a gift. Both of them are my gift, and I'll be damned if I let them go again."

Gabby's quiet; I'm sure processing my words. "You're going to be an aunt," Winnie says softly. "Can we focus on that? Let Harrison and me figure out the rest. This is our life, our future," she says gently.

"I've been here and I witnessed what losing him did to you." Her words cut deep, the pain slicing through my chest. "I don't want to see you go through that again."

"I survived. I made it through, and if that happens, we still have the best part of each other—this baby. You have to let us make our choices. Besides, you're the little sister," Winnie teases, trying to lighten the mood.

"I'm going to be an aunt." Gabby's smile is wide when it finally appears.

"Yes, and you have to keep it to yourself. No spilling the beans to Mom and Dad before we get the chance to. You're not supposed to tell anyone until after the first trimester in case of miscarriage."

"Wait? What? Are you okay? Do we need to go back to the hospital?" Panic floods my veins.

"No." Winnie's smile is soft. "It's just an awful fact that if you are going to miscarry, it's likely to be in the first trimester."

My mind races with how I can protect them. "How do we stop that? You need to take time off work, stay off your feet."

"Harrison."

I think back to what the doctor said at the hospital; he assured us that she was fine. "Wait, are you spotting? Is the cramping getting worse? We should go back." I start to stand, but she places her hand over mine and stops me.

"Harrison." Winnie moves her hand to my face. "I'm fine. No more spotting and the cramping is minimal, and they said that's normal, remember?"

I nod.

"I'm just spouting facts, that's all. Take a deep breath."

"Winnie." My voice cracks.

"We're fine." Her voice soothes me.

I pull her into me—as best as I can with the chairs between us. I bury my face in her neck and breathe her in. "Tell me what you need. Tell me what to do, and I'll do it."

"There is nothing we can do," she whispers. "It's all up to fate."

"Fate," I repeat. "That's what gave us our peanut."

"Oh my God," Gabby murmurs.

Pulling away, we turn to face her. Her eyes are swimming in tears. "You really want this." It's not phrased as a question, more of a statement, but I answer her anyway.

"More than my next breath."

"I can't say that I forgive you. You hurt her, and yes, I understand she had a part in the divorce as well, but she's my sister and my loyalty lies with her. However, with a confession like that, it's hard to not root for you."

"I can use all the help I can get." I wink at her to lighten the mood, causing her to roll her eyes. I stand from my chair and slide my plate in front of Gabby. A peace offering of sorts. Not to mention, I know she loves my grilled cheese sandwiches too. "I'm going to go and get the prenatal vitamin prescription filled. Is there anything that you want or need while I'm out?"

"No, I think I'm okay."

"Call me if you change your mind. I won't be gone long." I kiss Winnie's temple, grab my keys from the table by the door, and make my way to my truck. When I'm on the road, I hit the phone call button on my steering wheel. "Call Chase."

"What's happening?" he answers almost immediately.

"I need to make some changes."

"O-kay?" He drags out the word, unsure of what I'm up to.

"I want my wife back. I need to not work eighty hours a week to make that happen. She was in a car accident last night, and I'm staying with her."

"Is she okay?"

"Yeah, she's going to be just fine, but I need to be there for her. Not just when she's back on her feet, but forever. I pushed her away because I worked too much. Not because I didn't want to be around her, but I got lost in building something for our future. I see the error in my ways."

"What can I do?" No hesitation. His loyalty speaks volumes to our friendship. I know I can count on him, and he knows he can count on me. I'm lucky to have a friend like him in my corner, and a part of my business.

"I need to delegate, but I don't want to put all of this on you. I think I'm going to hire an admin assistant. Someone who can be the sole support for both of us. A lot of what I do is paperwork that someone else can easily handle. Maybe hire a payroll company instead of me doing it every other week. I don't really know the specifics, but that's where I'm hoping you come in. Help me cut back. Help me get my life back."

"You got it, brother. I'll be thinking. Can we meet this week? I can come there to the house," he offers.

"Yeah, that's probably best. I don't want to leave her for a few days. I'm only out now to get her— to go to the pharmacy."

"Need anything?"

"Just to get my shit in order at the gym. I can be what she needs and still own a successful business. If not, well, maybe it's time I let the gym go."

"What?"

I've shocked him. To be honest, I'm a little surprised myself, but that doesn't make my words any less true. I would give it up for my family. "Nothing matters to me more than Winnie. If I can't make this balance work, I'm going to sell."

"Just like that?"

"No contest."

"We'll make it work."

"I want that, but I'm prepared to let it go if not."

"What brought this on?"

"I lost her, Chase. Then last night I get a call that she's been in a car accident and it hit me that I truly could have lost her. I've been moping around missing her, loving her from a distance, instead of getting off my ass and fighting for her. The gym was a big part of why I lost her. If I can't make it work, if I can't figure out a way to work less and be with her more, I won't hesitate to let it go."

"That gym is your baby."

I smile at that. "Not anymore."

We agree to meet in a few days to brainstorm how to set my plans in motion. I drop the prescription off at the pharmacy, and they tell me it will be twenty minutes. While waiting, I wander through the store. I grab a bag of peanut M&M's which are Winnie's favorite and find myself standing in the baby aisle. It's a little overwhelming, but a smile still tilts my lips when I think of our baby. Slowly, I make my way down the aisle, taking it all in when something catches my eyes. The tag claims it's a onesie, but I'm not worried about what it is as much as what it says. *"If you think I'm cute, you should see my mommy."* I can't wait to see her face when I give it to her.

When I get back to the house, Gabby's car is still in the driveway. I find the two of them curled up on the couch watching reruns of *Grey's Anatomy*.

"I thought you went for my prescription?" Winnie asks when she sees the bag I'm holding.

"Yeah, I picked up a few things." I hand the bag over. I watch her closely as she reaches in and pulls out the M&M's.

She smiles up at me. "Thank you." She sets them to the side and pulls out the white pharmacy bag that holds her prescription. That too gets set aside. The next item she pulls out of the bag is a book. *"What To Expect When You're Expecting."* She reads the title.

"Yeah, that one's kind of for both of us. Probably more me, since I thought I should learn." I shrug.

"What's this?" She pulls the tiny outfit out of the bag. I watch as she reads what it says. "Harrison," she says breathily.

"It's black and white, so it's good for a girl or a boy, right?"

"It's perfect."

"Let me see." Gabby leans over to read what it says. "Aww," she coos. "You did good, Daddy."

My heart stutters in my chest.

I'm going to be a daddy.

CHAPTER 8

Winnie

He's driving me crazy.

Just a few hours into his self-imposed move-in, and he's completely making me insane. Sundays are usually spent catching up on laundry, grocery shopping, and getting my week ready for school. But not today. Today, I'm being held prisoner by my ex-husband, who won't let me move a muscle from the couch. Is it bad? No. I know he's doing what he thinks I need, but not letting me walk to the bathroom to pee is a little overboard, ya know?

I'm four episodes into a *Friends* marathon when I start to slide my feet out from under me. "Where are you going?" Harrison asks, glancing up from the book he's reading in the chair. He has a pair of readers perched on his nose, something that's new since our time together. A ping of longing slides through my body, and I can't help but wonder what else I've missed over these last several months.

"When did you start wearing cheater glasses?" I ask, ignoring his questions and asking my own.

He dog-ears the page he's reading, and I can't help but gasp. "What?" he asks, his entire body filling with tension as he starts to move in my direction. "Are you okay? What's wrong? Do you hurt? Is it the baby?"

Rolling my eyes, I reply, "I'm fine. Or at least I am physically. I think you just crushed a piece of my heart when you bent that page over."

Harrison glances down at the book he haphazardly tossed on the end table. "Shit, sorry. I forgot you hate that."

"You're a monster," I tease, fighting the grin that wants to slip out.

He glances my way and smiles. "A monster, huh?"

"What'd that book ever do to you?"

"That book didn't do anything to me, except maybe offer up a little too much information about birthing the placenta," he says, shivering with disgust as he takes his glasses off and runs his hand down the side of his face.

I slide off the couch, and his eyes are on me like laser beams. "I'm okay, you know. I don't need to be held hostage on the couch."

"I'm just trying to keep you both safe."

I crouch down in front of him, noticing the moment his eyes start to dilate. "I know that, and I appreciate it, but sitting on my ass for hours on end isn't doing anything to help me."

"You heard the doctor. He said to take it easy."

"Easy, yes, but captive, no. I'm okay, Harrison. A little rest is a good thing, but I need to be able to get up and get a drink," I say until I'm interrupted.

"I'll get you a drink."

"But I'm perfectly capable of getting my own," I inform him, holding his gaze and watching the internal battle play out. I know he just wants to help, and I'm certain he thinks he's protecting both our baby and me, but it's too much. It's only been a few hours and it's already driving me bananas.

His shoulders sag in defeat. "Okay, I get it, but that doesn't mean I like it," he concedes.

I offer him a small smile. "I understand your position, and I appreciate your help, but I'm perfectly capable of walking down the hall to use the restroom."

He tenses and stares down at me. "I didn't want you to trip."

"I've never tripped over the bathroom rug before," I gently say.

"But there's a first time for everything. All it would take is one time for you to trip, and I'd never forgive myself. We should just get rid of it. All of the rugs, actually. They're a trip hazard, and—"

"Harrison." I grab his hands and give them a squeeze. "The rugs stay."

Again, his shoulders sag. "Fine."

I can't help but smile. It's a small battle, but I feel like I just won the war. Harrison has always been overly protective of me, and I wouldn't expect him to change now that I'm pregnant. However, that doesn't mean I'm going to remove all my rugs or start drinking organic milk just because he thinks it's better for the baby and me.

"To answer your question, I went to the eye doctor about a month ago and he suggested I wear cheaters. My vision for distance is fine, but when I'm reading, the words were a little blurry. It was just a small change, but it was enough to bug the shit out of me," he informs me.

"You're not even thirty," I remind him, though it's a moot point. I'm pretty sure he knows how old he is, which is a mere two months younger than me.

"I'm aware," he says with a small grin, but it's replaced quickly with seriousness. "I'm sorry your birthday was ruined yesterday."

I think back on the entire day, from the party to the accident, resulting in a hospital stay. "I don't really think it was ruined," I start. "It wasn't exactly a great way to celebrate my thirtieth, but the end result was pretty fantastic," I add, meaning the baby.

His eyes brighten with excitement. "Yeah, that's probably the best shocking news I've ever received," he says before sobering again. "I'm sorry I wasn't there."

A lump forms in my throat, making it hard to breathe. "Why would you have been?"

"Because I vowed that I always would be."

My eyes burn as I stare at the man I was married to. "Sometimes things change. People change."

"Sometimes they make mistakes and realize it when it's too late, but vow to make it right. I *will* make it right, Winnie," he whispers, my name a plea on his lips. I've always loved the personal nickname he gave me from when we first met. No one else calls me Winnie. Only Harrison.

I don't know what to say. It's not as cut and dried as he thinks, but I'm not completely against the idea either. The truth is: I love him. I've always loved him. From the first moment I saw him in the library, I knew he was the man I wanted to spend the rest of my life with. He was the one my heart would always yearn for. But somewhere along the way, we lost our way. We let work and lack of communication drive a wedge between us. I'm still not sure if we can get back what we once had, but I'm willing to try.

"Put the glasses back on," I state, changing the subject.

He gives me an odd look but does what I ask—though it was more of a statement than a question. Harrison doesn't move as I bring my hands up to his face. His strong jaw is tight with tension as I cup it and stroke the coarse skin. There's a definite five o'clock shadow, something I've always loved. I can feel his eyes blaze with fire as he watches me. I don't make eye contact, instead keeping my eyes locked on my hands. I slide them up his cheeks and hear his breathing hitch.

Using my pointer fingers, I straighten the dark plastic glasses on his face. "I like these," I whisper.

"Yeah?" His voice is hoarse and gravelly.

Instead of speaking words, I nod and make eye contact for the first time. My heart hammers in my chest as our eyes remain locked. A whole slew of emotions and memories flood my mind, some good and some bad. They weren't all the latter, though. Until right before the separation, there were far more of the good ones than the bad.

Harrison turns his face, kissing the inside of my palm. "I'll wear them all the time if you'd like."

A small smile plays on my lips. "That's not necessary, but I wanted you to know how handsome you look."

"More than just a gym rat?" he teases.

"You were never just a gym rat, but they do make you look more distinguished. Very debonair."

Now he snorts a laugh. "I don't think I've been called debonair a day in my life," he adds, taking my hands in his and bringing them to his chest.

"That's a shame," I tell him, loving the way my heart beats a heavy pattern in my chest. It reminds me of that first time I saw him, and the next several times we talked. With our busy school schedules, we actually talked on the phone for an entire week before our first date. Those days were filled with short conversations between classes and text updates while studying. I looked forward to our communications, and craved those late-night talk sessions.

"Have you called your boss yet?" he asks, interrupting my walk down memory lane.

"Uhh, no, not yet. I was going to send her an email later. I need to line up a sub for Monday."

"And Tuesday. Actually, just take the whole week off," Harrison instructs, leaving no room for negotiation.

"Umm, excuse me?"

"The doctor said to take it easy for a few days."

I give him my best "teacher" look and reply, "Yes, a few days; not an entire week. There's no reason for me to be off that long. I'm fine."

"Through Wednesday, then." Harrison steeples his fingers at his nose, as if he's in a business meeting. Well, sorry, buster, but I'm not a business arrangement or contract in need of negotiating.

"I'll take two days. I need to call my doctor tomorrow anyway for an appointment. Hopefully they can get me in Tuesday."

Harrison sighs deeply. "You're not going to budge on this, are you?"

I shake my head.

Again, he exhales. "Fine, through Tuesday. I'm going to the doctor though."

Smiling happily that he conceded, I squeeze his hands. "Thank you, and yes, I'll let you know as soon as I have an appointment set. I can call you," I add, getting up off my knees and instantly feeling the need to use the restroom again.

I head toward the hallway when he replies. "No need. I'll be staying here."

Well, that stops me in my tracks.

"Excuse me?" I ask, startled, turning around and staring at the man taking over my easy chair. He's reading the book again, or at least thumbing through it as if he were.

"I'm staying here," he comments casually, as if no big deal.

"For today."

"For a while."

"We've talked about this. I agreed to let you stay for a very short term. One night, tops. Remember?"

He smirks over the top of the paperback. "I recall." Then he returns his attention to the book, essentially dismissing me.

"You're not staying here, Harrison. We're divorced," I state, crossing my arms over my chest. No, it's not the end of the world if he stays here, but it just makes the muddy water even murkier. The problem is that I'll start to enjoy having him here again, and eventually, he'll head back to his place, leaving me behind. That thought is just depressing, really.

"We'll see," he says, giving his attention back to the book.

I groan in frustration and head to the bathroom to do my business. As I wash my hands, I can't help but stare at the reflection in the mirror. I don't look any different, but I definitely feel it. My hands instantly drop to my flat stomach, much like they did in the shower earlier. There's a miracle growing inside me. *Our* miracle, even though I thought that ship had long sailed.

I just pray we're strong enough to weather the storm this time around.

On Monday morning, after a quick phone call to my regular OB/GYN, I'm scheduled for an appointment that afternoon. As soon as I mentioned the accident and spotting, they insisted on squeezing me in as soon as they could. I'm thankful as I think this appointment will go a long way at calming my nerves. Sure, they'll still be there, but I'm hoping they'll be able to confirm that everything is going to be okay.

"Gwendolyn," the nurse says into the packed waiting room of pregnant women. They come in every stage of pregnancy, some not showing, like me, and a few very close to their due date.

Harrison stands up and places his hand under my elbow. He guides me through the room to where the nurse smiles warmly. Her eyes seem a little brighter now that she's gotten a good look at my husband—err, ex-husband. I want to tell her I get it. He's totally adorable. But I keep quiet, and maybe lean into him a little closer.

"Let's check your weight first, and then you can step into the restroom and give us a urine sample," she says, glancing over my shoulder once to check out the man behind me. Okay, now it's a little annoying.

I've never been self-conscious about my weight, but there's something unnerving about stepping on the scale in front of Harrison and the nurse with wandering eyes. That number is only going to keep going up. For good reason, mind you, but I won't dwell on it since the reason will be well worth it.

"I'll escort Dad into the room. You can step across the hall and give us a sample. When you're done, place it in the small door on the wall for us to collect. Come to exam room four when you're finished," the nurse says, smiling brightly.

I take care of business, place the cup in the little window, wash my hands, and head out to room four. As I approach the door, I can hear laughter. "I thought you looked familiar! I'll be sure to stop in on my lunch break."

"Do that. I'm sure one of our personal trainers will be more than willing to add you as a client," Harrison says. I push open the door and find him standing in the corner, his arms crossed over his chest in a guarded manner.

"You don't take on new clients?" the flirty nurse asks, not noticing I've entered the room.

"Not at this time. I have a great staff though, and I'm sure we can find someone who fits your needs," he replies, noticing me for the first time.

"His staff is wonderful," I say, entering the room completely and not closing the door behind me. "You're sure to find someone *else* who's amazing to work with."

The nurse gives me a sheepish grin and drops her eyes. "I'm sure. I'll stop by and sign up," she says, looking down at my chart. "Dr. Taylor will be in shortly to talk to you before she does the exam," she adds. Then she's gone.

"I hate her."

Harrison snorts. "Stop it. She was just asking about training since she saw my newspaper ads the other day."

"She was totally wanting *you* to train her... and not in exercise." He raises his eyebrow in response to my statement. I sigh deeply. "I'm sorry, I shouldn't have said anything. Who you train is none of my business."

And then he moves, caging me against the exam table with his arms, wrapping me in the comfort of his scent. "Anything to do with me *is* your business, Winnie. I'm not training her because I just don't have the time, but I'm also not training her because she makes you uncomfortable. End of story."

"It's really none of my business," I repeat, averting my eyes and trying to hop up on the table, which is difficult considering how close he's standing. He grabs me by the armpits and lifts, setting me effortlessly down on the table. I hate that I feel so jealous. I've never been a jealous woman, mostly because, when we were together, I knew he only had eyes for me. But now, I have no right to feel jealous about anything or anyone, not when I was the one who initiated the divorce.

Still doesn't make that bitter pill any easier to swallow.

As soon as I'm situated on the table, he leans forward, placing his hands on either side of my hips, and lightly brushes them with his thumbs. "Do you know why it matters?"

I can't answer, so I shake my head.

"It matters because you're the *only* one who matters. The. Only. One. The fact that you're a little jealous only reiterates the fact that we belong together, baby. You and me. And Peanut. Ever since I saw you in that library, I've only had eyes for you. Nothing has changed, even after we split. So don't think that any of that was none of your business, because it most certainly is. *You* are my business. My priority," he whispers, running his nose along my jawline. I can't believe how quickly my body starts to heat at the slightest touch.

"I wasn't jealous," I whisper, my words all breathy.

Harrison snorts a laugh. "Were too."

"I wasn't, but *if* I was, it's only because you're so pretty to look at and everyone notices you."

"Guys aren't pretty," he clarifies. "But *if* I was, it wouldn't matter, because my eyes are on you, the most gorgeous woman in the world, who just so happens to be carrying my baby."

"And is your ex-wife."

"Semantics."

I give him a small smile, feeling slightly better at that ugly green monster that reared its head a few moments ago. He doesn't move, just stays standing between my knees and touching my face with his. It's comforting and familiar. After a few minutes, I relax into his neck, missing the way his body was seemingly made for mine. We fit, like puzzle pieces.

"Oh, Gabby is bringing dinner over tonight. She's stopping by after work."

"Fine. Chase is coming over too. We have some business to discuss, and he's stopping by my apartment to grab me some clothes."

"Chase and Gabby in the same room? Together? We better hide the breakables," I tease, though it's not really much of a joke. For some reason, Harrison's best friend and my sister have never really gotten along. It's like mixing oil and water. From day one, they've butted heads. At first, it was annoying, but now it's almost comical. They both seem to do everything they can to push each other's buttons.

"They'll be fine, babe. Besides, nothing short of a nuclear attack is going to dampen my mood. Today, we get to find out more about our baby," he says. Harrison has always had a way with words. He knows just how to make me melt like butter.

He places a kiss on my forehead just as a knock sounds on the door. "Good afternoon, Gwendolyn. Are you ready to check on your baby?" Dr. Taylor asks as she enters the exam room.

Before I can answer, Harrison turns to face her, extends his hand, and says, "Harrison Drake, father. And yes, we're definitely ready to see our baby."

CHAPTER 9

Harrison

Dr. Taylor shakes my hand and then turns her attention to Winnie.

"Gwendolyn, congratulations." She smiles kindly. "How have you been feeling?" she asks, glancing from the computer on the small counter.

"Good. Some mild cramping—" Winnie starts to explain, and I stop her.

"What? You told me you were feeling better?" I knew I should have refused to let her do anything for herself. Not even two days into knowing about this pregnancy and I'm already failing her.

"Hey." Her voice is soothing as her small hand cups my cheek. "I'm okay. Promise." Green eyes stare back at me, imploring me to trust her. "As I was saying," she drops her hand and turns to look at Dr. Taylor, "some mild cramping, but the spotting has stopped," she says. Immediately, I take a deep breath, releasing some of my tension.

Unable to help myself, I lean in and kiss her temple.

"That's wonderful news. Some cramping is normal during pregnancy, especially with your first. Says here you are about five weeks along. We're going to do another transvaginal ultrasound today to make sure everything is still looking good. We'll run some blood work as well. Your urine sample came back positive." She laughs. "But we already knew that. Then we'll use the Doppler and see if we can hear your baby's heartbeat. Don't be alarmed if we can't. It's still early. Usually, it's around the ten-to-twelve-week mark when we can start to detect it. We always try though." She smiles at both of us. "Go ahead and get into your gown, lay the blanket over your lap. I'll be back in a couple of minutes." She stands and leaves the room without another word.

"Uh, Harrison," Winnie says hesitantly once the door is closed.

She's nervous. "I've had my lips on every inch of your skin. There's not a single curve I don't have memorized." Her eyes turn molten as she bites down on her bottom lip. "When I told you I was going to be here, I meant it. I'm not leaving." Stepping between her legs, my hands grip the hem of her shirt. "Arms up, baby." She raises her arms and lets me remove her shirt. Hands under her arms, I lift her from the exam table and set her on her feet. My hands go to the button on her shorts, my eyes never leaving hers. "Step," I say, once I have her shorts and panties around her ankles. My voice is thick as I battle with my hormones. I'm a randy teenager anytime she's near. Resting her hands on my shoulders, she steps out.

Unable to help myself, I place my hands on her bare hips and press my lips just above her belly button. I feel her hands in my hair, so I look up to find her watching me. She's smiling down at me. My heart rate kicks into overdrive. She takes my breath away. I thought I'd lost her, and now here we are. Something passes between us. It's not anything that I can name, but it's strong and steady.

Just like us.

I'll make damn sure of it.

Standing back to my full height, I grab the gown from the table and help her into it. My hands find their way to her flat belly, and it's surreal that our baby is growing inside her. I can't seem to stop touching her and can't wait until she starts to show. The proof of the life we created evident. She takes her place back on the exam table, pulling me out of my thoughts. Reaching for the thin white blanket, I cover her up, but not before tracing her naked thigh with my index finger. She sucks in a breath, and that alone fuels my desire.

Knowing the doctor could walk in any second, I pull away and move to stand next to her, trying like hell to forget about her naked body under the thin material.

"This was a bad idea," she whispers as my lips connect with her forehead.

"Why's that?" I ask. I know why it was a bad idea, but I want to hear her say it. I *need* to hear her say it.

"Because Dr. Taylor is going to come back in here and she's going to know that I'm turned on."

Son of a bitch. Her confession ramps up my desire. "If we're not careful, she's going to know we both are," I say, shifting my stance to make room for my growing erection.

"Seems fair." She giggles.

Unable to resist, I bend down and kiss the corner of her mouth. "When we get home, I'll make the ache go away," I promise.

"Harrison…" My name is a whispered plea, doing nothing to douse the desire coursing through my veins. She meant it as a warning but missed the mark. Why should we both suffer? I can take care of her, in every way.

"Winnie," I counter.

"Knock, knock," Dr. Taylor says, entering the exam room and leaving Winnie no time to reply. "This is Kim, and she's going to be performing the ultrasound. Do either of you have any questions?"

Winnie looks up at me and I shake my head. "No, we're good," she replies to Dr. Taylor.

The next few minutes are a flurry of activity. Dr. Taylor tells Winnie to lie back on the exam table and place her feet in the stirrups. Then she tells her to move farther down on the table. Her legs are spread wide, as are my eyes. My grip on her hand is strong as I watch Dr. Taylor pull back the blanket, which is more of a thin sheet, and expose my girl to them.

"This might be a little cold," Alison says, holding up what looks like a dildo.

"Uh—" I start, but Dr. Taylor is quick to assure me that it's completely safe for both my wife and our baby. I nod and after a quick glance at Winnie, decide to keep my mouth shut. She's not worried about what they're doing to her. No, her eyes are glued to the screen, the one that will show us our peanut. It's not that it's unsafe, but that has to be uncomfortable for her. I know they used the same method at the ER, but I just thought that was because they just found out she was pregnant. Obviously I have a lot to learn.

The room is quiet, except for Alison clicking buttons on a keyboard. "A little pressure," she warns Winnie, but it's as if she doesn't hear her. Her eyes are still glued to the screen.

"There," Dr. Taylor speaks up. "See that small flutter—" She points to the screen. In the center of a little black blob is a tiny flutter. "That's your baby's heartbeat."

"Wow." I bring our joined hands to my lips and kiss her knuckles, all while leaning in closer to get a better look at the screen. The blob is small, but the flutter is fast. The last time we were in this position, I was still processing the fact that we were having a baby. This time, I'm soaking it all up like a sponge.

"That's normal, right? For the heartbeat to be that fast?" I ask her. I know the Emergency Room doctor assured us, but babies aren't their specialty. Call me paranoid, but it never hurts to get a second opinion.

"Yes, currently it's one hundred and forty-six beats per minute. Right in the middle, nice and strong," she assures me.

"Measuring right at six weeks," Alison says. She pushes a few more buttons. "I took some pictures for you," she adds, removing the wand from between Winnie's legs, and the screen goes black. Winnie pulls the cover back over her lap so that she's no longer exposed.

Dr. Taylor reaches under the table and extends it. "You can take your feet down," she instructs Winnie. She does as she's told. "Now, the fun part. As I said, don't be alarmed if we don't hear the heartbeat. It's still early, but I like to try, it's an experience you will always remember."

We already heard the heartbeat at the emergency room, but I don't tell her that. I want to hear it again, so I keep my mouth shut. I watch with rapt attention as she pulls down the sheet, and pulls up Winnie's gown, just enough to expose her belly. "This might be cold," she warns as she spreads gel all over Winnie's belly. "Our warmer has been acting up," she says, taking a small machine and moving the gel all around.

Glancing down at Winnie, I don't think either of us are breathing, for fear we might miss it. Dr. Taylor moves the wand this way and that. But still, I hear nothing. Until I do. The fast whooshing sound flows from the tiny speaker, and I swallow back the emotion clogging my throat. I was scared when she couldn't find the heartbeat, but there it is. Fast and strong.

"Nothing's wrong? Right?" I ask for clarification.

"Nothing. Mom and baby are perfect." Hearing those words lifts a ton of bricks from my shoulders, and the happiness now outweighs the fear. Fear of losing one or both of them.

Leaning down, I press a soft kiss to Winnie's lips. "Thank you. I love you so fucking much." My voice is thick with emotion, and my eyes glassy with tears.

"We're going to step out, give you a few minutes. You can go ahead and get changed," Dr. Taylor says. Neither of us acknowledges her. We only have eyes for each other.

Reaching up, Winnie runs her thumb under my eye. "This is unexpected, but I'm so happy, Harrison. I don't know how we're going to do this. Everything is so messed up, but this baby..." She swallows hard.

"This baby is a blessing," I finish for her. "Peanut brought you back to me, and I will never take you for granted again. I don't know what the future holds, but you have given me a gift. A piece of you." I place my hand over her belly. "And a piece of me to love for a lifetime." I kiss her again because I can't *not* kiss her. "I'll love you both with everything in me until the day I take my last breath."

She nods, wiping her eyes. "I should probably get dressed."

I help her off the table and into her clothes. Once she's fully dressed, I pull her into my arms and bury my face in her neck. It feels damn good to hold her in my arms again.

"You ready?" Dr. Taylor cracks open the door and asks.

"Yes," I say, pulling away.

"Everything looks great. We'll see you back in four to six weeks." She hands Winnie a stack of papers. "Here's a prescription for prenatal vitamins, and of course the pictures of your baby." She smiles at us. "Congratulations. If you need us for anything in the next few weeks, please don't hesitate to call."

"Thank you, Dr. Taylor," Winnie says with a blinding smile. She doesn't tell her that we don't need the prescription since the ER gave us one as well. I decide to keep quiet too. It doesn't matter. My wife and baby are both healthy. That's all that matters.

Once we're in my truck, I turn to face her. "Do you care if we stop by my place to get some things? That will save Chase a trip."

"Harrison, I'm fine," she assures me.

"I know that, but I still want to be with you. Both of you." I nod to her belly. "You're my family."

Her eyes well with tears. This has been an emotional day for both of us. "O-kay," she agrees.

Reaching over the console, I take her hand in mine and don't let go until we're pulling into my apartment complex.

"I'll just wait here."

"Nope. You're coming with me." I climb out and walk to the passenger side, opening her door. "It won't take me long." She hesitates, but removes her seat belt, and takes my offered hand to help her out of the truck. I don't release her hand. Instead, I hold tight until we're in my apartment. "I'll be just a minute." Dropping a kiss on her cheek, I head to my room to pack some clothes.

Pulling my suitcase out of the closet, I gather everything I think I might need this week, and a few extras. In the bathroom, I grab my razor, shaving cream, body wash, all the necessities. Snagging my phone charger from the nightstand, I zip up the suitcase and wheel it to the living room.

"Hey," I say when I see her standing in the small living room, staring off into space. "Everything okay?"

She blinks a few times and then turns to face me. "This place, it's bare, Harrison."

"I don't need much."

"You've been living here for months."

"See, that's where you're wrong. I've been sleeping here, but I haven't been living. I stopped that the minute I packed a bag and left you crying on the couch." The memory haunts me still to this day.

I've never been more wrong.

A tear slides down her cheek. "I've missed you," she whispers.

Releasing the suitcase, I wrap her in my arms. "I'm right here, Winnie. I'm not going anywhere." I hold her, letting her work through the tears, all while fighting back a few of my own. When she pulls away and looks up at me, I wipe her cheeks. "Ready to go home?"

She doesn't hesitate. "Yes."

A few hours later, we're sitting on the couch. Winnie is on one end, while I sit on the other with her feet in my lap. She's watching a movie on the Hallmark Channel, and I'm pretending to do the same. Instead, I'm watching her, only glancing at the TV when she catches me staring. That's how Gabby finds us.

"Well, isn't this cozy," she comments.

Winnie looks at me, and I expect her to pull away; instead, she surprises me. "We think so. What's in the bag?" She cranes her neck to look at her sister.

"KFC," she says, turning to walk to the kitchen.

"Ready to eat?" I ask, keeping the moment light.

"I don't know if I want to move." She laughs. "I never realized how comfortable this couch was."

"Then don't." I slide out from under her, resting her feet back on the couch. "Chocolate milk?"

"Yeah, but I can—"

I stop her by bending to place a kiss to her lips. "Let me take care of you."

Another surprise, she nods, accepting my plea. I find Gabby in the kitchen, setting everything up. "Winnie's going to eat in the living room. I'll get her a plate made up."

"I can do it," she counters.

"So can I." I cross my arms over my chest and stand tall. I know she's pissed, but I'm not letting her push me out, not when I'm finally exactly where I want to be.

Where I belong.

"Fine," she grumbles.

I can see in her eyes she wants to no longer be mad at me, but it's still too soon for her. I get it. I know she'll come around eventually. I busy myself making Winnie a plate. I make sure to grab two packets of honey for her biscuit; I know how much she loves it. I pour her a big glass of chocolate milk, grab a few napkins, and head back toward the living room.

"Hey, babe, you ready?" I ask her.

She sits up on the couch and grabs a pillow, placing it on her lap. I hand my girl her plate before moving the coffee table closer, so she doesn't have to stretch to reach her glass.

"You keep this up, I'm going to be spoiled and as big as this house by the time this baby arrives," she jokes.

"Good. I want you spoiled, both of you, and I can't wait until you start to show." I confess my earlier thoughts.

She laughs. "Right."

"I mean it," I tell her. "To know that a part of me is growing inside you, that's..." I shake my head, unable to find the words.

"Some sappy shit," Gabby says, plopping down in the chair with her own plate.

"You're just jealous," I tease her. Her reply is to stick her tongue out at me.

"So, what did the doctor say?" she asks before taking a huge bite of fried chicken.

"Everything's perfect," Winnie says happily. "We're six weeks. Oh, and we have pictures." She goes to set her plate down.

"I'll get them," I tell her. I want to kiss the hell out of her for saying *we're* six weeks, not *I'm* six weeks. It's the little things that can make a difference, and that statement tells me all that I need to know. Winnie and I are going to be okay. I make my way to the kitchen where we left them on the counter. I'm surprised Gabby didn't see them. Then again, she was pretending to be pissed that we were so cozy. I take a minute to stare at the grainy ultrasound pictures. It's hard to believe that's our baby.

When I get back to the living room, Gabby holds her hands out, and they're covered in grease. "Don't touch," I tell her.

"What the hell?"

"Your hands are covered in chicken grease."

"Sheesh, Harrison. If you're this protective of a grainy image that you can't even make out a baby, how are you going to be when the kid actually gets here?"

Winnie laughs. "Welcome to my world."

"Get used to it." I lift her legs and set her feet back in my lap. I see no point in denying it. I've always been protective of her, and now that she's pregnant that protectiveness is heightened.

"You have no one to blame but yourself. You're the one who's letting him stay here," Gabby tells her sister.

"He's waiting on me hand and foot. Can you really blame me?" Winnie laughs. "Besides," she looks at me, "Peanut needs Daddy close."

"I love you." The words are out of my mouth before I can stop them. Not that I'd want to.

"Gah, not while I'm trying to eat." Gabby breaks the moment, making us all laugh.

"Speaking of, Harrison, are you not going to eat?" Winnie asks.

"Yeah, I'm just waiting on Chase."

"Chase?" Gabby asks.

It's not lost on me that she almost sounds hopeful. Sounds like my sister-in-law has been missing my best friend since the divorce. They do say that there's a thin line between love and hate.

"Yeah, we have some work to do, so he's stopping by." I expect her to offer to stay with Winnie so I can go meet him at the gym, but she doesn't. Instead, her eyes peer over at the front entrance as if she can't wait for him to walk through the door.

Luck is on her side as there's a loud knock on the door. "You need anything?" I ask Winnie as I stand from my seat on the couch.

"No, I'm good, thanks."

"We'll be in the kitchen," I say, passing by her to answer the door.

"Hey, man," I greet Chase.

"Hey, is that Gabby's car in the driveway?"

"Yep."

"Gabby!" he calls out, already en route to the living room. "You have to stop stalking me. It's getting embarrassing."

Gabby's face turns red. "Waste of sperm," she mutters, shaking her head.

"You," I point to Chase, "kitchen." I push on his shoulder to get him moving. "Ease up on her, man," I say once we're out of earshot.

"What? It's Gabby. It's what we do."

"Maybe that's what you used to do. It's been months since you've seen her."

"I know. I've missed it." He grins.

There's no point in trying to reason with him. Instead, we make our plates and sit at the island. He fills me in on what's going on at the gym, and the new location. I was worried that stepping back like I have would get to me, but it's nice to have the break. If I had the choice, I'd choose more time with Winnie any day of the week. For the first time in ages, I feel like we've got this worked out, and everything is going to be okay.

CHAPTER 10

Winnie

"Is there a reason you keep glancing over your shoulder toward the kitchen?" I ask, unable to hide the smile on my face. She's only looked his way ten times in the last ten minutes.

"I'm not," Gabby argues fruitlessly. It's written all over her face.

"Liar."

My sister rolls her eyes. "He's just so frustrating. I wish he wasn't so good-looking. I can deal with cocky and arrogant, but the good-looking part? That's maddening. Jerks shouldn't be allowed to be hot too."

I set my empty plate on the table, surprised I ate it all so quickly. I guess I was hungrier than anticipated. "He's not really a jerk," I say, taking a drink of my yummy chocolate milk.

Again, my sister rolls her eyes. "Of course he is. He snapped my bra the last time I saw him! In the middle of the supermarket!" she bellows loudly, evoking two chuckles from the kitchen.

"I didn't realize you could snap a training bra like that!" Chase hollers from the other room.

"See? Jerk!" she yells boisterously. "I stopped wearing a training bra in sixth grade," Gabby says a little quieter, looking directly at me. Of course, because her eyes are on me, she doesn't see Harrison's best friend enter the room.

Chase crouches down behind where Gabby sits. "You're gonna have to whip them out so I can see, sugarplum. It's for research purposes."

Gabby glares icicles over her shoulder. "Your mama should have swallowed and saved us all the pain and suffering."

I burst out laughing, quickly followed by Chase. He just throws a wink and a grin at my sister and strolls back into the kitchen. Gathering up my dirty dishes, I follow in his wake, not wanting to interrupt but curious as to what they're discussing.

"You're right," Harrison says when his friend takes the seat across the table. "Everything is right on track."

I try to steal a peek at the papers he's reading, but after catching a glimpse of him wearing those dark readers, my focus is pulled elsewhere. He's wearing worn light-colored jeans that mold perfectly to his thighs, an old college T-shirt, and his feet are bare. How is it that a man can take off his shoes and socks and still be completely mouthwateringly sexy?

When my eyes finally meet his, there are small laugh lines crinkling around his big brown eyes, holding humor. The corner of his lip turns upward in that totally kissable way, and he doesn't call me on my obvious gawking. Thank God. How embarrassing to be caught staring at your ex-husband while he's working with his best friend, but in my defense, he's totally yummy and completely doable.

It must be the pregnancy hormones.

"How's it going?" I ask casually, averting my eyes.

Harrison's hand snakes out and grabs me. He gives me a gentle tug, causing me to stumble onto his lap. Instantly, I'm assaulted with the scent of his body wash. It's been so long since I've been this overcome by his smell that it brings tears to my eyes. It's so familiar, yet so foreign at the same time.

Rapidly blinking them away, I keep quiet as Chase continues. "The contractor is two days ahead of schedule and thinks he'll be done soon on the west property. It'll be complete and ready to open before the south site."

"That's awesome. How about the plumbers?" Harrison asks, keeping his hand on my hip. I try to get up, but he just tightens his hold. When I glance his way, he holds me close and places a kiss on the side of my brow.

Since I'm apparently not going anywhere, I listen as they go through papers, discussing the upcoming opening of his new gym. When we were married, Harrison had purchased a large abandoned building two towns to the west with the intent of converting it into a new gym. Many of their residents drive to Fair Lakes to work out. They had a gym, but it was small and outdated, and once Harrison's gym took off into the stratosphere, the small gym eventually closed down. Harrison saw the writing on the wall before it had actually closed the doors, however, noting the need in their community, which is why he's expanding. He also purchased a location to the south, which was in a little worse shape. Its remodel appears to be taking a little longer.

"We're on track." Harrison exhales loudly, relaxing back into the chair.

"We are. I'm headed there Thursday and Friday to meet the rep from Ultimate Fitness. He's going to help me with the layout of the rooms and get us a list of materials and equipment."

"Thanks for taking care of that for me," Harrison says, stacking the papers and placing them back in his folder.

"No problem. I only had to rearrange two clients," Chase says, moving his folder aside.

Something in the way he says that draws my attention. I glance at Harrison, narrowing my eyes as I wait him out. Finally, he gives me the answer to my unspoken question. "I was supposed to go, but I'm not leaving you. So Chase is going in my place."

"What? No, Harrison. You can't skip appointments just to babysit me," I argue. "Besides, I'll be back to work, so there's no reason for you to not go."

He clears his throat, takes off his glasses, and gives me a pointed look. "You were just in a major car accident, Winnie. I'm not leaving town right now in case you need me."

"First off, I'm more than capable of taking care of myself. And you're like thirty minutes away," I reason. "If I need you, I'll call."

"I'm not going out of town right now, Winnie. End of story," he maintains, his eyes boring into me with intensity and authority.

"I'm pregnant, Harrison, not helpless."

A loud gasp sounds across the table. My eyes fly to Chase's as he gapes at us with question. I quickly look back at Harrison, his body tense beneath mine, and confirm my suspicions. "You hadn't told him?" I whisper.

"We decided not to tell anyone yet," he replies quietly. True, we did, but I never thought he wouldn't tell Chase. They tell each other everything, as friends do.

"You're knocked up?" he asks, his eyes wide with shock.

Before I can answer, Harrison confirms. "She is." There's so much excitement in his voice as he pulls me against him, hugging me into his body.

"How the hell did this happen?" Chase asks, dumbfounded at this little twist in the story. Our rather *unusual* story.

"Well, you see, Chase, when two people love each other, they make a baby. First, they both get completely naked," Gabby says in a gentle voice as she enters the room, as if she were talking to a young child. "When a man gets excited to make a baby, his penis gets hard," she adds, taking her finger and sticking it up in the air.

"My penis is hard," Chase mumbles, his eyes laced with humor and mischief and so completely focused on my sister.

"Oh, well, then this is you," she states, putting her finger down and sticking up her pinky.

Chase barks out a laugh. "Oh, young Gabby, how I've missed you," Chase says with a rueful shake of his head.

My sister smiles sweetly. "I've missed you too, Chase. But at this range, I'm sure to hit my target."

The look on Chase's face is priceless. It's part shock, part admiration, and maybe even a little part turned on. I don't want to think about the latter, though.

"What's this?" Gabby asks, picking up a manila folder from the table.

"That's a handful of resumes that Chase got from an employment agency," Harrison replies, slowly moving his hand up my hip and bringing it around to rest on my belly.

"Resumes?" I ask, suddenly feeling a little breathless. I should probably move from his lap, but I can't seem to find the strength or the gumption to make my legs work.

"Yeah, I'm hiring an admin assistant. We've got the front desk covered, but I want some help in back. Filing, payroll, and some of the daily duties for both locations. I have a baby on the way, and want to be as much a part of it as possible," he says, flexing his hand over my abdomen and pulling me back into his chest. The hug is warm and comforting, even though I'm pressed against a wall of hard muscle.

"What about Chase?" I ask, glancing over to his best friend. *Our* best friend. For almost all my adult life, Chase has been there, a part of it. When I started dating Harrison, I inherited Chase too. I didn't realize how much I've missed him until this moment. Until he's back here, laughing and carrying on with the rest of us. It goes to prove how hard divorce is. You not only lose your spouse, but everyone they're connected with as well.

"You okay?" Harrison asks, placing his finger under my chin and turning my face.

I can't answer without risking tears, so I just nod and swallow the emotions. I can tell he doesn't buy it. This man knows me, probably better than I know myself. "I've just missed this," I finally whisper, hopefully low enough that no one else but Harrison hears.

He seems to understand right away and gives me a small smile. "You're not the only one," he whispers back, kissing my cheek and moving my head to rest on his shoulder.

"To answer your question, I'm not going anywhere. I'm still manager, but my focus for a while is going to be the new locations. I'll drive back and forth, but I'll be spending most of my time in Dalton. It's only a thirty-minute drive. Plus, I'll have some of my clients to take care of here," Chase adds, referring to the Fair Lakes location of All Fit. "And when the Lakeview location is further along, I'll do what I have to there too," he adds, referring to the location to the south.

"I know her," Gabby says, pulling a resume out of the pile and sliding it over to Harrison. I glance down and see the name Gina Laughlin. While it sounds vaguely familiar, nothing immediately jumps out at me. Chase reaches over and grabs the paper, glancing at it, as Gabby continues. "We went to college together. You remember, right, Gwen? She came home one Thanksgiving with me when her parents were off on some trip."

My mind digs for the memory and comes up with a shorter brunette with a pleasant smile and big dark eyes. "I think so. She stayed the holiday weekend with you at Mom and Dad's, right? Short dark hair and brown eyes?"

"Yep, that was her. I've only seen her once or twice since college. Our jobs just took us in different directions, but I remember she was working for her dad. I think he owned a gym, actually," she says, grabbing the resume from Chase's hands and giving it a quick glance. "Yep, Al's Gym in Dalton."

"That's the one that closed down when we started our plans for the expansion," Chase confirms, leaning toward my sister and glancing at the paper over her shoulder.

She stills just as he rests his chin on her shoulder. "Did you just sniff me?"

"You smell like fruit pie," he whispers back, taking another big whiff of my sister's neck.

Gabby rolls her eyes, places her hand on his forehead, and pushes. Hard. Chase flies back, but stays in his seat, laughing at the rise he got from my sister.

"Are you two done?" Harrison asks, unable to mask the humor in his voice.

"Nope, never. I'll torture her until the day I die," Chase states, a proud smile on his face.

"That'll be a lot sooner than expected if you keep that shit up," Gabby points out, giving him a glare. Chase winks at her, but lets her finish reviewing the resume. "I think she'd be a great candidate."

"I agree. She has experience, and it's in the same field. And it doesn't look like she's found a job yet, so she could be available to start right away," Harrison adds, adjusting me on his leg. When he does, my rear comes in contact with his erection. His very large, very hard erection. My entire body tightens, and I can tell the moment he notices. "See what you still do to me?" he whispers in my ear, his warm breath sending my body into hypersensitive overdrive. Suddenly, I can feel everything. His hands, his leg, his erection, and it's all too much. Too much want, too much desire, too much confusion, because even though we've discussed trying again, at a much slower pace, I can't deny the way my body reacts to him. How it has always reacted to him.

I stand up quickly; he lets me go this time. Without trying to draw attention to myself, I go to the cabinet and retrieve a glass, filling it with water. After a long drink, I turn back to the table and find his eyes on me. Instead of discussing Gina and the rest of the applicants, he's watching me with so much need and desire that my knees almost buckle right then and there.

The truth is, I'm not sure how much longer I can deny the way I feel for him. As confusing as this is, I just want to go back to the way things were. Back when love was easy and everything was right in the world. Now, everything is hard and confusing, and I realize just how weak I am when it comes to Harrison Drake. He's always been my biggest weakness. He's practically moving in with me, fighting to get his life and family back.

Me.

He's fighting for me.

And I don't want to fight him anymore.

I don't want to deny it.

I want that life too.

With him.

Us.

I just pray we don't destroy us in the process.

It's Friday and my afternoon class all works to finish their Letter X worksheet, outlining the letter and writing it repeatedly on the lines provided, as well as coloring the large X-ray picture. I continue to watch, helping my little students make sure they properly hold the pencil and execute the letter correctly. We've been working hard on keeping the letters within their respective lines, but sometimes it's fruitless when it comes to four-year-olds.

A knock sounds at my door, pulling my attention away from Riley and her super big X's that spill off the pages. When I glance up, I see our school receptionist, Miss Courtney, carrying a big bouquet of flowers and a bright smile. "These just arrived for you, Mrs. Drake," she says proudly as she enters my classroom and sets them on my small desk.

"Oh, uh, thank you," I reply, praying she doesn't question the flowers.

I know how it looks. Recently divorced woman receives flowers at her job. She must be seeing someone new, right? Little do they know these aren't from someone new. I already know who they're from. He was always sending me flowers for my birthday, our anniversary, or just because, especially in the beginning. When I landed my first teaching job, he sent me flowers every Monday for the entire year, even though we really couldn't afford it. They were smaller bouquets than this one, but the message and meaning were always the same.

"Are you seeing someone new?" Courtney asks, a beaming smile on her face.

Yep, called it.

"Oh, no no. I'm sure these are from my... parents," I reply, taking the card and sticking it into my pocket. I know the moment I lift the flap her eyes will be peeking over my shoulder in anticipation.

"Your parents sent you red and white roses with gorgeous orange lilies?" Courtney rolls her eyes. "Okay, fine, keep your secret, but just know that this is a small town. We'll find out who he is soon enough," she replies with an ornery grin before heading out of my classroom, closing the door as she goes.

My stomach rolls and I can't be completely sure it's from the pregnancy. The truth is this is a small town and it won't be long before everyone knows. Knows about Harrison. Knows about the baby. Knows that he's been living in my spare bedroom since the weekend and is showing no signs of leaving. Ever.

I fight the urge to pull the card from my pocket and return to my kids. Most of them have lost focus on their worksheet and are either talking or dancing in their chair. It takes me a few minutes, but I regain control of my class following our interruption, and they're all finishing up their worksheets.

"Mrs. Drake, who are those from?" one of my students, Kimber, asks.

"A friend," I reply with a smile.

"Is your friend my daddy? He sends flowers to my mommy," she adds, handing in her finished worksheet.

"No, not from your daddy. I'm happy that your daddy sends your mommy flowers, though. I bet that really brightens her day."

Kimber nods frantically. "She brings them home and puts them on the table. Then Daddy kisses her when he comes home," she tells me, giggling.

"Kisses are gross!" Thomas declares as he sets his sheet in the tray. "Girls have cooties!"

"We do not," Kimber argues, placing her hands on her hips and stomping her foot.

I fight the smile that threatens to spread across my face. "No one has cooties," I tell them gently. "Why don't you both go over to the reading rug and pick out a book. As soon as everyone is done, we'll have a snack and take our restroom break."

The kids scurry off, each picking a book to look at while they wait for their classmates. Before long, the entire group has completed their worksheet and is sitting on the rug. I get today's snack ready, setting the cheese and crackers at each chair, as well as a carton of milk. I give them my full attention, but it's hard. The small envelope and card are practically burning a hole in my pocket. I'm dying to know what he wrote, but I won't give in until my students are safely tucked away in their parents' vehicles and on their way home.

Finally, at 3:10 p.m., the bell rings. I make sure all of today's work is in their take-home folders and placed in their book bags. When the final child is released to their ride, then and only then do I finally give in to the excitement. With my classroom door firmly shut, I head over to my desk, taking my first real opportunity to smell the gorgeous blooms that were delivered this afternoon. Roses and lilies—two of my favorites, and he knows it. A smile breaks out on my lips as I pull the card from my pocket and take the seat behind my desk.

My dearest Winnie,
I hope your day was as amazing as you.
Your presence is requested at The Corner Grill.
Six o'clock.
Date night with my two favorite people in the whole world.
You and Peanut.

Until I see you, my love.
H

I can't help but notice he's already referring to our unborn child as a person. *Our* little person. The one we created together. Yeah, the circumstances of the conception are a bit scandalous for this small town, but it doesn't matter. Nothing matters. Just us.

Our little family.

I shove the card into my desk drawer and gather up my belongings, all while wearing a smile on my face. The Corner Grill has always been a favorite of mine. That's something he'd remember too. I have to admit, Harrison is doing quite well on this whole "dating" thing. My favorite flowers, and now my favorite restaurant.

It's hard to juggle my bag and the vase of flowers, but I manage and slip out the side door of the school, effectively avoiding any of the other teachers at our small preschool through fifth-grade school. Lady luck must be on my side as I belt in the vase to the passenger seat of my newly acquired rental car, hop behind the wheel, and pull out of our lot. Surely word has gotten around to my colleagues that I had a special delivery this afternoon. It was only a matter of time before everyone and their brother "dropped in" for a friendly Friday after-school chat.

Slowly, so that I don't spill the water, I make my way to my house, loving the fragrant scent of flowers that fill the car. You couldn't scrape my smile off my face with a putty knife. When I pull into the driveway, I notice Harrison's truck is gone. Since I went back to work Wednesday, he did as well, but he's almost always arriving home at the same time I have been.

I park in my spot and climb out. I slip around and unlock the back door of the house, leaving it open to let the spring breeze in, and head back out to retrieve the vase. My nose instantly drops down as I inhale such a wonderful scent. Oh, yes, he definitely earned a few bonus points for this one. They display beautifully in the center of the table, especially when the sunlight hits the pink glass.

Heading back to my bedroom, I think about tonight. What does my ex-husband have planned? Is it just dinner or will there be something afterward?

And then my mind goes to *afterward*.

Our relationship hasn't progressed past a few stolen pecks on the cheek or brushes across my lips. He's held my hand and has welcomed me into his arms for snuggling during a movie last night, but that's it. I know he still wants me—the proof was plastered on my leg earlier in the week—but he hasn't acted on anything or led me to believe *more* is coming soon.

Do I want more?

I'm pretty sure that answer is yes, but how soon, and will I regret it when it happens?

I never really regretted it when we fell into bed mere minutes after our divorce was final, but how can I regret something that created something so wonderful? Even after we got past the awkward stage and he left, I never felt an ounce of guilt or remorse. Instead, I felt a slight bit of comfort and a little bit of closure.

Of course, all that has been thrown out the window now, hasn't it?

After making sure the door is locked, I head to my bedroom, strip off my work clothes, and move to the bathroom. The garden tub is calling me, and I'm fortunate to have plenty of time to get ready for the evening. The room starts to fill with the calming scent of lavender as I drop a bath bomb in and grab a fresh razor. Making sure my hair is up and won't get wet, I slowly slide into the warm water, grateful for this extra time. I can't stay in long, knowing I had to give up hot baths when I became pregnant, so I make sure the water is at a slightly cooler temperature than normal. Just enough that I'm still able to relax. It's heaven.

Before I finish my bath, I take a few minutes to shave my legs, armpits, and other lady bits, as well as run my loofah and body wash over every square inch of my body. When I deem myself finished, I carefully step out, mindful of the baby nestled in my lower abdomen. After smearing lotion everywhere, I head to the closet for tonight's outfit. What exactly does one wear on a date with her ex-husband, with whom she happens to be having a child with?

Yeah, I don't know either.

I settle on a pair of fitted jeans, wedge heels, and a blue flowy top. It has short sleeves, so I make sure to grab a black sweater too. By the time I'm completely ready, the alarm clock on my nightstand says 5:45. I also notice I haven't heard Harrison come home. After securing my watch and throwing in the stud diamonds he bought me for our first anniversary, I head off in search of my date.

His room is empty.

Panic starts to set in.

Did he change his mind?

Move out without letting me know?

But when I spy his deodorant and aftershave sitting on top of the spare dresser, I know that he's still here. Well, maybe not *here* here, but living here. Staying here. Whatever.

When the clock hits 5:50, I realize I have a choice. I can wait here for him, assuming he's coming to pick me up, or I can head out and meet him at the restaurant. His card didn't indicate how I was getting to The Corner Grill, just that it starts at six. That must mean I'm supposed to meet him there.

Grabbing my purse and sweater, I lock up the house, head to my rental car, and back out of my driveway. It's only a few minutes to the restaurant, so I arrive with just enough time to get inside before the stroke of six. With my shoulders square and a flutter of nerves tickling my stomach, I head inside.

To the man in the corner booth.

To our first official date.

I can't wait.

CHAPTER 11

Harrison

I arrived early to ensure we could get a booth with privacy. This one in the corner is exactly that. I have a clear view of the door, and yet still tucked away in the back corner. Speaking of the door, I've had my eyes glued to it for the last fifteen minutes. Glancing at the clock, I see it's six o'clock exactly. Wiping my sweaty palms on my jeans, my nerves kick in. What if she doesn't show? Damn it, I knew I should have gone to the house and picked her up. I'm just about ready to reach for my phone to call her like the crazy stalker ex-husband that I'm becoming. What if she's sick, what if something happened to the baby? I'm making myself sick with worry when the door opens and she walks in.

Winnie.

My eyes drink her in, taking notice of her fitted jeans, and the blue top that makes her tits look incredible. Not that they're not already in a league of their own. I've read that with pregnancy, they're going to get bigger. I bite back a groan just thinking about it.

Shaking out of my thoughts, I stand to greet her before my cock makes it so it's impossible to do so.

"You look beautiful," I say, leaning in to place a kiss on her cheek. "How are you feeling?" I ask, my hand resting on her still flat belly.

"It was a good day. A bout of nausea, but not enough to ruin my day or anything." She slides into the booth as I take my seat across from her.

"Good."

"Thank you for the flowers."

"You're welcome," I say awkwardly. I don't know why I'm so damn nervous. This is Winnie, my Winnie. Shaking off my nerves, I forge ahead. "I ordered you water. I wasn't sure what sounded good to you, and I know you mentioned limiting caffeine because of the baby."

"Water is perfect. Although, I might order a chocolate milk. You think they have that here?"

"They do, I asked our server. I just didn't want the milk sitting and waiting for you."

"Look at you," she smiles brightly, "looking ahead."

"I've been doing that a lot lately, Winnie. So much, in fact, that I feel like I'm living in the future. In our future."

"Harrison." She whispers my name softly.

"We can do this," I assure her. "I know we can." Reaching across the table, I place my hand over hers. "I never once stopped loving you. We shouldn't be here. Divorced." I shake my head, disgusted with what I've let us become.

"I miss you," she confesses. "I miss us."

"Are you ready to order?" our waitress asks.

I motion for Winnie to order and she rattles off a burger, fries, and chocolate milk. "I'll have the same, but sweet tea for me," I say, handing her our menus. "I could have ordered for you." I chuckle. "You always get the same thing."

"Why mess with a good thing. Their burgers are so good." She moans.

"They are." I reach under the table and adjust my dick. I can't even listen to her talk about food and not get turned on. "So," I say, changing the subject. "When should we tell our parents?"

"I don't know. I was kind of wanting to wait until we reached the twelve-week mark."

I nod. "You think Gabby and Chase will keep it under wraps until then?"

"I do. They know the position we're in."

"We did nothing wrong."

"No, I know that. It's just... awkward. I'm pregnant with my ex-husband's baby. My ex-husband of only a matter of weeks."

"Does that bother you? Are you... ashamed?"

"No," she rushes to say. "I just want us to enjoy this a little longer without judgment or expectations."

I can understand that. "Okay, you tell me when you're ready."

"Harrison?" a female voice says from beside me.

Turning, I see a blonde. I can't remember her name for the life of me. I know I worked with her a few times at the gym. She was a little too handsy, so I passed her off to Chase who was all too willing to take her off my hands.

"I haven't seen you at the gym," she says, her voice high and whiney. It grates on my nerves.

"I've been busy," I tell her. I'm short with her, but it pisses me off that she's interrupting our dinner to talk shop. I'm not even her trainer.

"Chase is great and all, but I was hoping that you could start training me again too. Maybe even the three of us?" she says, licking her lips.

"I don't do much training these days. Have you met my wife?" I motion to Winnie sitting across from me. "Gwen, this is... I'm sorry I seem to have forgotten your name," I say as polite as I can, but still getting my point across. It's an asshole move, but this chick deserves it. She's being rude as hell. A simple wave or hello is okay, but she's clearly butting in on purpose. I don't like it.

"Nice to meet you..." Winnie pauses, waiting for the blonde to fill us both in.

"Michelle," she spits out.

"Nice to meet you, Michelle," Winnie says politely.

"I thought you were divorced?" she asks me.

"Nope." I hate that she's right, which only serves to piss me off even more.

"Since when?"

"Since the day I married the beautiful woman sitting across from me," I say, looking into Winnie's green eyes.

"I guess I'll see you around, Harrison," Michelle says, in a way that lets you know she has no intentions of backing down.

"I own the gym, so I'm sure that you will. However, let me make something clear with you, Michelle. I'm happily married and plan to stay that way. I would hate to have to pull your membership." Her eyes flare and I can tell she's now good and pissed too. Good. I couldn't care less if she stops coming to the gym. I won't stand for her trying to come between me and my wife.

"You wouldn't."

"That's up to you. On a professional level, we're good. You disrespect my wife again, in any way, you're gone."

"That's no way to run a business." She places her hands on her hips as if she's edging for a fight.

"I couldn't care less what you think or anyone else for that matter. My wife, that's who I care about. So watch yourself, Michelle."

"Whatever." She tosses her long blonde hair over her shoulder and storms off.

"That was... unexpected."

"Uncalled for is more like it."

"You were kind of rude."

"Good. That's exactly what I was going for."

She studies me. Our food is dropped off before she says anything. "That's different."

"I've tried life without you. It's not something I ever want to experience again. I'm not going to let the Michelles of the world be the reason."

"I can see right through her, and I know you, Harrison. Cheating was never the issue."

"Good. I'm glad. Regardless, I have zero patience for her, or anyone like her. You're sitting across from me. She acted like you weren't even here."

"But I am," she says soothingly.

"Damn right, you are. I intend to do whatever it takes to make sure that never changes."

"Harrison."

"Yeah?" Her green eyes are bright even in the dim light of this corner booth.

"I'm not going anywhere."

Four words. Four words that seem to ease my soul and lift the bricks off my shoulders. We've only just started this dating thing, but I have her assurance that she's with me in this. That's more than I could have hoped for this soon. I'll take it.

"I love you, Winnie. I love our baby, and if it takes being rude to any woman who thinks that she can come between us to prove that, I'm all over it."

She laughs. "Eat your burger." She reaches across the table and steals a fry, even though she has a plate full of her own. I put my arm around my plate, protecting my food, and she laughs even louder, the sound surrounding me.

It's beautiful.

Musical.

"I am eating for two," she teases.

"In that case..." I act like I'm going to slide my plate to her, and she holds up her hands to stop me.

"Tell me what's going on at the gym. Have you hired an admin assistant yet?"

I nod, holding up a finger letting her know I need to finish chewing before I can answer. "Yes. Chase and I interviewed the woman Gabby knows. We offered her the job earlier today. Just waiting to hear back."

"Good. It sounds like she'll be a good fit."

"Yeah, seems like she has the industry knowledge." I grab a fry and smother it in ketchup. "How about you? Any interesting stories from your kids?" I ask, popping the fry into my mouth.

"Every day. Today, it was show-and-tell. Jess brought her clogging shoes and showed us how she's learning to clog. She's just learning, so she's basically just bouncing around making noises with her shoes. The class all clapped for her and cheered her on. Anyway, when she was seated, Joey raised his hand. He wasn't on the list for show-and-tell, but I called him up to the front of the class. When I asked him what his talent was, he said: "I can clog too." I was intrigued so I asked him to show the class even without his shoes. He said, 'Mrs. Drake, I clog toilets.' He fell into a fit of giggles as did the rest of the class."

"Where do these kids come up with these things? I don't know how you keep a straight face."

"It's hard at times. Luckily on days like today, they're too busy laughing. I have time to compose myself before getting them in order."

"I can't wait." I place my crumpled napkin on my plate. "I can't wait for our baby to get here, and witness all the crazy things he or she says and does. I mean, Chase and Gabby alone are bad influences enough. Not to mention, other kids," I say jokingly.

"Maybe we should only allow them supervised visits?" she suggests.

"You might be onto something."

A moment later our waitress appears. "Can I offer you any dessert?"

"Winnie?"

"I'm stuffed. Thank you." She pushes her plate away with still over half of her fries remaining.

"Can I get you a box?"

"No, thank you."

"Just the check, please," I tell her. I pay the bill, and with my hand on the small of Winnie's back, I lead her out of the restaurant. "You feel like taking a drive? We can come back and pick up your car." Again, I'm kicking myself in the ass for not going and picking her up. I guess I just assumed since we're both going to the same place at the end of the night, it wouldn't matter. Regardless that we're sleeping under the same roof, I intend to give her a goodnight kiss.

"Where are we headed?" she asks once we're in my truck and on the road.

"I have somewhere I want to take you."

"So you're not going to even give me a hint?"

"Nope."

"Fine, but I get to control the radio." She leans forward and messes with the dial until an old Daughtry tune comes on. "I love this song. It's been forever since I've heard it."

Keeping my eyes on the road, I reach over and tangle her fingers with mine, resting our combined hands on her thigh. The drive is quiet. We're both lost in our own thoughts, letting the radio fill the silence. It's comfortable and normal, or what used to be our normal. We're working our way back there.

"Where are you taking me?" she asks when we pass the corporation limits to the town next to ours.

"I thought you liked surprises?"

"I do, but I want to know more." I hear the excitement in her voice.

"Where do you think I'm taking you?"

"I don't know. There are too many possibilities."

"Well, I have two places. This is the first," I say, pulling into the parking lot of a small independent baby boutique. "I know we're keeping it to ourselves, well, other than Chase and Gabby, but it never hurts to look, right? I mean, we're going to need lots of stuff for Peanut."

"Harrison." She squeezes my hand.

I turn off the truck and chance a look at her. She has tears in her eyes. "Hey, I thought you'd like this. We don't have to go in."

"Are you crazy?" She smiles. "Of course, we're going in." She leans over and kisses the corner of my mouth. "Thank you for this. It's sweet and thoughtful, and I'm so glad I'm not doing this alone."

"Never." My voice is firm. "You will never be alone in anything as long as I'm breathing." A tear slides down her cheek, and I catch it with my thumb. "Now, let's go take a look."

"Wow," she says breathily as soon as we enter the small store. "I don't even know where to start."

"Welcome to the Baby Boutique," an older lady greets us. "Is there something I can help you with?" she asks kindly.

"We're new at this," I tell her. "My wife and I are expecting our first."

"Oh." She claps her hands together. "How exciting. Don't worry, I'm here to help. I actually have a checklist of things for new parents. I've added to it over the years. But don't go buying it all up. You'll need to save some for the shower. The list contains a section for the big items most parents buy, and then the items you should register for. It's great to have in case you don't get something at your shower, you will know what you still need."

"That's... amazing. Thank you," Winnie tells her.

We follow her around the store as she points out things we'll need, and things that are not a necessity but nice to have. It's overwhelming, but I can't remember the last time I looked forward to something more. We're strolling down the aisle with clothes—tiny little items—and one amongst them all stands out to me. It's a bib that says: "*I love my daddy.*" It's green and yellow, so it should work no matter what we're having. I stand here, staring at it. I'm a daddy; it's surreal. Winnie stops next to me and follows my line of sight. Without saying a word, she grabs the bib and continues on down the aisle.

"Thank you so much, Judy," Winnie says as we make our way to the counter.

"You're welcome, dear. This is the list." She hands us a packet of stapled paper.

"Thank you. We'll get out of your hair. I just need to pay for this." Winnie sets the bib on the counter. I add the one I grabbed that matches it. Only this one says, *I love my mommy*.

"I thought we were waiting," she asks, unable to hide her grin.

"For what? It's yellow and green. Gender neutral." I grin back, proud of myself.

Her smile falters. "Is it too soon? We said we would wait. Now here we are buying bibs. What if something happens?" She whispers the last part.

My heart aches at the fear in her voice, and the thought of something happening to either of them. "Baby." I cup her cheek in my hands. "Nothing is going to happen, and in the event that it does, we'll have it for the next one."

"The next one?"

"This isn't a one-and-done thing, Winnie."

I turn my attention to Judy, who rattles off a total, and I insert my card into the machine. She bags up my purchase and we're on our way. We step outside onto the sidewalk and I clasp her hand. "I mean it, Winnie. I'm not here because you're pregnant. Sure, that might be what gave me an in. What gave me a chance to slither back into your life, but regardless of the baby you're carrying, I'm here. For this one, and the next one, and as many after that as you want."

"I love you, Harrison Drake." My heart flips over in my chest. After losing her, and never thinking I would hear those words again, every time it's as if it's the first time. They're words I will cherish always.

"That's good, baby." I lean in close. "Because you're stuck with me." I kiss her forehead. "Now," I say, pulling back. "Ready for our second stop?"

"Yes, but I'm not sure you could top this one."

"Oh, ye of little faith." I open the door for her.

It doesn't take us long to get to the next stop. It's just a couple of blocks down the street. "Is this where we're going?" she asks, hopeful, as I pull into the lot for the new bookstore.

"Yep. You said you've been wanting to go, right?"

"Yes, but I didn't expect you to take me."

"Why not?"

"You're not exactly a big fan of bookstores."

I shrug. "I'm a Winnie fan. Besides, I need a book myself."

"Oh, really? What book would that be? We've known each other for years and I've never seen you read a book."

"Well, maybe there was never anything important enough, or interesting enough to hold my attention. Besides, this is my second. I already read the first one, but this one is dad specific, so I'm going to read it too."

"Oh, I have to hear this. What book are you after?"

Pulling my phone out of my pocket, I go to my pictures. I took a screenshot of the book a "new dads" website said for me to get. I rattle off the title, *"The Expectant Father."*

I close out of my images and lock the screen before looking at her. Again, there are tears in her eyes. "Pregnancy hormones." She smiles. "No, that's not it. It's you. You're so confident about this. About us."

"Of course I am. But I'm also scared and nervous, and anxious that I'm going to be a bad father."

"Never," she says firmly. "We're in this together, right?"

"Yes." That's all the answer she needs. She collects her purse and climbs out of the truck, with me scrambling to do the same and catch up with her. "Don't get lost," I tease her as we enter the building.

"No promises."

"You got your phone, right?" I ask seriously. My girl loves books, so I might need it to find her in this place. It's a huge two-story facility. She waves over her shoulder, already heading off to explore. I ask for help, and I'm directed to the parenting books. I find the two that I had taken pictures of and then venture into the children's section. They have toys, books, and some clothes. I scan the books. I find one with a green monster on the front. *Because I'm Your Dad* is the title. I skim through it and it looks good to me. I add it to my pile and head off to find Winnie.

I make my way to the section that has romance hanging in big letters from the ceiling. If I know Winnie, this is where she'll be. I spot her at the end of the aisle, book in one hand, reading the back. A mesh bag over her shoulder already holds a few books. Her other hand is nestled over her still flat belly.

My heart trips over in my chest. I knew the minute I first laid eyes on her that she was special. I wanted her then, but now it's more than just want. It's as if I need her to breathe. My eyes drop to her belly. I bet she has no idea she's subconsciously protecting—cradling—our unborn child.

I step quietly down the aisle. She doesn't look up from the book she's pondering. Sliding my arms around her, I rest my hands over hers. Over our baby. "Marry me, Winnie."

"Oh my, Javier, what would Harrison think?"

"Harrison thinks you're pressing his buttons," I growl, kissing her neck.

She turns in my arms, green eyes smiling up at me. "I love you, Harrison Drake. There is no doubt in that. I still think we need some time."

"Time for what? We love each other. We've always loved each other. We shouldn't even be having this conversation. The divorce never should have happened."

"Just time. There have been a lot of changes, the divorce, the baby... all in a matter of a couple of months."

"I'm not going to stop asking," I promise her.

She nods. "I know. I just... want things to be settled a little more. Besides, I thought you were going to woo me." She grins.

"Baby, I have the rest of my life to woo you."

"Yeah?"

"Promise." I kiss her softly on the lips.

She steps out of my hold, effectively breaking the kiss. "You have what you came for?"

"Other than that smile on your face, yes." I point to my stack of books I set on top of the shelf before pulling her into my arms. "How about you?"

"Yes."

"Thank you for tonight," Winnie says a few hours later. We're sitting on the couch, her feet resting on my lap, a blanket thrown over her legs.

"I had a good time. I miss it... spending time with you."

"You see me every day," she reminds me.

"I do. It's not the same. Tonight was different. It was time carved out just for us."

"We used to do that all the time."

"I'm sorry." I've said it a million times and it never feels like enough.

"It's in the past."

"It's not. Not really, unless you've changed your mind?"

"Changed my mind about what?"

"Marrying me."

"Harrison." She sighs.

"Winnie."

She pulls her feet from my lap and the cover falls to the floor. I watch as she climbs to her knees and settles in close to me, resting her head on my shoulder. "I love you. That's never been an issue."

"What is the issue?"

"You're here because I'm pregnant."

"No. I'm here because you're my wife. I was a fool to let you go. Even before I found out about the baby, I was planning how to get you back. I missed you," I say, kissing the top of her head.

She sits up to look at me. She's close, so close I would just have to lean in the slightest bit to have my lips on hers. "I just don't want either of us to have any regrets."

"Too late." I cup her face in the palm of my hands. "I regret with every breath that I let you go."

"Me too." She leans in, her lips hovering over mine.

"Tell me not to kiss you right now."

"No," she whispers. "I can't do that."

I close the distance and press my lips to hers. She climbs onto my lap, straddling me. My hands find their way to her hips as she rocks back and forth. "Winnie," I growl.

"Hmmm?" she asks, kissing me, sliding her tongue past my lips, all while rocking her center against my straining cock.

"I want you," I mumble against her lips.

She pulls back, her green eyes dark with desire. "Then take me."

I react immediately. "Hold on tight." I stand, my hands clasping her thighs. Her legs wrap around my waist as I do so, and her arms lock around my neck. "Your room or mine?"

"Ours."

Leave it to Winnie to pick a time like this to extend me yet another olive branch. I don't know what she means by ours. Does that mean I get to lie next to her at night? Wake up with her in my arms in the morning? Was it just the heat of the moment? Whatever it is, we'll figure it out together.

Entering the bedroom that we shared, the one she still sleeps in, I set her on the bed. "I need you naked. Now."

She nods, pulling her shirt over her head and tossing it behind me. Next is her bra. "Harrison," she says.

"Yeah?" I say thickly, my eyes refusing to blink, not wanting to miss a second of this.

Of her.

"I need you naked. Now." She throws my words back at me.

"Right." I get to work stripping out of my clothes, taking a step back, allowing her room to stand and slide out of her jeans. She kicks them off and they go flying through the air. "I don't know where to start," I say huskily. Reaching out with both hands, I cup her breasts, testing their weight. It's been too long. The last time I was with her like this we were frantic. I didn't get to take my time and appreciate her. Not like I plan to tonight.

"I think we should start here." She wraps her hands around my cock.

"I want to take my time with you," I tell her, placing my hand over hers. My intention is to stop her mid-stroke, but it feels too damn good to stop her. Instead, I help her as a groan rumbles from deep in my throat.

"Can we save that for round two?" she asks.

"What do you want, Winnie?"

"You."

"You have me."

"I want you inside me. Now." She sits on the bed and moves back toward the headboard. She's a vision, lying there naked in the moonlight. "Harrison." She holds out her hand for me, and I take it, placing a kiss on the inside of her wrist.

Climbing onto the bed, I settle between her spread thighs, and she immediately wraps her legs around my waist. My hands are flat on the mattress, on either side of her head. I rotate my hips, teasing her.

"Two can play that game." She reaches between us and aligns my cock with her entrance.

"No games. Not with you." I push forward and am immediately surrounded by her warmth. "So good," I say, bending to kiss her lips.

"Y-Yes. There," she says, sliding her hands under my arms and gripping onto my back. "Don't stop, please," she begs. Her eyes are closed, and her head is tilted back.

I give her what she wants, setting a rhythm with every thrust. I can feel her body's reaction and know she's getting close, so I stop.

"What? No. Don't do that." She squeezes her legs tighter around me, trying to get me to move. I hold strong. Finally, her eyes open and she's staring up at me in confusion. "Why'd you stop?" she asks hesitantly.

"I want your eyes on me. When you come, I want you to know it's me."

"Who else would it be?" she says sassily.

Pulling out, I slide back in nice and slow. "Don't want you thinking about Javier," I tease, using the name she dropped earlier tonight.

"I have a secret," she confesses as I slowly thrust in and out, joining our bodies as one.

"Oh, yeah?"

"Mmm hmm." She lifts her hips. "I made him up."

"No!" I act appalled.

"True." She moans. "Story."

"I like stories. Want to hear one?"

"Now?" she asks, exasperated.

"Why not?" I thrust deep, and still.

"Harrison." My name is a plea from her lips.

"It's a good one."

"Fine. Just don't stop moving."

I grind my hips and bend my lips to her ear. "They lived happily ever after," I whisper, nipping her lobe.

"Who did?"

"We do." I don't wait for her reply as I unleash months of missing her. With every thrust, I think about the nights I spent alone, wondering what she was doing. I'll make damn sure that scenario never becomes my reality again.

"T-there," she mumbles, closing her eyes.

"Eyes on me, Winnie."

She forces them open. "You are the love of my life." My words are clipped as her walls squeeze my cock like a vise.

"Harrison," she calls out, and it fuels my orgasm. With one more deep thrust, I'm spilling inside her. I fall to my elbows on either side of her head, careful not to crush her. Her arms and legs are wrapped around me like she's afraid I might disappear.

"I liked your story," she whispers. "I love you, Harrison Drake."

"I love you too."

I don't ask her if I can stay. Instead, I clean us both up and climb back in bed beside her. She comes willingly when I open my arms for her. Her body relaxes against mine, and her breathing evens out.

"Yes," she mumbles.

"What's that?" Her only reply is a soft snore that she'll swear never happened. It's adorable, and completely Winnie. I'm looking forward to many more nights like this in our future.

CHAPTER 12

Winnie

The last several weeks have flown by. My days have been spent wrapping up the school year, which ended just last week, while my nights included plenty of time in the arms of the man I love. It's crazy to think we're here: pregnant, living together, and planning a future. Not that we made anything official, as far as the moving in part. Harrison just never left. He sort of transitioned from sleeping in the room across the hall to sharing my bed at night. Not that I'm complaining, though. Hell no. It feels good to have him there, his arms around me and his naked body pressed against mine.

Harrison continues to ask me to marry him—or remarry him—almost daily. I've come to expect it, actually, at some point during the day. Sometimes it's over breakfast or right before I drift off to sleep, while other times it's through text. No, he knows I won't actually agree to remarry him via text message, but he's making a point. He won't stop asking until I finally say yes.

Today is my twelve-week appointment. Last night, over chicken

Parmesan, we agreed to tell our families after today's appointment, so I'm doubly excited. Harrison is meeting me at the doctor's office since his workdays are busy with the gym. The west expansion in Dalton is almost ready, which means he'll work long hours as he helps train staff and gets everything ready for the grand opening. Chase has been a big help, doing a lot of the heavy lifting during the day, but now they're to the point where they need Harrison on-site more.

The crazy part is, now that the newer site of All Fit is nearly ready and the southern location in Lakeview is rolling full-steam ahead, another location to the north has presented itself as a golden opportunity. That's four total All Fits. When Chase brought it to Harrison last week, his first reaction was no. He didn't want to take on another project, especially with the baby on the way, even though that was his master plan all along. But we sat down and talked about the opportunity, which is a solid investment. It's another old gym. The guts are there, but it's in desperate need of rehab. I agree with Chase that it's a great fit for them. The problem is, with Chase running the Dalton location that opens soon and still overseeing the Lakeview site, that leaves Harrison to have to refurbish the new location in Porter. Sure, Chase will be available to help, but his focus will be on the other two sites. That means this one will be mostly Harrison.

"Gwendolyn." My name is called, pulling me from my thoughts.

I glance around, realizing Harrison isn't here yet. As I approach the door, I say, "I'm expecting someone."

The nurse isn't the same as the one from my first appointment, which leaves me feeling a little relieved. "Okay. As soon as they arrive, I'll escort them to your room."

"Thank you," I state, following her down the short hallway. We stop at the scale for a quick weight and blood pressure check, and then she hands me the small plastic cup. I know the drill at this point. Once I've peed in the cup and left my sample, I make my way back to my room, where I find Harrison waiting.

"Sorry I'm late," he apologizes quickly, pulling me into his arms and kissing my forehead.

"It's okay. You're here now," I remind him, reveling in the feel of his arms and scent surrounding me.

"My conference call went longer than expected, and Gina is still learning the ropes. I told her to interrupt when it was time for me to leave, but she didn't."

"I'm sure it's difficult for her to know when to interrupt and when not to," I tell him, pulling myself from his arms and taking a seat on the table.

"I get it," he starts, running his hand through his hair. "But I told her to interrupt me. Anything to do with you comes first."

Even though it makes me smile on the inside, I don't let it spread across my lips. "I get that, Harrison, but when you're there, you have to focus on work. You have a lot to do now that you're purchasing that fourth location," I remind him.

His eyes bore into me with that same focus and determination that I've always loved and admired. "You. Come. First."

My heart skips around in my chest, the same way it always has when he's demonstrating his possessive side. Harrison has always let me be my own person, but he's not afraid to show me (or in this case, tell me) that I come above everything else. Well, except for when I didn't, but we're not going there, not reliving the mistakes we made the first time around. Then my mind flits to the fact that I always, and I do mean always, *come* first, if you know what I mean. Sometimes more than once. I can feel the flush spreading up my neck and burning my cheeks.

He seems to notice immediately, his laser-sharp focus drinking me in and reading my dirty thoughts. The corner of his lip turns upward as he slowly moves closer, never taking his eyes off mine. That warm blush turns into a full-fledged inferno as blood and heat roars through my veins. "Care to share what has you all *flushed*?" he whispers, his larger body caging me to the table.

"I'd rather not," I whisper, in a voice that barely sounds like my own.

"Hmmm," he hums, sliding his nose against my jawline. "I guess after we leave here, you'll just have to show me."

My body screams in agreement. Yes, that! I want to show him. So bad.

Before I can say anything though, a knock sounds at the door. Harrison doesn't move right away, so when Dr. Taylor steps into the room, a coy smile on her face, my heated blush quickly transforms from need to embarrassment. I feel like a teenager who was just busted by her parents sneaking a boy out of her room.

"Well, good afternoon, Gwen. Harrison," Dr. Taylor says, the smile evident in her voice.

"Hi," I squeak over my very dry throat.

"Dr. Taylor," Harrison adds, in a voice that does crazy things to my panties. With a quick kiss to my forehead, he finally pulls back and takes the empty seat across the room.

"How have you been feeling this month?" she asks, washing her hands at the small sink.

"Well, actually," I verify.

"No more spotting?" She glances over her shoulder for confirmation.

Shaking my head, I reply, "None."

"And the morning sickness?" she inquires, writing a few notes down on my chart.

"Completely gone. It was like as soon as I hit twelve weeks on Tuesday, it just stopped."

"I'm happy to hear that," she adds, making a few more notes. "It looks like your urine came back clean for sugars and your blood pressure is normal. Everything is looking good." She sets down my chart and opens a drawer. She pulls out a tape measure and a small handheld Doppler instrument, and approaches the table. "The good news is that we shouldn't have a problem picking up the baby's heartbeat today on the Doppler. Go ahead and lie back," she instructs, adjusting the small pillow at my head.

I lie completely still as Dr. Taylor pulls up my shirt and exposes my abdomen. I feel Harrison's presence beside me as the doctor unsnaps my pants, places a paper towel at the opening, and gently pulls them down. She takes a few quick measurements with the tape measure before setting it aside and reaching for the small bottle on the counter. With a small dollop of warm goo, she moves the Doppler over my lower stomach, adjusting and turning it as she goes. It tickles a little, but my concentration is completely on the noise. It sounds like an old movie, something from a reel, until suddenly, a loud gallop fills the room. It's a little fuzzy, but there's no mistaking what it is: a heartbeat.

Peanut's heartbeat.

My eyes instantly fill, burning with unshed tears, as a hand grabs mine. I turn and take in the look of wonderment on Harrison's face. His eyes are trained on mine as the sweetest sound fills the room. He's holding something in his hand, and I realize it's his phone. He's recording the heartbeat, a small smile playing on his lips.

The rest of the appointment flies by. Dr. Taylor orders lab work to be completed before my next appointment in four weeks, gives us the opportunity to ask questions, and sends us on our way. As I approach the reception counter to check out, the flirty nurse from my first appointment is standing there, talking to the receptionist. "Oh, hey, Harrison!" she coos, her eyes lighting up as she catches a glance at the man at my side.

"Hello," he says politely, but doesn't embellish his greeting. His hand at my elbow tenses just a little, a sign that he's uncomfortable.

"I've already got results from my first month," she tells Harrison, ignoring me completely. The receptionist takes my folder and starts to make my next appointment. However, my focus is torn between listening to her offer me appointment times and eavesdropping on Miss Flirts A Lot. "...I saw you the other day, but you were so busy. I didn't want to interrupt."

"Yes, I've been extremely busy lately," Harrison comments as the receptionist hands me my reminder card. "And I'm happy you're seeing results. Keep up the good work, and have a good day," he adds, pulling me from the office and out to the sidewalk.

"Everything okay?" I ask as he walks me to my car.

His reply is immediate. "Yeah. Perfect." The tension in his shoulders says otherwise.

When we reach my car, I turn to face him. "Are you sure?"

Harrison takes a deep breath. "I just... I guess I don't want you to worry about Clara. I don't want anyone like her to come between us."

I gaze up at my husband—err, ex-husband—and notice the worry lines around his gorgeous eyes. "Clara? Is that the nurse's name?"

"I've seen her a few times at the gym. She's working with Ray in the evenings, but she comes in sometimes on her lunch breaks. I only know her name because I know *everyone's* name who comes into my gym. She's one of those flirty women, but that's it, Winnie. You have nothing to worry about."

Without giving it a thought, I reach up and run my thumb over his frown. "I know, Harrison."

"It's just that there's always someone there, someone a little too flirty or handsy. I might notice because, hell, I'm a guy, but I've never acted on it. I've never wanted anyone. Only you."

A smile spreads across my face. "Have you seen you? You're gorgeous. Stunning, actually. I've witnessed grown women losing their minds when they're around you. But do you know what? While it might bother me that someone has the balls big enough to openly flirt with you in my presence, I knew in my heart that it was just that: a flirt. I knew, at the end of the day, you were coming home to me. Not them. Me. So, please don't worry about me. I know your job and I know some of the women you train, but I also know you would have never stepped outside of our marriage."

He visibly relaxes as he reaches for my side and pulls me into his hard chest. "That includes now."

My hands slide up his back as I rest my cheek against his pec. "We're not married now," I remind him.

"Maybe not on paper, but we'll remedy that. Soon. As soon as you agree to marry me again." I smile, inhaling the intoxicating mixture of his body wash and the detergent in his shirt. "You've always been my wife, Winnie," he whispers, tightening his arms as if I might somehow slip away. "You always will be, even if you never say the word."

My heart pounds in my chest with the intensity of a drum. I'm sure he can feel it slamming against his torso, but he never says anything. As I gaze up and our eyes meet, I only see happiness reflecting in his, and I know we're going to be okay. Sure, this may be a little unconventional, but it's our story and no one else's.

We write our ending.

"Ready to go tell our families they're going to be grandparents?" he asks, a wide smile on his full lips.

"I am," I confirm, trying to pull away from the hug, but not getting very far.

Instead, Harrison lowers his lips to mine, giving me a slow, soft kiss. My body hums with energy, excitement racing through my veins. Even though we share a bed, Harrison isn't rushing anything between the sheets. We've actually only made love a few times, and those have seemed more out of desperate need than anything. He still treats me like I'm made of glass. I honestly think it's because he's trying to take this slow—*dating*, as he likes to call it. Well, I remember when we were first dating all those years ago. We couldn't keep our hands off each other and practically went at it like rabbits.

Something I wouldn't mind repeating in the near future.

"I'm going to stop by the gym, finish up a few things, and grab some work to bring home. I'll meet you there by five, and then we can head to the restaurant together," he says.

"Sounds good," I confirm, reaching for my door handle and giving it a tug.

It's warm for the first week of June, and I can already tell the inside of my new car is sweltering. Harrison found a great family car with the best safety rating for me. I slide onto the seat and crank the engine. It fires to life instantly, the air pumping through the fan warm and sticky. Harrison reaches through the open door and cranks on the air conditioning. Before he removes himself completely from the vehicle, he places both hands on my cheeks and puts his lips on mine. Again, the kiss is slow and sweet, but there's a fire smoldering just below the surface. I can feel it, and if the look in his eyes is any indication, he can too.

"See you soon," he whispers, his lips dancing one last time against mine. I shudder, craving his hands and his lips *other* places on my flushed body.

"Soon."

That's a promise.

Harrison and I walk through the front door together of another favorite restaurant of mine. It's not lost on me that he chose this place to share our news with our families. This is where we told them we were getting married and where our rehearsal dinner was held. A lot of memories were made within these walls, that's for sure.

As soon as the door closes behind us, we find both his parents, as well as mine, already chatting by the hostess stand. The confusion is clear when they see us enter together, as if them both meeting their child for dinner at the same time is more than just a coincidence. The light bulbs seem to turn on. My mom glances at his, then to my dad. There's no missing the look of question on their faces.

"Honey, good to see you," Harrison's mom, Sarah, greets her son with a hug.

"Dear, look who we ran into when we arrived for dinner," my mom adds as she pulls me into a hug of her own, glancing over my shoulder at her ex-son-in-law. "Is something going on?" she whispers in my ear.

"Let's grab our table, and we'll explain," Harrison says, heading to the hostess stand. "Drake, party of six."

My dad is watching me, his all-knowing eyes assessing and dissecting. I can feel all their questions rolling off them in waves.

"All right, let's have a seat and I'm sure the kids will explain why we're here together," Sarah agrees, taking her husband's hand and falling in line behind the hostess. Their eyes burn into my back as Harrison places a hand above my rear and guides me to our table. My heart is about to leap from my chest with nervousness, and I can't even drink to take the edge off.

Harrison takes the seat beside me, something the four sets of eyes around our table notice immediately. No one speaks as menus are placed in front of us and the hostess promises to send our waiter over immediately. I glance over tonight's specials, but already know what I'm ordering. I'm sort of a creature of habit like that.

Our waitress arrives and I recognize her immediately. She's worked here for years and has served Harrison and me many meals. She also knew about the divorce, like everyone else in town, so there's no missing the curious look she gives. "Good evening," she greets, setting glasses of water down at each plate. "Can I start you off with some drinks?"

Our parents order first, alcoholic beverages for each one. When she gets to me, I state, "Just water, please."

"Same," Harrison adds, closing his menu and setting it to the side.

"So, how's work?" Sarah asks, glancing across the table to her son.

"Good. Busy. We're getting ready to open the second location, and the third should follow later this summer. I also purchased a fourth location, which should be ready to go by the end of the year. It needs some cosmetic work to the building, but the structure is sound," Harrison tells his parents.

"Good deal, son. Happy to see it taking off like this," his dad, Adam, compliments.

As soon as our waitress returns with our drinks and takes our orders, all eyes fall on us. My nerves have me ready to jump out of my skin and I can't stop my hand from thumping the tabletop and my legs from bouncing uncontrollably.

"Okay, spill," my mom finally demands.

I clear my throat and open my mouth. "We have some news."

"You're back together," Sarah states, her eyes full of happiness.

"Well—" I start, but am cut off.

"Yes," Harrison answers, reaching down and taking my hand in his. The touch instantly calms my nerves. "We're back together," he adds, glancing my way and giving me a warm grin.

"Oh, I'm so happy!" my mom coos, clapping her hands victoriously as Sarah's eyes fill with tears.

My dad just stares at my ex-husband, not voicing his pleasure like the women. When I glance at Adam, he's doing the same. Both men look like they want to say something, or at least ask a question, and it's my dad who speaks first. "What's different about this time around?"

I sober instantly and sit up straight. My mouth opens, but nothing comes out. I glance at the man at my side to find his gaze locked on my father's. "Everything," Harrison reassures. "I openly admit that I messed up last time. I shouldn't have let it get to the point it did. I shouldn't have agreed to a divorce when I wanted anything but. That was entirely on me. I won't make the same mistake a second time," he adds, bringing my hand to his mouth. "I have too much at stake now." He says the words to my dad, but I know they're for me too.

"You don't get all the blame," I remind him, knowing full well I played a part in the demise of our marriage.

"But I take it. All of it. I should have fought harder for the things I loved and valued most in this world." His eyes are intense and speak volumes for the sincerity in his voice. I know he takes full responsibility, even though that's not where it lies. It's placed at both our feet, though no matter how much I try to reason, it's a bit difficult to get that through his thick skull.

Risking a glance across the table, I see both our moms wearing a tearful smile, while our dads still watch us closely, silently observing.

When my dad finally speaks, he says, "I believe you, son. Just know that I won't let you hurt her a second time."

"Me either," Adam states, "but I have to admit, I don't see it happening a second time. I saw firsthand how bad that separation and divorce tore him up. Poor Chase took the brunt of his bad moods for several months."

Harrison huffs. "Don't *poor Chase* anything. He deserves every ounce of shit thrown his way," he teases with a grin.

Adam lets out a hearty laugh. "Well, you may be right there, but still. You've been a bear with a thorn in your paw for months. If it takes returning that pretty lady beside you to your side, then I'm all for it." Adam lifts his glass and salutes.

"Thanks, Dad," Harrison replies before turning to my dad. "Dwayne, you have my word that I won't hurt your daughter ever again. My purpose in life is to make her smile, not cry."

And because I'm a hormonal mess, I start to cry. My mom reaches over the table and squeezes my arm. "Good tears are okay," she adds with a wink.

"I suppose," my dad grumbles, offering me a wink over his glass.

Our entrees are delivered a few moments later, and even though we haven't shared our *other* news yet, I've crossed the first big hurdle of the evening. I can't imagine anyone having any issues with the fact we're bringing a baby into the world. Well, unless you take into account the fact we're not married, have recently divorced each other, and are just now rekindling our relationship.

You know, besides that.

My linguine smells amazing. The perfect blend of light garlic and cheese mixes with the cooked shrimp. I'm a huge seafood lover, so I made sure to do my research on what I can and cannot have while pregnant. The good news is, as long as my shrimp is cooked, I can still enjoy it in moderation. The best part is their linguine sauce isn't made from wine—another huge plus, considering the bun in my oven.

Just before I dig my fork into my noodles, Harrison grabs everyone's attention. "If I could take a quick moment to share one more piece of good news before we eat, I think now is the time."

Setting my fork down, I turn to face him. "Now?" I whisper, my mouth watering and my stomach growling for food.

He gives me a smile and wink and confirms, "Now." Harrison takes my hand once more and brings it to his lips. His eyes remain locked on mine as he opens his mouth. "Winnie and I wanted to share that we're making you grandparents at the end of the year."

I hear the gasp first (undoubtably from my mother), followed quickly by the squeal of excitement. Chairs scrape on the floor, but I keep my eyes on the man beside me, lost in the sea of emotion we seem to be riding on these last few months. I'm pulled into a pair of arms, wrapped in the familiar perfume that belongs to my mom. Finally, Harrison lets go of my hand and I quickly stand, engulfed in a fierce hug.

"I can't believe this! Grandma!" my mom bellows, loud enough that I know the entire restaurant has heard.

Before I can even respond, I'm tugged into another pair of arms, this time belonging to my former mother-in-law, Sarah. "I've always wanted to be a Mimi," she whispers, her tears of happiness sliding effortlessly down her cheeks.

When she finally lets go, it only takes a moment for her arms to be replaced with the ones that offered me continual support and congratulations throughout my childhood. My dad pulls me in tight, and there's no missing the wetness pressed between our cheeks. "Congratulations, baby girl."

"Thanks, Dad," I whisper, holding on just a little longer to the man who has been by my side my entire life. The one who accepts the direction my life is headed, even if he wants to step in to protect me.

"You're gonna be an amazing mama," he reassures, kissing me on the cheek before finally letting go.

When I step back, I'm surprised to see so many tears of joy. Even Adam's eyes glisten under the low lighting. "Well, let's not let our food get cold," Harrison's dad says. "I'm sure our grandbaby is hungry."

As if on cue, my stomach growls, making everyone chuckle. I take my seat, anxious to dive back into my food. Before I can shovel in my first bite, my dad raises his glass. "I'd like to make a toast. To Harrison and Gwen. May their future be filled with love and laughter and may they find happiness in each other's arms. And to the unborn baby they will bring into this world and nurture. Well, there will be no baby loved and cherished more than this child. Cheers."

"Cheers."

CHAPTER 13

Harrison

Time is flying by at a rapid pace. Seems like just a few weeks ago, we were hearing our peanut's heartbeat for the first time. Now here we are sitting in the waiting room for Winnie's sixteen-week appointment. Sixteen weeks and my girl has a noticeable baby bump. Seems like overnight Peanut has made an appearance, and I can't keep my hands off her. Luckily, Winnie humors me and just grins every time my hands or my lips attach themselves to her tiny bump.

"How are you feeling today?" I ask.

"The same as when you left for work this morning," she teases.

"That was four whole hours ago. A lot can change in four hours. Look what four weeks have done." I reach over and place my palm flat on her tiny bump.

"Four weeks and four hours, the same but different, right?" She laughs.

"Exactly." I wink, letting her know I get it. I know I'm a crazy man when it comes to my wife, yes *wife*, and unborn child. I own that and make no apologies. They're everything to me. Sure, we're not technically married, but I don't need that piece of paper saying so. I know it in my heart.

"Gwen," the nurse calls.

I stand quickly and offer Winnie my hand. "I don't need help out of chairs, just yet," she reminds me.

"Doesn't matter. If I'm here, you're getting my help."

"See what I deal with?" She points over her shoulder at me as she talks to the nurse.

"He's one of the good ones," she assures her.

I place my palm on the small of Winnie's back and follow her down the hall. "I know the drill. Which room?" I ask the nurse as we stop at the scale.

"Room two."

"Love you." I don't bother lowering my voice as I say the words, and kiss her temple before leaving her to step on the scale, and pee in a cup.

As soon as I'm sitting in the room, my cell rings. Pulling it out, I see that it's Gina. I silence the call, making sure my phone is on vibrate, and slide it back into my pocket. There's nothing at work that can't wait twenty minutes for this appointment. Immediately my cell rings again, but I ignore it. The third time, I slide it out of my pocket.

"What?" I say, irritated.

"Harrison, the contractor for the Lakeview location just called. He needs your final paint choices," Gina says, clearly ignoring my irritation.

"Gina," I say through gritted teeth, just as the exam room door opens, "I told you not to bother me, that Winnie and I had an appointment today. The contractor can wait. I don't consider paint colors to be an emergency." She starts to speak, but I hang up on her. I don't care what her reasons are; they're not good enough.

"Gina?" Winnie asks.

"Unfortunately," I say, running my fingers through my hair. "I told her not to call unless it was an emergency. She called three times back to back, so I answered."

"And?" she prompts.

"Paint colors."

"Not an emergency," she agrees.

"Not even close. I swear she tries my patience. Did I tell you she had a meeting scheduled for this exact time today with the equipment company? Had I not been paying attention I would have stood them up. I caught it and called them myself to explain and reschedule."

"She knew about the appointment?"

"Yes. It's on my calendar, the one she has full access to."

"Knock, knock," Dr. Taylor says, entering the room. "How are Mom and Dad?" she asks politely.

My heart squeezes in my chest at being referred to as Dad. It's something we talked about, and I know it's happening—I see the proof in the changes in my wife's body, have heard our baby's heartbeat—but to be called Dad, it's surreal and exciting.

I sit down while Dr. Taylor goes through the same routine as our last checkup four weeks ago. Asking Winnie the usual questions, she takes measurements. The doctor pulls the Doppler from the cabinet and I can't stand to sit here this far away from them. Standing, I go to Winnie, kissing her temple and clasping her hand in mine, while we listen to the steady thunderous beat that is Peanut's heartbeat.

"Everything looks great," Dr. Taylor says, handing Winnie paper towels to wipe off her belly. I intercept them and do it for her. I can't explain it, but there's something inside me that swells with pride at the chance to take care of them. When I think about getting to do it every day for the rest of my life, it's humbling.

"So, we'll see you back in four weeks. We'll do an ultrasound at that appointment and get some images of your baby. We can usually determine the gender at that time as well if that's something that you're interested in."

Winnie looks up at me with question in her eyes. "Whatever you want, Winnie."

She bites down on her bottom lip, trying to hide her smile. "I'd like to know, so we can paint the nursery and be as prepared as possible," she says.

"Then we find out." I kiss the top of her head. I've always had a hard time keeping to myself when she's near, but this time around, it's worse. So much worse. I have to be near her, to be touching her. It's almost as if I'm fearful she'll disappear if I don't. I know that's irrational as we're in this together. Stronger than ever. But the constant worry of her and the baby, of losing either of them again, eats me up inside. I never want to be without her. Ever.

"Do you have time for lunch?" Winnie asks as we walk out of the doctor's office.

"I'll make time," I assure her, leading her to my truck.

"Harrison, we don't have to. I know how busy you are. It was just a suggestion."

"A great one at that. I'm taking my wife to lunch." I open the door for her and motion for her to climb in.

"How about we eat at the restaurant around the corner from the gym? You can then go straight to work after."

"Winnie, it's fine."

"I'll see you there." She waves over her shoulder and turns to her car. Quickly closing the passenger door on my truck, I rush to catch up with her. "What are you doing?" she asks, laughing.

"Walking you to your car."

"You know it's literally fifteen feet away, right?"

"And?"

"*And* I can manage to get there safely."

I shrug. "I'm sure you can, but I'll be by your side when you do it."

"What am I going to do with you?" She shakes her head with a smile playing on her lips.

"Marry me." I throw it out there, knowing it's not a true proposal.

Knowing she's going to laugh it off like she has the hundreds of other times I've asked her since getting her back.

"You know, just because we're having a baby, you don't have to keep asking me. We're still doing this together."

We're standing beside her car. She's staring up at me, with so much love and a hint of worry in those green eyes of hers. My hands cradle either side of her face. "I'm asking you because I should have fought harder for us. I'm asking you because the divorce never should have happened. I'm asking you because you are the love of my life and I want nothing more than to grow old with you."

Her eyes well with tears. "I love you, Harrison Drake."

"And I love you, Gwendolyn Drake. Now drive safe, and let's get my loves fed." I kiss her lips and pull open her door. I wait until she's settled and strapped in before shutting her door and jogging back to my truck.

"So, how're the plans for the third location coming?" Winnie asks once we've placed our order.

"It's coming along. We're at the part where the construction crew is ready to start painting. We're on schedule for the grand opening a month from now."

"I'm so proud of you, Harrison. You took a dream and turned it into a reality."

"Thanks, but I would trade it all, every location for another shot at this," I say, motioning between us. "I never should have let it get between us like I did."

"We were both at fault, and stop bringing it up. It's done. Over. We're past it and moving forward. We are doing this together," she says with a soft smile as she rests her hands on her small bump.

"Harrison," a female voice says. Looking up, I see Gina, my new admin assistant, standing next to our table.

"Gina," I greet her, not bothering to hide the irritation in my voice.

"I wish I'd have known you were going to be here. I would have brought the samples so we could go over them."

"Gina, you remember my wife, Gwen."

"Ex-wife I thought," she says, holding her hand out for Winnie to shake.

"Enough." My voice is low and menacing. "She is my wife, and you will refer to her as nothing but. Do you understand?"

"Harrison." Winnie slides her hand across the table and places it over mine. "It's fine." She turns her attention to Gina. "Yes, on paper I'm his ex-wife, but we are very much together and raising this baby together."

"Of course." Gina is quick to backpedal.

"I'll be back at the office later." I dismiss her.

"Sure, then we can—"

I hold up my hand cutting her off. "Later, Gina. I'm having lunch with my wife."

"Harrison, I—" I give Winnie a look that tells her this isn't up for negotiation.

"Right. I'll see you in a little while. It was good to see you again, Gwen."

"You too, Gina." Winnie gives her an apologetic smile before she's turning on her heel and walking out of the restaurant. "Harrison," Winnie says, grabbing my attention. "You were hard on her."

"That's my job. Not to be her friend, I'm her boss. The boss that has told her more times than I can count that you come first. If I'm with you, she's not to interrupt, unless it's an absolute emergency. Paint is not an emergency. Not to mention, I'm still pissed off that I almost missed our appointment last month."

"Almost," she says gently. "She's learning; cut her some slack."

"No." There's something about Gina that rubs me the wrong way. I can't put my finger on it, but it's there all the same. "She needs to know her job and what's expected."

"Okay," she concedes, obviously seeing that this conversation is going nowhere fast.

Our waitress brings us our food, and we both dive in. There is a lull in conversation as we eat. "I was thinking," I say, taking a drink of my sweet tea. "Maybe we should look for a new house."

"What? Why would we do that?" she asks, swiping her french fry through ketchup.

"Something with a bigger yard, and a couple more bedrooms."

"We have three bedrooms."

"I know, but once Peanut arrives, that leaves us with one spare for guests. And then when peanut number two arrives, that leaves zero."

"Number two?" she asks, barely containing her smile. "Just how many peanuts are there going to be?"

"At least two, but I'll take as many as you'll give me."

"Let's start with this one." She glances down at her belly. "I like our house, but the idea of a bigger yard is appealing."

"A fresh start of sorts."

"The house we live in now, we bought it together. It's not like we had other people there."

"It was just a thought. We don't have to."

"I'm not against it. I guess if something were to come up, then we could consider it."

"Consider a house and marrying me?" I ask, trying to lighten the mood a little. I know I overreacted with Gina, but I can't seem to help it.

"I'll take both requests into consideration," she agrees, pushing her plate away from her.

It's not a yes, but it's the closest thing I've gotten to a yes since we've been back together. I'll take it.

"What are your plans for the rest of the day?" I ask, not wanting to end my time with her.

"Mom has been on me to register for a baby shower. I'm thinking about making a list of things we're going to need."

"I can go with you. Tell me when and I'll be there."

"You sure?"

"Absolutely. I want to be involved every step of the way."

"You're a good man, Harrison Drake."

"Good enough to marry?"

"I did once."

"Yes, but will you do it again?" I counter.

"Hmmm, it's a possibility."

"A damn good one," I say, standing from the table. "As much as I hate to say this, I need to get back to the gym. I have a few things I have to do today, and then when I get home tonight, we can go over that list. Maybe even go to the store and start a registry?"

"Let's just see how the day goes," she says, not committing.

I know why, and it pains me. I used to make plans to be home early, or on time even, and then never make it. She's used to the old Harrison, the one who didn't put the love of his life first. The new Harrison, the man I am now, the man who knows life without her refuses to ever go back.

"I'll be home at five thirty," I assure her.

"I'll be there." She smiles up at me. "Thank you for lunch."

"My pleasure, baby." With my hand on the small of her back, I walk her to her car. I steal a kiss—okay, I steal two—before opening her door for her and waving her off. Once I can no longer see her taillights, I climb into my truck and drive around the block and park in the staff parking behind the gym.

"Finally," Gina says as soon as I walk through the door. "I've been waiting all day with these." She holds up a swatch for paint.

"Gina, let me make something clear. My wife and my unborn child are my priority. Not paint samples, unless it's Gwen asking for suggestions. When I tell you not to bother me unless it's an emergency, I want the gym to be on fire. Got it?" I know I'm being a dick, but I can't seem to find the will to care.

"Sorry, I just know you've been moving full force ahead on this project, and I wanted to make sure that I wasn't the delay." She says the words, but her body language tells me something different. She's not sorry. She's just telling me what she thinks I want to hear.

"Thank you. You're not, and I appreciate your effort, I do, but nothing comes before them. If she calls you, find me. I don't care who I'm with or what I'm doing. You find me and tell me it's her. If she shows up here or any of the locations, you find me. Send her back to where I am. I don't give a fuck who I'm training or who I'm in a meeting with. Gwen trumps all."

"Got it." She nods her acceptance.

"Now, what has to be done today? I'm leaving here at five."

"That's only four hours from now. We have paint for the Lakeview location, reception, and office furniture, plus signage."

"We'll work through what we can today and finish the rest tomorrow."

"I thought we would just order in some food and work through it all."

"You thought wrong. I have plans with my wife this evening that I don't plan on breaking."

"Surely, your *wife*," she says it as if she has a bad taste in her mouth, "understands that you have a job to do."

"She does. Gwen is very supportive of the gym, and my commitment to the gym. However, I am supportive of her and our baby and my commitment to them. I lost her because I didn't have a good balance. I won't let that happen again. I'll sell this place first."

"You can't be serious." She gives me a look that tells me she thinks I'm insane. Maybe I am, but I'm owning that shit.

"Very," I confirm. I don't know why I'm explaining myself to her. She works for me. I guess it's my innate need to tell the world what Winnie and our baby mean to me.

"You'd just give all of this up?"

"You make it sound like this is the be-all end-all of life. Sure, I've worked my ass off to make All Fit what it is, but you have to understand something, life isn't anything without her by my side. So, yes, Gina, if I have to choose between my wife or this gym, she wins every time. Hands down."

"Are you going to propose?" she inquires.

"That's none of your business, but since I love Gwen and couldn't give a fuck who knows, yes, I am."

"Oh." She looks as if someone just kicked her puppy.

"Now, paint, let's start there," I say, not wanting to go any deeper into this conversation with her than I have to. We spend the next four hours going over paint and furniture.

"That's good for today," I say, glancing at my phone. "I'm heading out, we can wrap up the signage in the morning."

"If we don't get it ordered today, it's going to add another week to the install."

"Why would you not tell me that four hours ago?"

"You said you wanted to start with paint." She shrugs.

"Fine. Since you failed to tell me all the necessary information when you knew I had to leave, you can handle pushing the opening back a week since we won't have signage."

"What? That's going to take days."

"Not my problem."

"Harrison." She stomps her foot like a child.

"Gina, you knew I was leaving, and I'm not staying because of your mistake. You fix it."

"But you wanted to open in four weeks."

"It's a week," I remind her. "Not the end of the world. We open when it's ready."

"But I have vendors scheduled, and refreshments ordered."

"Reschedule them."

"An hour tops," she says.

"Not happening. I'll see you in the morning. Oh, and I want a report by the end of the day tomorrow where we are with rescheduling everything."

"What if I walk?" she asks, crossing her arms over her chest.

"Are you?" I counter.

"You didn't answer my question."

"We're all replaceable, Gina. All of us. You want to walk? I'm not going to stop you."

She steps close, too close. "You could let me go that easily?" she asks, her voice dropping low, almost as if she's trying to be sexy. It might work for some guys, but not on me. She's not my wife.

"Yes." My one-word answer is not what she wanted to hear. I can see her eyes grow dark as anger takes hold. "If you're here tomorrow morning, I'll see you, if not, I'll mail your last check." I turn and walk away from her

"Harrison." I hear her stomp her foot again. I don't have the time or the energy to deal with her bullshit today. She's running on thin ice. She interviewed well, and she's a friend of Gabby's, but I've had about all I can take.

"I told you I'm leaving at five. It's three minutes after," I call out, not bothering to turn and look at her.

"Fine," she calls out. "See you in the morning."

I wave over my shoulder and keep on walking. She can try to play games all she wants. It's not going to work with me. The drive home is short, and as soon as I pull into the driveway, my mood brightens. I make a mental note to get the rest of my clothes from my apartment this weekend, and let it go. I'm exactly where I need to be. Climbing out of the truck, I make my way to the house, pushing open the front door. "Honey, I'm home!" I yell out.

I hear laughter, more than just Winnie's, and I follow it. I find her and Gabby sitting at the kitchen island, Winnie's laptop open between them. "How are my girls?" I ask, bending to kiss Winnie on the lips.

"Not your girl," Gabby fires back.

"Good thing I wasn't asking about you, now, was I?" I reach over and give her a one-armed hug, and she doesn't protest—that's progress.

"What?" she screeches. "You're having a girl and didn't tell me?"

"No," Winnie rushes to tell her. "Harrison just thinks we're having a girl. We find out at our next appointment."

"You." She pokes me in the side, causing us all to laugh.

"What are we doing here?" I ask Winnie.

"Registry. Well, kind of. We're making a list." She points to the notebook paper in front of her.

"I tried to get her to let me register her online, but she said you were taking her."

"Babe, you do it however you need to. If online is easier, then we'll do that."

"No, I like the idea of going to the store and strolling up and down the aisles."

"We going tonight?"

"Yes." Her eyes light up with excitement. "I wasn't sure if you'd be home early enough," she comments.

"Told you I would be." I know it's going to take some time for her to get used to this, to get used to the fact that she can trust my word, and I hate that. I never once stepped out of our marriage, but not keeping my word is just as bad in my eyes.

"Can I go?" Gabby asks.

"That's up to you, Winnie. I'm going to go grab a quick shower while you ladies figure it out. We'll grab dinner while we're out."

"Harrison," Winnie calls, and I stop in my tracks turning to look at her.

"Welcome home."

"No place I'd rather be." I race upstairs and strip out of my clothes while the water heats. I rush through the shower and dress in shorts and a T-shirt. My feet thunder down the steps to find my wife and sister-in-law waiting by the door. "Ready?"

"Yes." They both clap their hands and wiggle around as if they are toddlers and I just told them that I was taking them to Disneyland.

"I'm so excited," Gabby says as we make our way to my truck.

"This is really happening," Winnie says, stopping at the passenger side door.

"Peanut will be here before we know it," I add, placing my palm over her small bump.

"I never thought I'd see the day," Gabby quips, pulling our attention from one another to her.

"See what day?" Winnie asks, reading my mind.

"The day Harrison and Gwen were... you again. This is how you were before things got bad, and it's inspiring. I want a love like that someday. One like the two of you, and Mom and Dad. You two finding your way back to each other gives me hope that there's someone out there for me."

"There is." Winnie leans into me, and I wrap my arms around her. "You're going to find him, and then you'll understand," she says softly, her gaze meeting mine.

"Understand what?" Gabby asks, but Winnie's eyes stay on me. Green orbs shining with happiness and love, all directed at me.

"Understand that when you give your heart away, when you truly find the one, you'll never get it back. No matter the circumstances."

"I love you." I bend and press my lips to hers.

"Come on, you two, we've got a baby to shop for." Gabby pulls open the back door of my truck, and climbs inside.

The girls chatter back and forth during the drive about the items on the list, and everything a baby needs. From clothes to bottles to diapers, they cover it. I chime in when I can, but I'm content to just be here with them. Soaking up all the baby information that I can. Soaking up as much time with Winnie, and hell, even Gabby, as I can. She's always been a big part of our lives, and I missed her too. She's been a little sister to me. I lost my second family, not just my wife.

The girls insist on the baby store first, so that's what we do. Aisle after aisle, we scan so many items it's hard for me to believe one tiny human needs so much. Then again, some of it I know is overkill. Like the jazzed-up swing I scanned. That thing has like fifteen functions, and the reviews online said it was the best. Yes, I checked. I'm that dad who stands in the middle of the aisle checking safety and parent-approval reviews online before scanning. It's my job to keep Peanut safe, and I'm taking it seriously.

CHAPTER 14

Winnie

"What time does the boat set sail?" I ask my sister as I slide out of my car and head toward the front entrance of All Fit.

"Ten in the morning. Dad says it's gassed up and ready to go," Gabby confirms.

Tomorrow is supposed to be an amazingly beautiful August Saturday, and my sister has been bugging me to take our parents' pontoon boat out on the lake. Our town was built around Fair Lake, and during the summer months, everyone congregates to their boats and rafts for weekend fun. Harrison and I used to take the boat out often, after he'd get off work on Saturday afternoon, but when his dreams of expansion started to take off, our weekend getaways were put on hold, much like our relationship in general.

"I'm just getting to the gym. I'll talk to Harrison and see what he thinks," I say as I pull open the glass door. The deep pulse of rock music sweeps through my veins as I use my keycard to open the second interior door.

"I'll text you a confirmation in just a bit," I tell my sister, hoping that my husband—er, ex-husband—has a light enough day tomorrow that he can take a few hours off to enjoy the sun and the lake. We've only been out on the boat one other time this summer, and if we don't seize the moment, summer will pass us by.

"Don't let him say no, Gwen. Use your womanly charms. And your vag. Use that if you have to," Gabby encourages with a giggle.

I roll my eyes at my phone, even though she can't see me. "I'll text you in a bit," I repeat, waving at the front desk employee and heading back to the hallway where the offices are located.

"You better text me a yes," my sister grumbles.

"Bye, Gabby," I say as I enter the office area and hang up my phone.

Gina is sitting behind an old worn desk and gives me a friendly smile when she sees me. "Hey, Gwen!" she greets, standing up and coming around the desk. She's wearing a tight pencil skirt that hugs her curves like a second skin and a ruffly top that dips dangerously low, revealing plenty of cleavage. It's one of the things I've noticed about Gina, her provocative attire that borders on inappropriate, but Harrison has never said anything.

What guy would?

"Hi, Gina," I greet, pasting a bright smile on my own face and stepping into her arms. Gina's a hugger and has been since day one. The first time I stopped by with lunch, she greeted me with a warm smile and open arms. She seems sweet, which is why I'm not sure why Harrison seems hard on her. "Is he busy?"

"Just wrapping up a conference call with the event planning for next week's grand opening. Chase had a few things he wanted to discuss with the organizers, a few suggestions to make it run smoother," Gina says with a shrug. "You look fabulous, by the way," she coos, just before putting her hand on my belly. Not that I have an issue with people touching my stomach, but I wasn't prepared for the amount of people that would do it without asking first.

"Thanks." I smile, placing my hands on the bump. At twenty

weeks, there's no missing the small bump protruding from my abdomen. It's like overnight I went from a small swell to a small ball that moves and kicks. "We find out next week what we're having," I add, barely able to contain my excitement. Harrison and I have had the conversation many times. Neither of us care what we're having; we just pray for him or her to be healthy and have all their little fingers and toes.

"So exciting! Are you leaning one way or the other?" she asks, leaning back and perching on the corner of her desk.

"I've been on both sides of the fence, but Harrison says girl."

"Aww," she coos. "He's going to be such a great daddy!" Her excitement seems genuine. I know Harrison has had a little trouble with her, jobwise, but she always seems pretty friendly and happy when I'm around.

"So, while I wait for his call to end, can I ask about his schedule tomorrow?" I take an empty seat across from her desk.

"Sure, let me pull it up, but I'm pretty sure tomorrow is light," she says, heading back around her desk and typing on her computer. "He has two training appointments early, one at seven and one at eight. I think he was hoping to get some last-minute stuff done before next week's grand opening in Lakeview."

"But nothing definite on the schedule," I say aloud, though mostly to myself. Harrison has been bringing work home with him when it doesn't require him to remain in the office, especially on Saturdays.

"Nothing definite. Why? Do you have plans?" she asks, her eyes sparkling.

"Well, I'm hoping to enjoy the day on the boat," I tell her, relaxing in the seat as Peanut kicks my bladder.

"Oh, how fun! I haven't been on a boat all summer." She pouts a little face that probably makes most men fall at her feet. Gina is a beautiful girl, that's for sure. Especially when she's revealing all her God-given assets in a tight top and skirt.

Before I can stop myself, I'm saying, "Well, if you don't have any plans tomorrow, you're welcome to come with us."

I feel bad not asking Harrison first, but she seems so eager to go and we have more than enough room on my parents' boat. It seats fourteen comfortably, and since it's just us and Gabby, we have the space. Plus, she's a friend of Gabby's (or was, at least), so I'm sure they'd enjoy catching up.

"I'd love to! What time?"

When I finish giving her the details of tomorrow's excursion, the door to Harrison's office opens. I glance that way as Chase strolls out. The moment he sees me, a large wolfish grin plays on his face. "Well, if it isn't my best friend's girl and the love child we made behind his back," Chase croons, knowing full well the reaction his words will evoke.

"I will kill you slowly and feed you to the damn fish," Harrison growls. His words precede him as he steps through the doorway, just as Chase pulls me up and into a big hug.

"You don't scare me, Drake. Pregnancy has made you soft," Chase teases, giving me a wink.

"You're playing with fire, buddy. Be careful before you get burned," I remind him with a grin.

He laughs, bending down and placing his hands on my hips. It's not sexual in any way, but I can see the fire in Harrison's eyes as he watches his best friend put his hands on me. "Hey, little one. It's Uncle Chase. You remember who the cool one is, you hear me? Uncle Chase will buy you whatever you want. Aunt Gabby is boring. You remember that," our friend says to my stomach, making me laugh. His words bring a smile to Harrison's face, but it isn't until he lets go of my hips that my ex-husband finally seems to relax.

"This is a nice surprise," Harrison states, coming over and pulling me into his arms, as if staking a claim.

"I was on my way to get some groceries when Gabby called."

"Gabby? What did your sister want? Was she asking about me?" Chase teases, his eyes full of mischief and delight.

"Nope, she didn't ask about you once," I tell our friend. "But she did ask us to join her on the boat tomorrow," I add to the man who still has his arms around me.

"Tomorrow?" he asks, almost absently, as if mentally running through his day.

"I've already checked your schedule, and you have two sessions in the morning, but nothing else the rest of the day," Gina confirms.

"But with the Lakeview location grand opening Friday, I'm sure there are a lot of last-minute details to tie up," Harrison states.

"Most of them are confirmations that I can do Monday," Gina adds.

"Gabby's gonna be on the boat? I'm in," Chase boasts, clapping his hands together and giving me another wolfish grin. I can tell he's already planning five ways to torture her by noon. He quickly turns to Harrison. "We're on schedule, man. Everything is ready for next Friday. As Gina said, she'll make the confirmation calls Monday and we'll be all set. We'll be there Monday through Wednesday anyway to make sure the staff are trained. Why not take a day and just relax and enjoy the sun?"

Harrison seems to think it over. Part of me expects him to back out. As he gets close to the opening, I know his mind works overtime to make sure everything is right and ready to go. This opening is no different than the ones before. Knowing he could really use a few hours to decompress, I decide to take matters into my own hands. I step into his side, pressing my swollen belly into him, and wrap my arms around his body. "I think he's right. We need a little fun in the sun," I tell him. He turns his gaze my way, and that's when I go for the kill. "And besides, I really want to wear the new bikini I just bought," I whisper, so that no one else can hear me.

His eyes darken with lust. There's no missing it. Harrison turns me so we're facing each other and bends down until our lips are a hairbreadth apart. "Okay, let's go. I think a day on the lake is just what the doctor ordered."

"Yay! I can't wait!" Gina cheers, clapping her hands and bouncing on her high heels.

Harrison gives me a look. "I, uh, invited Gina to go with us," I whisper.

Besides the tightness of his jaw and the tic of his lip, he doesn't let on to how he feels about his personal assistant tagging along.

"The whole day to bug the hell out of Gabby?" Chase bellows with a grin. "I'm definitely in."

"Seriously? You brought Chase with you?" Gabby growls as I join her on the boat, her eyes watching as Chase and Harrison unload the cooler and bags of food from the back of his SUV.

"He was standing there when I asked Harrison. I couldn't *not* invite him," I argue. Though, I didn't really invite him to begin with. He just sort of invited himself.

Gabby throws her hands in the air. "That's great. He's going to give Roman a hard time," she grumbles, setting my beach bag on the floor.

"Who's Roman?" I ask, placing my large hat on my head and digging for the sunscreen.

"He's a guy I started seeing. He's an investment banker," Gabby says absently, her eyes glued to Chase as he carries the heavy cooler down the dock.

"And you invited him to go boating?" I ask, not missing a moment of how her eyes practically devour Chase's body as he reaches the boat.

"Who'd you invite to go boating?" Chase asks, setting the cooler of drinks down on the deck.

"Roman, the guy I'm seeing. Muscular. Smart. Big dick," Gabby states, crossing her arms over her chest.

Chase advances quickly, getting right in my sister's personal space. My heart hammers in my chest as they stare each other down.

He's imposing with his big frame, but my sister doesn't cower. In fact, she seems to spark to life, the challenge evident in her eyes. "Big dick, huh? That ain't nothing if he doesn't know how to use it, sweetheart. You ever want to know what *that* feels like, you let me know."

And then he turns and stalks off, that ever-present cocky swagger trailing behind him as he goes. "He wishes," Gabby mumbles, quiet enough that I almost don't hear her.

Something tells me that Chase isn't the only one who wishes.

Voices draw my attention to the docks, where I see Gina and Harrison heading our way. She's wearing a swimsuit cover-up, but I can already tell the bikini underneath is skimpy. And red. She has the body for it, though. Can't fault the woman for flaunting what she was given. I'm sure Chase will eat it up, considering that man bed-hops more than the Energizer Bunny does in those battery commercials.

"We all set?" Harrison asks, his body tense as he gets ready to untie the lines.

"No, we're waiting on Roman!" Gabby hollers from behind the wheel.

"Roman?" Harrison asks.

"Muscular. Smart. Big dick," Chase mimics, unable to keep his annoyance from his words.

Just then, a shorter guy with jet-black hair and a manscaped goatee approaches the dock. He's wearing expensive boat shoes and pressed Dockers shorts with his short-sleeved button-down shirt. Chase snorts beside me as the man approaches the pontoon.

"Hey, Roman!" Gabby hollers, heading over to where we stand.

The moment he steps on the boat, he pulls my sister into his arms and kisses her lips. Honestly, it surprises me, considering he hasn't even been officially introduced to any of us yet, and if the growl that slowly erupts from Chase's throat is any indication, I'd say he's not so happy about it either.

"Good morning, sweet Gabby," Roman croons, taking her hand in his and bringing it to his mouth, as if he didn't just have his tongue down her throat seconds before.

My sister just smiles, her big doe eyes eating up all the attention he's throwing her way. "Everyone, this is Roman. Roman, my sister, Gwen, and her ex-husband, Harrison," Gabby introduces.

Harrison steps forward, offering his hand to the shorter man. "Soon-to-not-be *ex* any longer," he greets, pulling me into his side.

Roman just glances toward my sister, as if he's missing a big piece of the story. "Long story. I'll tell you later," Gabby confirms. "This is my friend Gina," she adds, pointing to Harrison's assistant.

"Nice to meet you," Gina greets, her large boobs pressing against Harrison's arm as she slides forward to shake Roman's hand. I can feel Harrison tense beside me and gently move us away from the boobs. In her defense, Gina's boobs have their own zip code. She can't exactly help that they get in the way all the time, right?

"Come on, Roman. We'll get situated in the back," Gabby says, tugging Roman's arm.

Before either of them move, a throat clears just over my shoulder. "Don't forget me, Gabby Goose. I'm sure you want to introduce Roman to me, right?" Chase asks, his voice sugary sweet as he steps into the group and offers his hand to the short man at my sister's side.

"Chase Callahan. *Friend*," he states, reaching his hand out for the other man. There's tension in spades right now, and I'm not sure why. It's like a pissing match is about to ensue. Yes, Chase and Gabby like to tease each other, but they've never crossed any lines from frenemies to... more.

Right?

Suddenly, I'm not so sure.

Roman takes Chase's hand and gives it a squeeze in return. "Strong grip, Mr. Callahan. I like that," Roman says to Chase with a grin that holds a hint of smugness. "Roman Tatro. Pleasure to meet you."

"Likewise," Chase replies before throwing his trademark cocky grin back in place. "We ready to hit the water?" he asks, clapping his hands together and defusing the weird tension that settled over everyone.

Harrison steps behind the wheel as Chase releases the ropes from the dock. Within a few minutes, we're settled in seats and heading out of the small marina on the lake. I can already see tons of boats littering the large lake, ensuring the waters will be busy today. We'll spend our day putting around, enjoying the sun, and swimming by a few of the sandbars around the waterway. Some of the bigger, faster boats will spend the day tubing, but that's never really been my thing.

When we reach our first stop, everyone gets ready for a dip in the warm lake. Gina lost her cover-up pretty much the moment we left the dock and Chase seems to be enjoying the view. She's eating up the attention he's throwing her way, flirting and touching each other from the opposite side of the boat. Gabby and Roman remain in the back, and the few times I glanced her way, she seemed to be throwing eye-daggers at her friend and not paying Roman an ounce of attention, even though his hands are all over her.

Interesting...

As Harrison drops anchor, I quickly grab the sunscreen that I didn't get to put on earlier. I lather up my legs and feet, knowing my pale skin will burn if I don't, and add a little to my arms and face. I remove my blue cover-up, exposing the black and gold swimsuit underneath. A hiss pulls my attention to my right.

"Jesus, Winnie, how am I not supposed to have a fucking hard-on all day with you in that?" Harrison growls, taking the empty seat beside me. His hands instantly fall to my stomach as his lips softly caress mine. "Let me help with the sunblock."

I turn to give him my back as he squirts a large blob into his hands and starts to rub it on my skin. My body starts to heat as desire races through my veins. There's something almost magical about having his hands on my body. Maybe it's the fact that we've done nothing but cuddle over the last two weeks or perhaps the extra hormones in my body, but this dangerous and definite need I feel consumes me. Suddenly, it's all I can think about. All I want.

And the cuddling? Well, we've both been so exhausted and by the time we snuggle on the couch, I'm falling asleep in his arms.

"Are you being naughty, Winnie?" he whispers in my ear, the warmth of his breath caressing my lobe. If he were to kiss me behind the ear right now, I'm sure to burst into flames.

His large hands continue to work their way down my back and eventually around my waist. He squats in front of me and grabs the bottle once more. With his eyes locked solely on mine, he applies sunscreen to my abdomen. His fingers tease the waistband of my bottoms and then dip under the cups of the tops. My entire body is an electric wire, alive and fully charged, and the worst part is, he knows it. His eyes burn with desire, much like mine, as he watches the way I respond to his touch.

Leaning forward, he whispers, "I'm going to let you rub down your chest, angel. If I touch you there, I'm going to end up taking you right here in the middle of the boat deck and I'm sure that's not the memory you want to give our family and friends." Harrison sweeps a gentle kiss across my lips, and then quickly backs away. Of course, there's no mistaking the way he hides what's happening in his pants from the rest of the boat.

"Hey, Harrison, need some ice, buddy?" Chase teases loudly, drawing everyone's attention. He's putting the stairs over the edge, wearing nothing but his trunks and a smile.

"Fuck off," Harrison growls and continues to gaze out at the lake, willing his hard-on to subside.

Within the next few minutes, everyone is ready to jump in the water and enjoy the day of fun and relaxation. Though, I'm not sure how much relaxation will happen when you add in all the sexual tension that seems to be on the boat with us.

This trip just got very interesting.

"Are you fucking kidding me right now?" Harrison bellows into the phone. He's been pacing back and forth across the living room from the moment Gina called a few moments ago.

The calmness and relaxation of Saturday was quickly replaced with a busy Sunday making calls and finalizing plans for the gym's grand opening on Friday. Harrison just got home a few moments ago after spending the entire day training the new staff in Lakeview. He opted to skip going to the office after his return to town and just come home to me. We planned to throw steaks on the grill and watch a movie, but those plans were interrupted by the ringing of his phone. And if the way he's yelling is any indication, I'd say those plans are completely derailed for the evening.

I finish the pasta salad and stick it in the fridge, trying to give him privacy to conduct business, but it's hard when he's yelling at his assistant into the phone.

Everything seemed good Saturday evening. *Really* good for Chase and Gina, if you know what I mean. They couldn't keep their hands off each other the entire day, even though I'm pretty sure one of his eyes was constantly watching my sister. Harrison had brought it up, their connection on the boat, but there's nothing in his employee handbook that says anything about inter-office relationships. Not that he's ever needed any reason for something like that. By the time the sun started to sink and the boat was docked back at the small marina, Gina had her hand down Chase's trunks and they bolted from the boat as if their hair was on fire. Hopefully they made it somewhere private before ripping off their clothes (or swimsuits).

Gabby, on the other hand, seemed annoyed throughout the entire day. She wore a fake smile and doted on Roman as much as possible, but it seemed forced. The only time she seemed like herself was when she was sparring with Harrison's best friend—and those times were often on Saturday. Everything they did appeared to be for the sole purpose of getting a rise out of the other.

As for Harrison and me, well, we finally broke our two-week dry spell. After the sunblock incident and the fact that his hands were constantly on me while we swam, we barely made it home before we went at it like bunnies. Four times. That's how many times I screamed his name between sundown and sunup Sunday.

Now, here we are, Monday evening, and all that rejuvenation from the weekend is long gone. Harrison and Gina had gotten along fine, even though I could tell he was a little uncomfortable with her being there. Probably because she works for him. I can understand that. But she was super sweet and chatty with me the entire day. Well, until she decided to play street hockey in Chase's pants.

"How did this happen?" he says into the phone, his words much quieter and resolved. He stops pacing and stares out the front window. "Fix this, Gina. I can't miss that appointment," he barks into the phone, drawing my attention his way.

Appointment? I know he has many this week, especially with opening the third All Fit location, but I can't help the feeling of dread that slides down my spine and lands in the pit of my gut. Our ultrasound appointment is this week. Thursday at two o'clock, actually.

Harrison sighs deeply and turns to face me. "That'll have to do, I guess. But this is a huge mistake, Gina. I could fire you over this and would have no problem doing so," he says, stopping and watching as I enter the room and take a seat on the couch, "but someone once told me that people make mistakes. It's how they right that wrong that shows their character. I'm going to go to Lakeview tomorrow for the staff training. Chase will be with me. You have twenty-four hours to move everything else from Friday to Thursday. I'll take care of staffing. This can't..." He stops, shaking his head and closing his eyes. "This can't happen again, Gina. No more issues like this or you're gone."

He listens for a few more seconds before signing off, throwing the phone onto the chair cushion and giving me a look that tells me exactly how upset he is. I get up and walk toward him, instantly wrapping my arms around his chest. His entire body is riddled with tightness, but as soon as I lay my head on his chest, the anxiety seems to ebb from his body. He wraps his arms around my shoulders and pulls me in tight.

"What's wrong?" I ask, even though I know I won't like what he's about to say.

"Gina fucked up the invites for the grand opening. The Lakeview Mayor, council members, chamber of commerce, everyone received an invitation to attend our grand opening. On Thursday."

"Ouch," I whisper, hugging him tighter. My stomach presses into him. It's as if Peanut knows Daddy is upset and chooses that exact moment to give a hard kick, right into his daddy's lower stomach.

He pulls back and glances down, the anger from moments ago replaced with a look of awe. Harrison drops to his knees and takes my abdomen in his large hands. "Hey, little Peanut. You know just what your daddy needs right know, don't you?" he asks my stomach, earning another kick and a punch.

We both laugh, as if the baby inside me is responding directly to the question asked. "I think Peanut knows Daddy is upset and stressed and trying to tell him it's going to be okay," I say. "So tell me what happened so we can figure it out. Together."

He gazes up at me with those dark eyes. "So everyone is coming to the grand opening at noon on Thursday."

"And my appointment is at two on Thursday."

He nods. "I won't miss it, though. I'll be there."

"I can try to change it," I offer, running my hand through his hair.

"No, I don't want to do that. Our families are coming to dinner that night for the reveal. We'd have to push that back too, and that seems like a lot of unnecessary juggling. The grand opening and ribbon cutting should take about an hour. I'll be able to welcome everyone, give my speech, cut the ribbon, and be out of there by one or one thirty."

"What would you be missing after the ribbon cutting?" I ask, continuing to rub the top of his head.

His eyes close involuntarily as he lets out a little moan of pleasure. "You can keep doing that. Just the hobnobbing and tours. Chase can handle that stuff. Plus, the assistant manager will be there too so she can help."

"Are you sure? If you need to be there, I don't mind calling and rescheduling. It's not a big deal."

He opens his eyes and I can feel their intensity clear down to my toes. "It *is* a big deal. This is more important, Winnie. *You and Peanut* are my priorities. The rest is fluff. I won't let you change our big moment Thursday. I'll run to Lakeview and cut the ribbon and then make it back to town by two for our appointment."

"If you insist."

"I do." He places his hands on my stomach once more, earning another kick from the child within. "Do you hear that, Peanut? We're going to find out if you have an innie or an outie in a couple of days."

I laugh at his wording as excitement races through me. He's right. In just a few days, we'll know if we're having a son or a daughter. A boy or a girl. Either way, I can't wait, and I love knowing Harrison is just as ecstatic as I am.

"Gwen," the nurse calls into the waiting room full of expecting moms.

I glance toward the door once more and slowly get up. My heart is pounding in my chest as I make my way to the doorway, giving the entrance to the office one last look. He's not here. I know today was a big day for him and All Fit, but he promised to be here for this appointment. They're even running a few minutes behind.

"You know the drill," the nurse says as I prepare to step on the scale. When I do so, she moves the slide—and moves it some more. "Hmmm," she says aloud, though probably mostly to herself.

"Is everything okay?" I ask and then glance at the number.

Oh.

"No, nothing's wrong, per se. You've just experienced a bigger weight gain this month," she adds with a smile.

I know I've enjoyed my late-night popcorn with M&M's in it, plus the nightly big glass of chocolate milk, but I didn't think it would actually result in a seven-pound weight gain in four weeks. Ouch.

The nurse has me follow her to room four for the ultrasound. The uneasiness I felt a few moments ago about the results of the scale is quickly replaced with joy as I think about the ultrasound and finding out the sex of the baby. "Dr. Taylor will be in shortly. She'll do her normal measurements and then she'll send in the ultrasound technician," she informs before excusing herself from the room.

That excitement I was feeling is quickly replaced with sadness as I hop on the table. Alone. Has something happened? Why is Harrison late? He wouldn't miss this unless it was an emergency. That sadness quickly transforms into fear as all the horrible things that could happen on the roadway filter through my mind.

A knock sounds, followed quickly by Dr. Taylor. "Good afternoon, Gwen. How have you been feeling?"

"Okay," I reply, feeling anything but.

"Well, a few things today before we conduct the ultrasound. You've had a significant jump in weight gain since your sixteen-week appointment. We'll do the urine test as soon as the ultrasound is complete. That'll let me know where you sugars are. I'm just a little concerned about that. If you don't have any questions, I'll get the technician in here and we'll take a look at your baby."

That brings a wide smile to my lips. "I'm ready."

I glance toward the door one last time, a movement Dr. Taylor catches. "You're alone today?"

"He had a work thing." It's hard to keep the disappointment out of my voice.

She doesn't say anything, just nods as she steps out of the room. Fortunately, the ultrasound technician enters quickly, keeping me from thinking about all those horrible things that could have kept Harrison away from this appointment. It's the same woman as our first ultrasound, and it only takes her a few minutes to get everything set up and ready. My abdomen is exposed as she squirts a healthy glob of goo on my skin. Just as she sets the wand on my stomach, a knock sounds at the door.

"Come in," the tech says.

When the door pushes open, my entire body seems to sigh with relief. Harrison is there, a look of complete guilt and pain on his handsome face. When his eyes connect with mine, everything seems to just fade away. He's here. He's all right. Everything else can wait.

"Right on time, Dad. We're just starting to get a look at your baby," the tech greets as he enters the room, closing the door behind him.

Harrison immediately comes to my head, kissing my forehead with a lingering kiss. "I'm so sorry," he whispers against my skin.

"You're here now. We'll talk about it later," I assure him, reaching for his hand. It's large and warm and provides just the comfort that I need right now.

The diabetes thing kinda freaked me out, but I don't want to burden him with that now. Clearly, he's had a long, stressful day, and adding stress isn't what I want or what he needs. I'll tell him, eventually, just not now.

"Wow, someone's not shy," the tech says, pulling both our attention to her monitor. "See that?" she asks, pointing to the screen and clicking a few buttons. She takes a few still images, but the sight on the screen has me in complete awe. Our baby is there, all wiggly and perfect. My eyes burn with tears and the hand around mine tightens. I want to glance at him, to see his reaction, but I can't take my own eyes away from the monitor. I'm totally transfixed to the sight, to our baby.

"Harrison and Gwen, say hello to your daughter."

The rest of the appointment proceeds as if I'm floating on a cloud. A daughter. After the technician leaves, Dr. Taylor returns with a cup for a urine sample. As I get ready to head to the restroom, Harrison's phone rings. "Work," he says, excusing himself to step outside for a few minutes.

I do what's needed for the urine sample and return to the room. It only takes a few minutes before Dr. Taylor returns, a grim look on her face. "It's as I was suspecting, Gwen," she starts. "There are sugars in your urine, as well as the significant weight gain. Both of these together are signs of what we call gestational diabetes," she says, handing me a pamphlet. "Here's more information on it. As long as we monitor and treat, if necessary, everything should be okay. There are a few health risks that increase with gestational diabetes, like pre-eclampsia and depression, so we'll watch for those. Do you have any questions?" she asks.

I'm completely caught off guard. Gestational diabetes? No one in my family is diabetic.

"This condition develops in non-diabetic patients. It's fairly common, affecting about 6 percent of all pregnancies," she adds, letting me know I actually had asked my question aloud. "The good news is, if it is gestational diabetes, we've caught it early and will treat it, if necessary. Right now, I want to change your diet and add in a little exercise. Maybe a walk in the evening around the neighborhood or around the mall."

"Like all the old people?" I ask, a smile playing on my lips.

"Yes, well, those walking clubs aren't just for the elderly," she replies with a laugh. "We'll get your through this, Gwen." Dr. Taylor glances around. "Did Harrison leave?"

"Oh, uh, work call."

"Be sure to talk to him about this, okay?"

"I will," I reply on autopilot.

Tucking the pamphlet in my purse, I head to the lobby and schedule my next appointment. As I step outside, Harrison is tucking his phone into his pocket. "All done?"

I nod, not yet bringing a voice to the concerns in my head. I need to wrap my head around this before I tell Harrison. I know he'll instantly worry, and I don't want that.

"Let's go home."

CHAPTER 15

Harrison

I'm hovering between being asleep and awake, but when I feel the bed dip and Winnie's feet hit the floor, I'm fully awake. "You okay?" I ask her in the darkness of our room. We've only been in bed about an hour. It took me a while to relax, running through my to-do list at the office tomorrow. Things are crazier than ever with the new sites.

"Yeah, I'm thirsty, and I have to pee," she says, making her way to the bathroom.

"Chocolate milk?" I ask, because that's been her thing since she's been pregnant. Well, that's always been her thing, but more so since the pregnancy.

"No, just water," she calls out through the door. "I can get it."

I know she can, but so can I. Throwing the covers off, I pad down the hall to the kitchen and grab her a cold bottle of water from the fridge. By the time I make it back to our room, she's climbing back into bed.

"Thank you." Winnie takes the bottle and drinks greedily. She doesn't stop until the bottle is empty. "My throat was dry, and now I regret it because I'll have to pee again." She softly laughs.

"You have an entire gallon of chocolate milk that's about to expire. That's not like you," I tease her.

"Yeah, just haven't been feeling it," she says, burrowing under the covers.

I take my spot beside her in bed. Propping myself up on my elbow, my other hand caresses our baby girl. "Take it easy on Mommy," I whisper to her belly. "Is there anything I can do?" I ask Winnie.

"Just be you," she says, running her fingers through my hair. "Sorry, I woke you."

"You didn't, not really. I was just starting to doze off."

"You okay?" I can hear the concern in her voice. I missed these times with her. Just talking and being there for each other.

"Yeah, I'm good. Just running through my day tomorrow and mentally going over what still needs to be done to get this third location up and going."

"You open in two weeks."

"Yeah, when Gina messed up the scheduling, we had to push it back a little, but it ended up working out. Thankfully."

"Harrison, I know you're in this," she tells me. "Don't wear yourself out with worry about being home every night right on time. I know you're going to need to put in some work at the gym. I'll still be here when you get home."

"I've got it covered," I assure her. "I hired Gina for a reason. She's on thin ice, but the work is getting done."

"Are you being too hard on her?"

"No. I make her tasks clear. She knows what's expected; she just doesn't seem to care."

"Maybe she's having a hard time comprehending. Some people have learning disabilities they don't let show."

"Come on, Winnie. You and I both know that's not the case."

"I know you're worried about me, and about the baby. I know you have a lot on your plate. Maybe Gina is taking the brunt of all that frustration?"

"Hardly. Trust me on this; she deserves it. I'm at my wit's end with her. One more mistake and she's gone. She's stressing me out. The rest of it I can handle. I'm constantly watching my schedule, making sure our appointments are not sabotaged. It's almost as if she's doing it on purpose." I finally speak the words I've been thinking for weeks out loud.

"Harrison, come on, you don't really think that? She's harmless."

"I don't want to talk about Gina. You think you can get back to sleep?" I ask her. I don't want to upset her, but my gut tells me Gina is not who she wants us to believe.

"Yes." She pauses. "After I use the bathroom again."

"You just went."

"Well, *your daughter* must be lying on my bladder because I need to go again."

My daughter. I can't wait to meet her. "You need help?" I offer. I hate that she's doing all the hard work, and I'm just here watching, waiting to meet our baby that she's growing.

"I can manage." I hear the smile in her voice as her feet hit the hardwood floor and she pads her way to the bathroom.

When the bathroom door opens, I hold the covers up for her as she slides back into bed. My arms wrap around her, my hand resting on her belly. "Marry me," I whisper into the darkness.

"I love you, Harrison Drake."

"I love you too, Winnie. Night." I kiss the back of her head.

"Goodnight."

Today is our twenty-four-week appointment. That's something I've learned. Pregnancy is referred to in weeks. We heard the heartbeat at the hospital and again at our first appointment at the OB/GYN office and we told our parents at twelve weeks, we found out we're having a baby girl at twenty weeks. Winnie has this book about the stages of the baby's growth. It says that currently our daughter is the size of an ear of corn, and should weigh a pound. It's so hard for me to believe that my wife is growing a tiny human that we created.

Today's appointment is early, and a long one. Something about glucose testing. So I'm driving us and will head to the gym later today. Chase is there to keep Gina in line. Not sure what happened with them a few weeks ago. He said he drove her home, without going in, but that's not like Chase or Gina from what I can tell. They were all over each other on the boat, so it's hard for me to believe he just dropped her off. Chase swears that's all that happened, and I've known him for years; he's never been one to lie.

"Winnie!" I yell up the stairs. "You about ready?"

"Yes," she says, appearing at the top of the steps. She has on a pair of maternity jeans, that still make her look incredible, and a white tank top.

"Babe, it's a little chilly out. You might want to grab a sweater."

She holds up a pale pink sweater and grins. "I'm on it, Daddy."

Daddy. We've gotten in the habit already of referring to each other as Mommy or Daddy. Every damn time she says it, my heart trips over in my chest. Sixteen more weeks and we can meet our little girl. Weeks and I'll be responsible for a tiny human. Thankfully, I have Winnie. She's great at everything, and I have no doubt motherhood will be the same.

"You're beautiful," I say when she reaches the last step. My hands go to her belly. I can't pass up the opportunity to touch her, and our daughter. In the last four weeks, she's really started to show. She looks like she's swallowed a basketball. From the back, you can't even tell she's pregnant though.

She's glowing.

"You sleep beside me at night, I'm a given. You don't have to butter me up," she teases.

"Don't go talking like that and get me all excited. We have an appointment to get to."

"Yeah," she agrees.

"You okay?"

"Definitely. Just tired."

"Baby girl is taking all your energy. The last couple of weeks, you seemed to be tired all the time. Maybe we should mention it to the doctor today."

"I'm an incubator for a baby. Of course I'm going to be tired." She rubs her protruding belly affectionately. "Now, let me pee, and we can go."

"Get moving," I say, tapping her lightly on the ass as she clears the bottom step and heads in the direction of the half bath off the kitchen.

"So, where are we going?" she asks as I pull into the lot of the department store.

"Shopping."

"Shopping? What are we shopping for?"

"Baby girl."

"Harrison, we're going to have a baby shower. Our moms and Gabby are already all over it. She's going to be spoiled rotten as it is. Not to mention I have a doctor's appointment."

"There's nothing wrong with that. Besides, Mommy and Daddy get to spoil her too. And we're early. Come on, let's just take a look."

"I guess it won't hurt to look," she concedes. I can hear it in her voice. She's excited, as I knew she would be. Hell, I'm excited too. All of this is new to both of us.

Five minutes later, we're in the big chain baby store with a cart and a mental list of everything we're going to need. "What do you want to look at first?"

"Everything." She laughs. "There is so much stuff, and I know we've registered, but I just want to look at it all." She walks along beside me as I push the cart. "We need to pick out her furniture."

"We do. I assumed paint would be picked out first and then we could go with furniture. Are you still thinking white? I agree that seems like a good fit for a little girl."

"Yeah," she agrees. "White is good. Are we going to have a theme? You know like princesses or Winnie the Pooh?"

"Are we supposed to?"

"There is no supposed to. Some people have a theme for the nursery."

"What do you want?"

"I kind of just want to make it girly. Nothing cartoonish, just... feminine for our sweet little girl."

"I have no preference. You tell me what you want, and I'll make it happen." That's the least that I can do since she's doing all the work here. I'm just kind of along for the ride.

"What if I changed my mind?" she asks, picking up a small blanket. "This is the cutest thing ever." She holds it up so I can see it. It's a small blanket with pink and gray elephants on it. "I'm thinking light gray walls, white furniture, and pink, gray, and white decorations. I wonder if they have this bedding?" She walks further down the aisle. "Look." She points to a large bag of bedding. "It's the entire kit for the crib."

"You like it?"

"I love it. It's so cute."

Walking to stand next to her, I pick up the bag and place it inside the cart. "Now what?"

"Harrison, we shouldn't. We're having a shower."

"We didn't register for this, so we should be good to buy it. Besides, we need blankets and clothes, and bottles and toys, and all that other stuff that I can't remember. I think we're safe. You love it, so it's happening." I kiss the tip of her nose and go back down the aisle and grab the blanket she was just holding. "Winnie," I call out to her. "They have crib sheets and a mobile." I hold up the package that tells me the coordinating items to look for. "Do we need that?"

She grins. "Yes." She joins me and adds a few matching items to the cart. "Okay, I think we're good. We should wait to buy anything else."

"This is only the first aisle," I tell her. "We've got more to see."

"How much time do we have?" she asks, biting down on her bottom lip. I know my wife and she could get lost in here shopping for our baby girl. Hell, I could too. I'm man enough to admit it. This is an important time for us, and I want to share all of it with her.

"We have about thirty minutes before your appointment."

"I guess we can look at a few more aisle's, she says grinning."

"That's my girl. I figured we could browse a little, go to your appointment, which I knew was going to be a longer one, and then grab something to eat."

"Come on, Momma. Let's go see what else we can find."

She grins and turns on her heel, heading down the next aisle.

I toss in a rug, and a lamp that matches the bedding. I don't know if we need it, but it matches, and she needs decorations in her room, right? I really have no damn idea what we need, but it's putting a smile on my wife's face so regardless, it's worth it.

"We should go," she says, eyeing the cart that is now overflowing. "We just came in here to look." She eyes the cart. "It's been what five minutes and you have this thing overflowing."

"You might have just come to look. Why do you think I got this cart?" She gives me a beautiful smile, and her green eyes light up. Something I've not seen much of these past few weeks. She's been exhausted. "However, I agree we should get moving so we're not late getting to your appointment."

Checkout is quick, maybe because it's early morning, I'm not sure. The back seat of my truck is loaded down with lots of pink, and it brings a smile to my face. This weekend, we're going to go pick out the paint so I can get started. I just need to feel like I'm doing something. Like I'm contributing to our family. Sure, I work, but as far as the baby goes, it's all on Winnie. I need to do whatever I can to be involved and take the stress off her.

"So, I was thinking after your appointment we can go check out some paint colors for the nursery. I'd like to get started," I say once we are in the truck and headed to her appointment.

"Don't you have to get to the gym?"

"I do, but Chase is there today, so I have some time."

"Are you sure?"

"Definitely."

"You know, I've been thinking about what you said about moving. I think we're good where we are, for now at least. We're settled, and the thought of moving right now stresses me out."

"I'd take care of it, but I agree with you. I want to get her room all set up, so you can start your nesting."

"What?" Her giggle fills the cab of my truck.

"Nesting. The book I read said that new mothers begin to nest closer to delivery. I want to have the room ready, so you can do that."

"What am I going to do with you?" Her voice is muffled with laughter.

"Marry me?"

"We're getting there." She smiles.

"Yeah?" I ask her, because more and more she's hinting that she might be ready.

"I just want to make sure we do this for the right reasons."

"There is only one reason, Winnie. We love each other. I think we both learned what not to do the first time around, well, except for Peanut." I reach over and rest my hand on her belly. "We definitely need to do that again."

"Let's bring this little one into the world, and then we can see about siblings."

"Deal," I agree, parking my truck. We make our way inside, and before we are done signing in, a nurse is calling her name.

"You're going to see Dr. Taylor later. First we're going to start your glucose test," the nurse explains. "You'll have an hour before you see the doctor, so you can leave and come back. Just check in with the receptionist when you get back so we know." She twists the lid off a small clear bottle filled with orange liquid. "I need you to drink all of this, and then in an hour, we'll check your glucose reading."

"How bad is it?" Winnie asks the nurse.

"Meh, not too terrible. We keep it cold, which makes it easier to take. My suggestion is to just get it over with."

"Here goes," she says, placing the bottle to her lips. She takes a big drink and then cringes. "It's sweet." She scrunches up her face. I watch her as she takes a few more large gulps and finishes it off. "Ugh, that was nasty."

"What next?" I ask the nurse.

"Now we wait. I'll check back in with you in an hour and draw some blood. Dr. Taylor will see you after." She gives us a wave and is out the door.

"That was bad," Winnie makes a face that tells me she did not enjoy consuming that little bottle of liquid.

"I'm sorry, babe. So, we have an hour," I say trying to get her mind off of it.

"How are things at the gym?"

I go on to update her with the progress of all of our new locations, and how in the back of my mind I've thought of branching out even further. "More of a franchise," I tell her. "So I would sell the name and the operation procedures, but we wouldn't be running the facilities."

"All Fit is your baby, you sure you want to do that?"

"No, this," I reach over and lay my hand on her belly. "Is my baby, you are my wife, and I'm not willing to take on more and take more time away from either of you."

She smiles. "We'll work it out, Harrison."

We chat about our parents, and how they're taking to being grandparents. To say that they're excited is an understatement. We talk about the possibility of her staying home full time with the baby. Time flies as we can an hour just for us. We both know the communication is important and what it can do to a relationship if you lose it.

"How long does it take to get your results from this test they have to do today?" I ask her.

She shrugs. "Twenty-four to forty-eight hours, but she said very rarely is it longer than the next day before they get the results. Depending on how busy the lab is."

A knock sounds at the door before Dr. Taylor is pushing it open. "Good morning." She smiles warmly. "How are you?" she asks Winnie.

"Good," she says brightly. Way too brightly. "Aside from that nasty tasting drink."

"It's definitely not a fan favorite. How are you feeling otherwise?"

"She's been tired a lot," I chime in. Winnie turns to look at me, but I can't read her expression. "She's also thirsty all the time, and she seems to have to pee more frequently, but she tells me that the baby is lying on her bladder." I spill everything that I've observed since our last visit.

"Harrison, I'm fine," Winnie protests.

"Babe, it's better to ask just to make sure. We're both new at this, and we need to make sure everything is okay."

"He's right," Dr. Taylor says, lifting her eyes from the computer screen. "You've gained eight pounds since the last visit. We talked about gestational diabetes, and from what Harrison is telling me, your symptoms go hand in hand. Have you been watching your diet, and getting plenty of water and exercise?"

"Wait." I stand and walk to the exam table where Winnie is sitting, wringing her hands together. "You talked about diabetes? Where was I?" I'm running the details of our last visit through my mind, and nothing stands out to me.

"At Gwen's last visit."

"I don't remember that," I admit. Surely, I didn't forget something as important and critical as this?

"It was before you got here," Winnie confesses.

Fucking Gina. "Why didn't you tell me?" I question. "I could have been helping you. I thought we were in this together?" I'm stunned that she's kept this from me. I thought we were past that. I thought we were no longer hiding our feelings. "Winnie?"

"I'm sorry," she says, her voice breaking. "You were upset that you were late, and I know how much stress you're under with the gym, and the new locations. I did everything that Dr. Taylor suggested I do." Her eyes are glassy with tears, and those tears tug at my heart.

"Baby." I cradle her face in my hands. "I'm never too busy for you and our baby. Never. I know I used to let work come between us, but I promise you that's not going to happen this time. You have to tell me these things. How am I going to take care of you if I don't know what's going on?"

"I'm sorry," she says again, this time a single tear rolling down her cheek. I capture it with my thumb.

"We should have the blood results back tomorrow. I see here there is still a trace of sugar in your urine, not more than your last visit, but something to watch."

"What does that mean?" I ask her. I place my arm around Winnie's waist, where she sits on the exam table.

"The blood test will tell us more. Lots of women acquire gestational diabetes, which means the issue resolves with delivery."

"So she's okay? What about the baby?"

"Mom and baby are both safe. We typically see higher birth weight in babies of moms who have been diagnosed with gestational diabetes. It's important to eat a healthy balanced diet, drink plenty of water, and get some exercise."

"What kind of exercise? What's safe?" I'm already thinking of a workout I can design for her that's safe for both her and the baby.

"Walking is the best exercise."

"Treadmill? Elliptical?" I ask.

"Yes to both. A recumbent bike, swimming, and yoga are a few others that are completely safe. Nothing vigorous, and everything within moderation. You don't need to exercise all hours of the day.

Thirty minutes a day, with your heart rate up five times a week, is what we recommend."

I nod. "We can do that." I'm already working through a low-impact routine for her in my mind.

"What happens if the test comes back high? Then what?" Winnie asks. I reach out and take her hand, and her grip tightens. She's worried. I hate she's been handling this alone. Sure, it's only been four weeks, but that's four weeks that I could have helped carry some of the burden. It makes sense to me now why she's stopped drinking her beloved chocolate milk.

"If you fail the one-hour glucose, the test you took today, we then have you come back in for an extended glucose test. It's a three-hour test, where we draw your blood once every hour for three hours. You will have to be fasting for this one, and the drink is the same orange delicacy." She chuckles.

"Okay," Winnie says, straightening her shoulders.

My hand is gripping hers as the real fear of something happening to Winnie or the baby takes hold. I've never met our baby, but I love her all the same. And Winnie, she's been my world since the night we met all those years ago. I'll do everything I can to help her through this. To fight to keep them both healthy and here with me.

"Now, let's see how you're doing." She asks a few more questions, and I step back so that Winnie can lie back on the table and the doctor can get measurements. "Measuring bigger than you should be at this point, but that's okay. It's nothing that causes a red flag currently," she assures us.

We get to listen to the heartbeat, and my own thunders just as loudly. I love this baby. This tiny piece of me, and of Winnie. This tiny human that we created out of love. *Please, God, let them both be okay.* I send up a silent prayer.

"Everything sounds great. I'll call you tomorrow with your results, and we can take it from there. If need be, we'll schedule you in the next week or so for the three-hour fasting glucose test."

"Thank you, Dr. Taylor," I say, offering her my hand to shake. She takes it then offers hers to Winnie.

"You're welcome. You and your baby are in good hands. We see this all the time. What's important is you doing your part with diet and exercise. Do you have any more questions?"

I look at Winnie who's already looking at me. "No." I turn back to Dr. Taylor. "But that doesn't mean I won't think of more," I admit.

She smiles. "When you do, call us. That's what we're here for." She stands and walks to the door. "I'll call you tomorrow, and we'll take it one day at a time."

We say our goodbyes, and it's just the two of us. "Harrison," Winnie whispers my name into the quiet of the room.

"I love you." I pause, letting my words sink in. "I love you more than my job, and I need you to tell me that you know that."

"I do." She nods, tears again filling her eyes.

"Good." I go to her and wrap my arms around her. She buries her face in my neck and lets the tears fall. I don't say anything. I just tighten my hold on her, and let her work it out of her system.

"We should go." She pulls away.

"Yeah, you hungry?" I ask her.

"Not really."

"Okay. Well, I want to stop by the gym and pick up some contracts that I need to go over, then we can head home."

"You're not going to work?"

"No."

"Harrison."

"Gwendolyn," I counter. "I'm not going into the gym today. I need to be with you. I can't explain it, but I can't leave you right now. Please don't fight me on this."

"Okay."

I offer her my hand, and she takes it. I help her off the exam table and usher her out of the room. We stop at the desk and make our next appointment, then make our way to my truck. The drive to the gym is quiet. "I'll just be a few minutes. You coming in?" I ask her.

"No. Not right now. I'll just wait here."

Leaning over the console, I kiss her cheek. "I'll be right back." Climbing out of the truck, I jog into the building.

"Harrison," Gina calls out for me. "I didn't think you'd ever get here. We have a new client that wants you to train—" I hold up my hand cutting her off.

"No. I've told you I'm not taking on any more clients right now. Not with the baby coming."

"But—"

This time it's Chase who stops her. "He said no." He stops to stand next to her. "You good, man?" he asks. He knows me too well.

"I'm working from home today. Just stopped to pick up a few things."

"Anything I can do?" he asks.

"Nah, just got some news today. It's not terrible, but Gwen might have gestational diabetes. I'm going to look over the contracts, and then work on an exercise program for her."

"What, is she getting too fat for you?" Gina spits out.

"Enough!" I bellow. My feet carry me to her. We're standing toe-to-toe. "When it comes to my wife, you have nothing to say. Do you understand me? I don't have to defend my actions to you or anyone else. You know what, I'm done—" I stop when Chase's hand lands on my shoulder.

"Go get what you need. I've got this."

The words "you're fired" are on the tip of my tongue. I've had enough of her, but even I know that I'm on edge from the appointment. I nod once and turn my back to them, heading toward my office. I trust Chase to handle her. I shouldn't be making any kind of decisions with my emotions all over the place. Even if she's been on thin ice since the day she walked through the doors. Grabbing what I need, I don't bother saying goodbye as I walk out the front door.

"Everything okay?" Winnie asks when I'm back in the truck.

"Yeah, everything's fine," I say, then decide not to hold back. *"Never again"* is a promise I made. "Gina grates on my last nerve."

"How about some lunch?" she suggests. I know she's trying to turn my bad mood around, and it works. My focus is no longer on Gina or the gym; it's all her and our little girl.

"You change your mind?"

"She did." She rubs her belly with a small smile.

"What sounds good to you?"

"Anything."

"How about Twist of Lime?"

"Sure. Let's call it in and take it home," she suggests, already swiping the screen of her phone. "What do you want?"

"Grilled chicken salad, and some breadsticks."

"I love their breadsticks," she says, moaning. I listen as she orders us both a grilled chicken salad and extra breadsticks. "Ten minutes," she says, ending the call.

I start the truck and head that way.

Looking up from my laptop, I scan the room, searching for Winnie. I don't see her anywhere. Glancing at the time, I see I've been at this for a couple of hours so I gather the contracts and place them back in the folder. Grabbing the water bottle I've barely touched, I chug it back, spilling some all over my shirt. I finish off the bottle, and then pull my shirt over my head, wiping my mouth with it. Tossing the bottle in the trash and the shirt in the laundry room, I go in search of my wife.

I find her in our room, sitting on the bench at the foot of the bed. She's staring into space with her hands wrapped protectively around her baby bump. "Hey," I say softly.

She smiles, turning to face me. "Hey, you all done?"

"Yeah." I enter the room, taking a seat on the floor in front of her. "You okay?" I place my hand on her belly.

"I am."

"You sure?"

"Definitely. She was kicking up a storm, so I stopped to enjoy it. That sounds crazy, but I love this. I love being pregnant. If you say something, she'll kick. She loves the sound of your voice."

"No crazier than the fact I can't seem to keep my hands off your belly, or the fact that she knows my voice," I say, lifting her tank top to expose her to me. Winnie scoots to the edge of the bench, moving closer. I place my hands on either side of her belly and wait for a kick. Baby girl doesn't disappoint as she thumps against my hand. "Does it hurt?" I'm fascinated that my daughter is growing inside Winnie and kicking at the sound of my voice.

"No. Well, that didn't. Sometimes it's painful."

"Hey, baby girl, it's Daddy." Another strong kick.

"Told you."

"Maybe she'll be a soccer player."

She laughs. "Maybe. She can be anything she wants to be."

"Definitely, but she's not dating until she's thirty."

"Yeah, right. She's going to have you wrapped around her little finger."

"Maybe, but I'm not budging on the dating thing."

"We'll see." She laughs softly.

"Have you thought about names?"

"Yeah, but nothing has come to me that stands out. What about you?"

"I've thought about it, but like you, nothing that stands out to me. I mean, this is a big deal. She's stuck with her name for the rest of her life."

"Well, until she gets married. Then her last name changes."

"He can change his," I grumble, making her laugh.

"I changed mine."

"Damn right, you did." I think back to the day I met her, and I knew then that she was going to be important to me. I could never have imagined how much. I didn't realize how much she would bring to my life. And now, she's giving me a daughter. I have so much love bursting inside me for both of them. I don't know how to handle not being able to make it better.

"I love her." I rest my forehead against Winnie's belly, and she runs her fingers through my hair. "I love both of you. I know the doctor said that it was okay, that lots of women get gestational diabetes. I heard her say the words, but that doesn't quell the worry that consumes me. It doesn't diminish this demand for me to protect both of you. The only problem is I don't know how to do that. I don't know what to do to help you, and it's making me crazy."

"It's common. I just have to eat right and take care of us."

"What can I do, Winnie? I hate feeling helpless. You're going through all of this to bring our daughter into the world, and I'm just sitting by idle."

"You support me, Harrison. Every day you're here. You pushed yourself back into my life. You knew that what I needed was you. You've never once shied away from me or this baby. You love us unconditionally, and that's what I need from you. I need to know that you're here. That even though I'm carrying her, I'm not in this alone. I know I can lean on you and I'm sorry that I didn't. I don't want us to lose this, this newfound connection that we have. I love the life we're rebuilding, and I wouldn't trade it for anything. Sure, it's unorthodox, but it's only ever been you, Harrison Drake. You are the love of my life. You are the man who stands tall next to me, no matter what. The man who drills my doctor with questions for concern for me and our unborn child. That man is doing everything he can to take care of his family."

Lifting my head, I see the truth in her words. I see the love in her green eyes and know this is it. "Gwendolyn Drake, I want to grow old with you. I want you by my side, always. Will you marry me?"

Tears fill her eyes as she nods and says, "Yes." She bends down and presses her lips to mine. It's a soft kiss, mixed with the saltiness of her tears. "A thousand times yes," she says, pulling out of the kiss. "I don't want to make this a big deal. I just want to go to the courthouse and make what's in our hearts official."

"I never should have signed those papers." My heart is soaring, racing so hard I fear it might pound right out of my chest. Relief washes over me, knowing she's truly mine, for the rest of our lives. I'll never take her for granted ever again. She and our children—because baby girl needs siblings—will be my priority until I take my last breath.

"We were both stubborn and thought we were giving the other what we wanted. I never want to go back to that. I'm sorry for not telling you."

"Now I know, and we'll take this one day at a time together. We can sit down and figure out a good exercise regimen that is healthy for you and the baby, and meals, we eat healthy most of the time. Although, now I get why your gallon of chocolate milk in the fridge is still full and about to expire."

"Yeah, I miss it." She pouts. "But it's for her." She rubs her belly affectionately. "I can do and will do anything for her."

"It's for both of you. This affects more than just the baby, Winnie. This is about both of you."

"I know that. But Peanut and me, we have the key to success. Everything is going to be just fine."

"Oh, yeah, care to enlighten me?"

She cups my face in her hands. "We have you."

The emotions of the day, the fear, the worry, and now hope wash over me, forming a lump in my throat. I don't speak, but I wrap my arms around my family and hold them close, praying I can be everything they need. Now and in the future.

CHAPTER 16

Winnie

"I'm getting a little mad that you haven't asked for my help yet," my sister says when I enter the gym. The music is loud, a deep beat pulsing through my blood instantly.

"Mad? Why?" I ask as we sign in at the front desk and head toward the locker room.

"The wedding? Duh!" Gabby sighs dramatically.

I roll my eyes and open my locker, setting my purse inside. I grab one of Harrison's T-shirts and a pair of very unattractive pregnancy workout shorts (you know, the ones with the stretchy mesh over the stomach). "It's on hold. I'm not getting married like this," I state, pointing down to the very large protruding ball at my abdomen.

My sister immediately smiles. "I don't blame you there," she replies, greeting her niece with a friendly rub. "How was your appointment?"

"Fine," I reply, changing from my classic preschool teacher outfit into the clothes I keep at the gym.

At thirty-two weeks, the pregnancy is progressing quickly. I'm tired more frequently, which makes evenings like this, when I have to come to the gym, more difficult. All I really want to do is curl up on the couch with a book and rest. But with the confirmation of gestational diabetes after my twenty-four-week appointment, I know this is what is best. Harrison has a daily activity plan for me, which includes healthy meals. I started coming to the gym every day after work when school started again in August. As I get closer to my due date though, I'm finding it more difficult to do anything more than just walk.

"I'm going every two weeks," I confirm, slipping on my walking shoes and meeting Gabby at the door. She looks amazing, of course, in a tight tank top and skimpy little shorts. Something I wouldn't feel comfortable wearing six months ago, let alone now that I'm approaching blimp size.

We're quiet as we approach the treadmills. We take two side by side and fire them to life. My workout is much less strenuous than Gabby's. She'll run two miles before hitting the free weights. Me, on the other hand, will work up to a heart rate increasing brisk stroll that'll leave my calves burning and my feet aching.

"How's Roman?" I ask, trying to figure out what's going on with my sister's personal life. She seemed all about him, but then suddenly, nothing. Gabby hasn't mentioned the guy she was seeing for the last week or so.

She shrugs. "We ended it. There was no spark."

"Nothing?" I ask.

She glances around before her eyes connect with mine. "Not a thing. Kissing him wasn't even that good."

I glance at her, shocked as all get out. I thought they seemed to get along fine when they were on the boat. "And the sex?" I whisper so no one else around us can hear.

"Never got there. If the kissing isn't that great, that means his tongue-work isn't up to par. I'm not sure I want that subpar action for my lady bits," she replies with a decisive nod.

I can't help it, I laugh.

As soon as she finishes her warm-up and starts her jog, she asks, "So when is the big day anyway?"

"Yes, when is this very important big day, where you vow to love and cherish me for the rest of your life?" Harrison asks as he steps on the empty treadmill to my right. "Again..."

I offer a warm smile. He's wearing Nike basketball shorts and a T-shirt with the gym logo on the front. My entire body starts to hum, and it's not from the pace I've set on the treadmill. Harrison Drake is fucking hot, and the further along I get in this pregnancy, the more I want to take him for a ride. My hormones are out of control. Not that he seems to mind. I crave him morning, noon, and night, and he's all too accommodating to help with my little problem.

Trying to keep my eyes straight ahead, I risk one more quick glance his way. He gives me a knowing smile, as if he can read my mind and knows exactly what I want to do to him. On his desk. With my tongue. "Knock it off," he whispers, taking my hand in his. The warmth of his lips pressed against my palm spreads through my blood like lava, making me almost trip up. "Careful," he states, placing my hand on the handle and ensuring that I'm holding on.

"I'm fine," I assure him, but keep my eyes looking forward.

"Isn't this the point in the pregnancy where you want to hump day and night?" my sister asks, clearly throwing any trace of decorum out the window.

"I'm available for humping," I hear over my shoulder as Chase hops on the treadmill on the opposite side of Gabby.

"Puh-lease," she draws out, barely even breaking a sweat or breathing hard from her jog, "I'd rather hump a porcupine."

"Prickly," Chase replies, firing up his machine and immediately cranking it up to a fast pace. Gabby notices, of course, and bumps hers up a few more notches so she can one-up him on the speed. Chase just smiles and accelerates even more.

"So, about this wedding thing," Harrison starts, jogging at a much slower pace than the lunatics on the other side of me.

"I'm thinking next June," I blurt.

Harrison stops his machine and turns to face me. "June? That's seven months away," he grumbles, crossing his arms over his broad chest. I can't help but smile at the motion, so reminiscent of that of a toddler. All he'd need to do was stomp his foot.

I slow my snail pace to a stop and turn to face him. "I know I said I'd be happy with a quick trip to the courthouse, but I don't want that. I want a small ceremony at the lake. Or maybe the backyard. I want our close family and friends to be there and share in the joy of us remarrying. But most of all," I start, placing both hands on my stomach, "I want our daughter to be there and be a part of it all."

His eyes flare with heat and excitement, partly because of my finally agreeing to remarry him, but also at the prospect of our future and what it will hold. A daughter.

"June at the lake sounds perfect," he whispers, leaning over the machine and kissing my lips. His hands thread into my hair as he devours my mouth with his own. He's a master kisser, and the longer his lips are on mine, the more I want *other* parts of him on me.

"Awww," I hear behind me, the sugary sweet voice breaking through the sex-haze cloud we're surrounded in.

"Hey, Gina," I say, trying to turn and face Harrison's assistant, but he holds tightly to my head.

"Are we still on for Saturday?" she asks.

That catches his attention and finally turns to face her. "What do you mean? We don't have anything on the calendar for Saturday."

Gina giggles and rolls her eyes. "I know, silly. I was talking to Gwen. We're having lunch."

I can feel Harrison's eyes on me as I turn to Gina. "Yep, we're still on. I've been looking forward to trying that new salad at Twist of Lime."

"Me too! I'll meet you there at noon," Gina says, throwing a wave at the rest of the group and heading toward the front door.

"You're having lunch with Gina?" Harrison asks, the annoyance clear in his voice.

"Yes," I tell him, crossing my arms and staring him down.

"Why?" He seems genuinely confused by this revelation.

"Uhh, because we both need to eat. Last week when we were chatting, I mentioned that I wanted to try the new Cobb salad on the menu at Twist of Lime. She said the same, so we decided to go on Saturday. You're training most of the day, right, and lunch with a friend beats sitting at home," I tell him.

He continues to watch me. "I could get you that salad."

Smiling, I reply, "I know you can, but she offered and I accepted. What's the big deal?"

Harrison runs his hand through his hair. "I guess it's not a big deal," he mumbles. "I just didn't expect the two of you to hang out."

"It's lunch, Harrison. I'm not inviting her to be in our wedding," I sass.

"Damn straight you're not! That position is already taken," Gabby pants as she continues to run like her ass is on fire. Chase, who's running just as fast, almost trips himself up when he glances down and checks out my sister's ass.

Harrison and I each step off our machines. "I'm sorry, I'm not trying to be overbearing. If you want to have lunch with Gina, that's completely your prerogative."

I wrap my arms around his waist, pressing my large belly into his lower stomach. "I'm used to the caveman routine."

"It's not a routine," he teases, followed up by a gentle swat on the ass. His lips swipe across mine once again in a kiss that promises more to come, hopefully soon.

"Hey, Harrison, I was thinking of adding a few personal training sessions to my plan. I know you recommended Carlos last time. Do you think he's still available to work me over?"

Gabby asks as she slows her jog down to start her cool down.

"I'm sure he is. He stays late on Wednesdays now, and even takes a few clients on Sundays," Harrison tells my little sister.

"Carlos?" Chase asks, practically stopping his run and turning a wide-eyed face to Gabby.

She shrugs. "He seems more than competent to give me what I need," she coos, clearly insinuating something a little on the dirty side. I already know that's completely for Chase's benefit, to get a rise out of him.

And it appears to be working.

"Fuck that. You need someone to work you over, I'm your man, baby."

"I'm not sure you have the stamina to handle me, Callahan."

"Baby, I have stamina for *days*. No need to worry your pretty little head about that."

"Are they still talking about training sessions?" I whisper to Harrison, making him bark out a laugh.

"Of course we're talking about training! What else would we be talking about?" Gabby asks over her shoulder with a friendly smile on her face.

"Definitely. I'm the only man for the job," Chase responds, his eyes glued to my sister's ass as she walks on the treadmill.

"If you both say so," I mumble as Harrison entwines his fingers through mine.

"We're gonna leave you two to talk about your pending training, then. I'm gonna steal Winnie away to go over her schedule for next week," Harrison says, gently pulling me away from my sister and his best friend.

I groan aloud; I can't help it. I hate going over our own training schedule. Harrison always thinks he needs to add different Callanetics exercises into my routine, and then I spend the next ten minutes arguing with him about why I don't need to do them. He bores me to death with the added benefits, and I tune him out. It's the same routine we've battled for the last eight weeks, since my gestational diabetes diagnosis.

My legs are heavy as we make our way through the gym and down the hall toward the offices. With Gina gone for the day and Chase up front torturing my sister, there's no one back here. We enter Harrison's office together, and he quickly shuts the door. He throws the lock—not a good sign for me if we're about to argue over next week's schedule.

I open my mouth to try to head him off, when his lips slam against mine. With my mouth still open, his tongue easily dips inside my mouth, licking and tangling with my own. A groan spills from my mouth as his fingers thread into my hair and he pulls me tautly against his body. His erection is there, large and heavy in his shorts, and making the ache between my legs that much more intense.

"Fuck, you can't wear this anymore in public," he growls, tracing his lips along my jaw and down my neck.

"Wear what?" I ask, my brain struggling to catch up.

"My shirt. I know it's mine, Winnie, and when I see it stretched across your belly, it makes me want to do dirty things to you," he whispers, just before nipping at my earlobe.

Gasping my agreement, I throw my arms around his shoulders and try to climb him like a tree. It doesn't work, of course, considering I have a basketball attached to the front of my body. Harrison guides me backward until my ass hits his desk. His lips devour mine, stealing every ounce of breath and sanity I have left. I hear the sweep of his hand and the sound of things falling, but I pay no attention to it. I can't. All I can think about is the way he makes me feel.

The pleasure he gives.

Harrison lifts me up and sets me on top of the desk. My legs instantly wrap around his hips as I grind against his erection. My body is on fire, alive with reckless desire, as he makes a grab for my T-shirt. The moment it's gone, I internally groan at the image I must present. I'm wearing a no-frills sports bra, which does nothing but flatten my girls to my chest. But I've learned that the bigger my boobs get, the more I need the sports bra when working out.

"Fuck, Winnie," he barks, glancing down between us. You can clearly see his erection, tenting out his shorts, but also my swollen abdomen and my nipples, tight and aching in the confining material. He slowly pulls down my shorts, my hips lifting in assistance. "What were you thinking about earlier? You know, when you almost tripped on the treadmill."

Cool air kisses my heated flesh as he removes my panties right along with my shorts. "I was thinking about you. And this desk."

His nostrils flare and his eyes darken further. "What were we doing on this desk?" he asks quietly, relieving me of my sports bra next. Before I can answer, his mouth descends, greedily sucking one nipple into his warm mouth.

I gasp as pleasure shoots through my body. My pelvis tilts and I grind against his cock.

"What were we doing on this desk, Winnie?" he asks again, shifting to show my other nipple equal attention.

"You were sitting on the desk," I moan, my hand moving to his hair. "I had you in my mouth."

Harrison stops and glances up at me. "We can try that next."

"Yes, please."

He drops his head again and licks at my nipples. "So polite. I think that deserves a reward," he says, his hand dropping to remove his shorts.

"Yes, yes, definitely a reward," I beg, reaching for his hard erection. As soon as it's in my palm, I give it a few quick strokes. You know, to make sure he's good and ready.

It's his turn to moan now. "Fuck, you keep doing that and this won't take long at all," he bites out between strokes, grabbing the neck of his shirt behind his head and pulling it over.

"That just means we can get to round two quicker," I reason.

Harrison's eyes burn into mine with the same intensity I've always seen reflected in them when we're in this moment. He looks at me as if I were the only woman on the planet, the only one he wants.

I lean back and glance down, unable to watch this moment with my belly in the way.

"Close your eyes, Winnie. Close your eyes and just feel," he whispers, taking my hand in his. He wraps it around the base of his cock, his large, warm fingers around mine, and guides himself to my entrance. "I can already feel how wet you are, baby. I can already feel how badly you want this right now."

"So much," I whisper as, together, he starts to enter me.

My breathing stalls in my throat as I stretch to accommodate him. My legs wrap around his back and lock the moment he's fully seated inside me. I lean back on my elbows as Harrison places both his hands on my stomach. And then he moves. He thrusts his hips, filling me completely, stroke after stroke. The entire time, he never moves his hands, just lets his hips and legs do all the work.

"You look so fucking good on my desk, with my cock buried inside you."

I clench around him as his words and his dick continue to drive me closer and closer to the release I've been craving. I can't seem to find words as he pumps harder into my body.

"So fucking beautiful," he growls, his hands gripping me as he thrusts deep. "Mine."

My orgasm hits quick and fierce. Harrison pauses for a second, closes his eyes in euphoria, and then slams hard into me one last time when his orgasm follows. We're still for several moments before he bends down and takes my lips with his. "I love you."

"I love you too," I pant, trying to catch my breath.

"I love this," he adds softly, rubbing his hands over my tight stomach. His cock twitches inside me. "I love it so much," he says, pulling out and gently sliding back in. "I think you should stay pregnant."

"Well, we're on our way to achieving that." My giggle turns to a gasp as he flexes his hips and hits that magical spot deep inside me.

"You are the most radiant pregnant woman ever," he adds, lifting my legs and holding me in position. After a few slow, teasing strokes, Harrison pulls out completely, making me whimper in protest. "Come on, love. The shower in my bathroom is calling our name," he says, as he leads me toward the small adjoining room off his office for round two.

"I'm so excited that you made it!" Gina bellows as I enter Twist of Lime. It takes me a few seconds to adjust to the dim lighting in our favorite hangout.

"Me too. I was busy doing laundry all morning to keep my mind occupied, and now I'm craving this salad something fierce," I state, joining her in the booth.

"I went ahead and ordered for both of us," she says, nodding toward the water glass in front of me.

"Thank you so much. I'm so thirsty." I take a few greedy drinks before we launch into talk about the gym, one of the things we have in common.

"It's been so crazy lately. With all the new locations and staff, I can barely keep up."

I level her with a serious gaze. "If it's too much, Gina, don't hesitate to say something to Harrison. I know he doesn't want you overwhelmed at work."

She waves me off. "Oh, it's fine. I mean, he hired me so he could be with you more, right? If I complain, that just means he'll take back some of the duties he's given me, and you don't want that."

No, no, I don't want that, but I don't want her stressed and overwhelmed either. "Well, promise me that if it gets to be too much for you, you'll say something. Or let me say something to him if you'd prefer."

Gina grins. "That's sweet, but I'm good. I really enjoy my job. Harrison is a great boss."

I just smile in return. Even though she bugs Harrison daily and he's threatened to fire her on more than one occasion, she seems to really like what she's doing. She really has been a tremendous help with those office duties that he has always hated doing, even if she gets a few things confused from time to time. I mean, we all do that, right?

Right.

"Oh, I got your shower invitation the other day. I already put it on our calendar at work, so I made sure not to schedule anything on

December fifth. Harrison already has that entire week blocked out for the opening of the Porter location."

"Yeah, it'll be a busy Saturday, for sure, but my sister said that date was the only one open at the community center. With Christmas coming up and different things going on, it was sort of a take-it or leave-it date."

"What fun, though! You get to celebrate your baby girl right before Christmas. Plus, Harrison will be at the other gym all week, so he'll stay out of your hair," she adds with a giggle. Though, I don't really mind having him around. In fact, I sort of like having Harrison *in my hair*.

Our salads are delivered, and we both dive right in. There's a fresh mix of vegetables and nuts on the salad, and paired with avocado and chicken; it's everything I had been hoping it would be. In fact, I go ahead and order one to-go for Harrison. Since he's spending his Saturday training the few clients he kept and a couple for the trainer who is on vacation, he probably hasn't taken time to eat lunch.

"Well, I should probably get this over to the gym," I say to Gina as the waitress delivers the to-go salad.

"I had so much fun," she states as she pulls some cash from her pocket. "I hope we can do this again. With Chase gone most of the time to the Dalton and Lakeview locations, and knowing that Harrison is about to get super-crazy busy opening the Porter building, I get lonely at the office. I hope you'll stop by all the time!"

Pulling my own money from my purse for my two salads, I drop it on the table and gather my stuff. "I'm sure I will. I'm still on the strict exercise plan to keep the diabetes under control. We've managed it without having to medicate, which I'm grateful for," I tell her, sliding from the booth.

"Oh, I'm sure that's tough," she says sympathetically, touching my arm.

"It's not horrible, but I do miss my large glasses of chocolate milk." I chuckle.

"That is horrible!" she cries, with a laugh. "Almost as horrible as finding women's underwear under your boss's desk!"

As I reach the sidewalk out front, her words register and stop me in my tracks. "What?"

Gina seems to realize what she said, a cross between pity and mortification flash in her eyes. "Oh, nothing," she says, trying to laugh it off.

"No, seriously, what do you mean about finding underwear? When?"

Gina must be able to tell I'm not going to drop it. She shifts on her feet and averts her gaze. "Well, yesterday, when I got to work, I was on Harrison's computer, making sure to sync the calendars and I found them under his desk."

My heart hammers in my chest.

"I'm sure they're not from Harrison, Gwen. I mean, chances are, Chase had some gym bunny in there and she left them," Gina assures, her eyes still not showing me she's convinced of her own words.

And then it hits me.

Thursday night.

The gym.

The desk sex.

And suddenly, I'm laughing.

"Everything okay?" she asks, clearly thinking I'm losing my mind.

"Yeah, everything's fine. Those panties," I start, recalling how I didn't put them back on after our shower, "I'm pretty sure those were mine."

Gina just gives me a look before laughing. "Well, you little hussy, you."

Hussy? No.

Horny pregnant woman who can't keep her hands off her ex-husband, turned fiancé? Guilty.

"Yeah, I might have forgotten to pick them up," I reply, sheepishly.

"Well, I'm so thankful they were yours! I mean, after hearing Harrison tell Chase that you've really been putting on the weight, I was afraid he was stepping out on you! And it's not okay to step out on my friend!" Gina declares with a laugh.

But my mind focuses in on one part of her statement.

Putting on weight.

"He said I'm putting on weight?" I whisper, feeling the tears burn in my eyes.

"Oh, well... shit. I shouldn't have said anything. I mean, of course you're going to put on weight, right? You're pregnant!"

I give her a forced smile and nod, but in my chest, I feel like my heart was just dropkicked into December. I know I'm gaining weight. For a while, I gained more in a two-month span than some people do in their entire pregnancy. It's a sore subject for me, but I guess I never stopped to think about how this weight gain would affect Harrison. His business revolves around physical fitness, and here I am, blimping out like I just swallowed an Oompa Loompa.

My mind spins.

"Are you okay?" she asks, pulling me into her arms and giving me a tight hug.

"Yeah, I'm fine. This weight gain isn't forever, right?"

"Right! In about two months, you'll have a beautiful baby girl in your arms, and all this pesky weight gain will mean nothing."

I nod, though it's more for her benefit than my own.

"Well, I better get going. I'm grabbing groceries before heading home," Gina says.

"Thanks again," I say automatically, though my mind is already a million miles away.

Gina pulls me into her arms once more. "Keep your head up, sweetie. I think you look beautiful," she whispers before letting me go and heading off toward her car.

I'm left standing on the sidewalk, trying to figure out why I never realized that my weight gain would change the way Harrison sees me. Of course he'd see the extra pounds I've put on. He gets an up close and personal view of my swollen ankles and the extra-wide birthing hips I've developed in the last couple of weeks. He's always said he loves my growing body, but then why did he say something to Chase?

My heart drops when I think about him lying to me.

To make me feel better?

God, that makes me want to throw up.

On autopilot, I make my way to the gym to deliver lunch to Harrison. I guess if he's starting to get disgusted by my weight, I'll just have to keep it covered up more. Maybe make sure the lights are off from now on. The last thing I want is to make him uncomfortable, or worse, for me to see the look in his eyes when he catches just how big and fat I'm getting.

And I still have two months to go.

Joy.

CHAPTER 17

Harrison

With pregnancy comes hormones. Lots and lots of hormones which mean mood swings. My Winnie has had those in spades the last few weeks. We went from making love anywhere and everywhere to once a week if we're lucky, and only at night in bed. Don't get me wrong. I'm fine with that. I know that she's an incubator for our daughter and that the further along in her pregnancy she gets, the more uncomfortable she is.

I get that.

I understand that.

What I don't understand is the distance I'm starting to feel. Maybe it's all in my head, and maybe it's not. One way or another, I'm going to find out. We've come too far to let miscommunication come between us. If it's pregnancy hormones, bring it—I'm here and not going anywhere. However, if it's something more, I want to know about it. I can't fix it if I don't know. Regardless, she's stuck with me. There is no other option.

It's Friday, and I'm taking the day off. Winnie's last day of work for the Christmas break was yesterday, and I'm surprising her by spending the day together. Tomorrow is our baby shower, and her sister and our mothers will monopolize her time. Today she's all mine. She just doesn't know it yet. Chase is on call for the gym, and I've all but threatened Gina with her life not to call me. She's to contact Chase, and if he needs me, he'll call. Otherwise, it's just me and my girls.

I've been awake since five, my usual wake up time. My body is on a routine, and I can't seem to turn it off. I'm used to getting to the gym early for my workout before starting my day. It's now just before seven, and I'm still lying here wide awake. I have work I could do until she wakes up, but she's snuggled up next to me, and this bed is warm. Besides, no work today, or this weekend. I have to find a balance, and I feel like I need this time with her. Like we both need it.

We're lying on our sides, face-to-face, the dim light of the morning peeking through the blinds. She's peaceful and the most beautiful woman I've ever seen. I've heard of the "pregnancy glow" but never thought much about it. I take that back. I thought people who claimed it was a real thing were a few fries short of a Happy Meal. That's until my wife became pregnant. She really does have this... glow about her, and that's the best way I can explain it. I never thought of pregnancy as a turn-on, but when it comes to Winnie, it's exactly that. Her body is changing as our baby girl grows and it's the most erotic thing I've ever seen. To know a part of me is growing inside her... it's a definite aphrodisiac.

Reaching out, I push her long silky strands out of her face, and her eyes flutter open. "Morning, beautiful," I whisper.

"What time is it?" she asks, her long lashes fluttering against her cheeks.

"Around seven."

Her eyes spring open. "Why aren't you at work? Is something wrong?"

"No, baby." I cup her face in the palm of my hand. "Today is our day. I wanted to spend the day with you."

"You don't have to do that. I know how busy you are."

"That's exactly why I *want* to do this. I know I don't have to. I want to. I miss you. I feel like we've been distant the past couple of weeks."

"Crazy time of year."

She's right; the holidays are always a busy time of year, but it's more than that. I can feel it. "Yeah," I agree, not wanting to dig too far into anything just yet. "What do you want to do today? Anything you want." My hand that was cradling her cheek falls to her hip. I give it a gentle squeeze and then move in closer, aligning my body with hers. "It's hard to believe that in just four short weeks, or maybe even sooner we get to meet her," I say, moving my hand to gently rub over her belly. "How long do we have to wait to have another one?" I ask her. She's sexy as fuck.

"Right," she scoffs.

"Hey, what's that about?" I ask.

She closes her eyes and expels a heavy breath. "Nothing, just tired."

"You slept for over nine hours. What's going on, Winnie?"

"You can't be serious, Harrison. Look at me. I'm huge. My ankles are swollen, at least that's what Gabby told me. I can't see them. My boobs are swollen and tender. I waddle when I walk, and I've gained so much weight," she says, looking up at the ceiling.

"Look at me." I wait for her to pull her eyes from the ceiling. "Gwendolyn, look at me," I say again. This time, she slowly focuses her gaze on me, and there are tears in her eyes. "I'm dead fucking serious." My words are crisp and clear.

"Don't cuss around the baby," she scolds as a tear falls over her cheek.

"Then don't say things that make me cuss. How could you think that I'm anything other than serious? I can't keep my hands off you.

As of a few weeks ago, you couldn't keep your hands off me. What's changed?"

"Nothing. I just— I don't feel sexy." She pulls the cover up to her neck.

"Nope," I say, tugging it back down. "Let me show you."

"Harrison, we should go have breakfast."

"Oh, I intend to," I assure her. I place a gentle kiss to her lips before sliding down the bed. "Open for me." I tap her knee.

"Harrison, no. You don't have to do this."

I raise up on my knees so she can see me over her belly. "I want to do this, Winnie. It's been weeks since I've tasted you. I won't do anything you don't want, but I know you want it just as bad as I do."

"Maybe tonight," she counters, reaching for the covers.

"No. Fuck that. I want you now." I slide my hand up her thigh and don't stop until I reach her pussy. With my index finger, I trace her slit over her panties. She's soaking wet. "You want me," I tell her. "Lift your hips, baby."

"Harris—" Immediately she stops her protest when my fingers dip below her panties and push inside her.

"Tell me you don't want this and I'll stop." I gently pump my finger once, twice, three times before she lifts her hips. I make quick work of withdrawing, which causes her to whine. Grabbing either side of her panties, I pull them down her legs and toss them to the side. "Winnie," I say, running my fingers through her folds.

"Hmm?"

"Hold on to the mattress." I drop to my belly on the mattress and seal my mouth over her. She writhes underneath me, which fuels me on. I suck her clit into my mouth, tracing small circles with my tongue. Careful not to hurt her or the baby, I add one digit, then slowly as she draws closer to her orgasm, add another.

"Don't stop," she begs.

I don't bother with a reply. Instead, I pump my fingers a little faster, and swirl her clit with my tongue. Her walls tighten around me, and I know she's close. She gets tired easily these days, and I know getting another one out of her will exhaust her beyond measure. Pulling my fingers out, I climb to my knees. Wiping my mouth with the back of my arm, I align my throbbing cock at her entrance and push inside.

"Oh my God," she moans.

"I missed this," I say between thrusts. If you would have told me six months ago that fucking my pregnant wife was an aphrodisiac, I would have laughed in your face. Staring down at her, her belly between us, I feel my orgasm start to build. "I'm close, baby," I tell her, moving my hand between us and stroking her clit.

Her head moves from side to side, and her grip on the sheets is solid. I feel the moment she lets go, her body squeezing the hell out of my cock. I try to hold on, but I can't. With one final thrust, I release inside her. Pulse after pulse until I'm sated. I lie down next to her and pull her into my arms. I kiss the top of her head, and cradle one arm around her, the other resting on her belly.

"That is how we should start every day," I tell her.

"Mmm," she hums her agreement. I hold her, not wanting to let go, not wanting to lose this connection. Eventually, she looks up at me. "I need a shower."

"Let's get to it so I can feed my girls breakfast."

"No, you go ahead. I'll go next."

"Why not together?" I pout. Even my voice sounds like a child who was just told they couldn't go to a friend's house. I'm not ready to let her out of my sight just yet.

"It's a tight fit."

"We'll make it work."

"No, really it's fine. You go ahead."

"Winnie, don't make me carry you into the bathroom."

"You can't do that! I weigh too much."

"What? Are you fucking kidding me right now? You weigh nothing. You're all baby." To prove my point, I climb out of bed and lift her into my arms.

"Harrison! Put me down. You're going to hurt yourself."

"Stop." My voice is hard. "Enough of that shit, you hear me?" I get a subtle nod. I continue carrying her into the bathroom and set her on the counter. "Don't move," I say, pointing at her. I rush to turn the water on, then turn back to her. "Arms up." She doesn't fight me, but she's hesitant before she finally lifts her arms and allows me to remove her nightshirt. I rake my eyes over her. "Do they hurt?" I ask, tenderly tracing the swell of her swollen breasts with my finger. Bending down, I softly place my lips on the H tattoo.

"Sometimes. They're sensitive," she confesses softly.

I lift them, one breast in each hand, testing their weight. I feel wetness on my hand. Pulling my eyes from her breasts, I see she's blushing. "I'm sorry," she whispers.

"For what?"

"That." She nods toward my now wet hand.

"It's natural, right? I mean, I read that this could happen. That's how you're going to feed and nurture our baby girl. You have nothing to be sorry for."

"It's embarrassing."

"It's sexy."

"Right. Come on, Harrison, don't play games with me. Not after all we've been through."

"How am I playing games with you? I mean it. It's sexy to me. You're sexy to me."

"The water's going to get cold," she says, gazing off toward the shower.

I nod, knowing when to push and now isn't the time. I help her off the counter, leading her into the shower. I take my time, washing every inch of her body. I've read that some women have body issues during pregnancy, but I never thought that would be Winnie. She's fucking gorgeous, and I don't know how to make her see that. Maybe I should call Dr. Taylor and see if she has any tips for me.

Once I'm finished with her body, I move on to her hair. As soon as the suds are rinsed away, she climbs out, claiming she wants to get started on breakfast, while I quickly shower. Five minutes later, I find her in the kitchen, towel wrapped around her head, and a bathrobe on. "I need to go to the store," she says, peering into the refrigerator.

"We can do that today if you want. How about an egg and cheese sandwich?" I ask, looking over her shoulder.

"Yeah, that sounds good."

"Did you test your sugar?" I ask her.

"Yes, dad," she says and I can hear the roll of her eyes.

"Hey," I lean in and kiss her neck. "I'm just taking care of my girls."

"I know," she sighs.

"You go get dressed. I'll take care of breakfast."

She nods and heads for the stairs. "Winnie," I call out for her. She stops and turns to face me. "I love you."

Her eyes soften. "I love you too." She turns back around and slowly ascends the stairs.

"Thank you for breakfast."

"You're welcome. I have a surprise for you."

"I thought spending the day with me was my surprise?"

"Well, then I have two surprises for you."

"Gimme," she says, setting her bottle of water on the table.

I throw my head back and laugh. "Come with me." I stand from the table and offer her my hand. Slowly, I guide her upstairs. We stop just outside the room next to ours. The one we chose for the nursery.

"What? I get to see it?" she asks.

I had asked her to let me take care of the room, and to not peek until it was ready. "It's ready."

"How? You've been working so many hours, and I'm home when you're home."

"Well, you've been crashing early the last few weeks. I've been sneaking out of bed at night to work on it. It's finally done. Just in time to bring home all her gifts from the shower tomorrow. You can start your nesting." I kiss her nose.

"You and this nesting business. Do you believe everything you read?" she asks.

"When it's in those baby books, yes. I have nothing else to go on here."

She smiles up at me. "You're going to be such a great daddy."

"We've got this, Mommy. Now, close your eyes." She does as I ask. I open the door and guide her into the room slowly. "Open," I whisper, my lips next to her ear. I pull back and watch as her eyes flutter open and well with tears as she takes in the room around her.

The walls are painted a light gray, which stands out nicely with the white trim and white furniture. I picked up a few canvas prints that are pink, white, and gray that stick with our elephant theme. The bedding we bought is placed in the crib along with a new pink-and-gray stuffed elephant. The rug is in the center of the room, and the lamp is on a side table next to the white rocking chair, with gray cushions. Our daughter's crib sits on the opposite side of the room, and wooden letters, that I personally hand painted pink, are hung on the wall with white ribbons spelling out her name.

Sophia.

I watch Winnie as she slowly turns in a circle taking it all in. I know the exact moment she sees it. Her battle with tears is lost as one slides down her cheek. "When did you—" She swallows hard. "When did you take that?"

I know she's referring to the black-and-white picture I framed and set on the dresser. It's next to another black-and-white picture of the two of us that Gabby took one night when she was over. I'd handed her my phone, and she'd snapped a few. The one on the dresser is my favorite. We're standing side by side, arms around each other. Winnie is looking at Gabby, giving her a beautiful smile. I'm looking at Winnie. The other one is a picture I took of her a couple of weeks ago. She was sitting on the bed, her nightshirt pulled up, rubbing lotion on her belly and talking to our daughter. I snuck up on her and took the picture. Her hands are resting on her bump, and there is a smile playing on her lips.

"A couple of weeks ago."

"Why would you put that in here?" She turns to face me.

"Because she needs to know how much we love her."

"But that picture of me, it's... I don't want her to remember me like that."

"Like what?"

"Big and fat," she says, her voice breaking on a sob.

Taking her hand, I guide us to the rocking chair and sit, pulling her onto my lap. "Tell me what's going on, Winnie. What's going through that beautiful head of yours?"

"Nothing." She sniffs, but I know better.

"Tell me, baby. I'm right here," I say, wrapping my arms around her and resting my hands on her belly.

"I know, okay. I know what you told Chase."

"I tell Chase lots of things. You care to enlighten me?" I ask.

"About me being fat, gaining too much weight."

"What the fuck are you talking about? I've never said those words a day in my life. Who told you that?"

"You can tell me, Harrison. It's fine. I get it. My body's changed."

"Yes. Your body has changed, but it's because of our baby girl. You're beautiful to me, Winnie." She starts to speak, but I place my finger over her lips. "I can't keep my hands off you, baby. You being pregnant with our daughter is a huge turn-on." I take a deep breath, bracing myself for what I'm pretty sure I already know. The timeline adds up. "Who told you that?"

"Gina."

"When?"

"That day we had lunch at the Twist of Lime. She said she overheard you talking to Chase about all the weight I've gained."

Fury. I'm not even sure fury describes the rage I'm feeling toward Gina at this moment. "Look at me," I say gently, which is a contrast to the storm brewing within me. "I've never said those words. Never even thought them. You are gorgeous to me, inside and out. I'll never think anything different. Tell me you believe me."

She nods.

"I need to hear you say it, Winnie. I need your words."

"I believe you. These past few weeks have been so hard," she cries. "You make me feel so loved and so special, but then in the back of my mind, I wondered if you were just saying that because you thought that's what I needed to hear. I was so confused, and I missed you."

"I missed you too. I felt the distance, but I was trying to give you space. I know I've been a caveman when it comes to your eating and exercise, but, baby, it's not because of how you look or the number when you step on the scale. It's the diabetes. I want you and baby Sophia to be healthy. I don't know how else to help you through this. I'm sorry if my actions made you think otherwise."

"I'm sorry too. I should have confronted you. No, I shouldn't have believed her. I know that's not the kind of man you are. We've been through so much, and I was already feeling self-conscious about the weight."

"Don't. You're perfect." I kiss her lips and rest my forehead on her shoulder. I think about the last two weeks. Her keeping her body covered, not wanting to make love unless it was in the dark of night. I should have caught on sooner.

Fucking Gina.

"Baby, I know I said no work today, but I have to make a phone call. You want to sit in here for a while?" We stand, and she takes my seat on the rocker.

"Yeah, wait." She pulls on my arm. "What are you doing?"

"Firing her," I grit out.

"No, I don't want her to lose her job."

"Sorry, but it's too late for that. She's had one foot out the door since the day she started, and now this? What purpose does she have trying to come between us like that? I refuse to stand by and let it happen. Nothing, and I mean, nothing is going to keep us apart again. She's gone. End of discussion."

"Okay." She nods. She knows me well enough to know that when my mind is made up, it's a done deal. There is no going back on this decision. She's done.

"I'll be back in a few minutes." I leave the nursery, shutting the door behind me, my phone already at my ear.

"Why are you calling? Aren't you supposed to be sexing your baby momma?" Chase answers.

"Is Gina there with you?" I ask him.

"Yeah. What's up?" he asks, all traces of humor gone from his voice.

"Fire her."

"What?"

"You heard me. Fire her. Now. If you can't handle it, I'll be in to do it myself."

"Can I get a little more intel?" he asks. I go on to tell him the conversation I just had when Winnie.

"Consider it done. How is she?"

"My wife is in tears thinking I don't want her."

"Fuck," Chase murmurs. "I'll handle it. See you tomorrow for the shower."

"Thanks, man."

"None needed. You take care of your girls. I've got this."

It's times like these that I'm glad to have my best friend as my right-hand man. I could fire her, but I know with the way my blood is boiling at the moment, I would say things that were far from professional. It's best to let Chase handle this.

I should have fired her ass a long time ago.

It's Saturday afternoon, and most of our guests just left. My parents, as well as Winnie's, along with Chase and Gabby, remain.

"Does my niece really need all this stuff?" Chase asks, picking up a small pink fuzzy blanket and caressing it with his thumb and forefinger.

"Definitely," Janet says while my mom nods in agreement.

"Babies go through several outfits a day sometimes, and that includes sheets and blankets and burp cloths." My mom ticks items off, raising a finger for each one.

"Is there anything that we still need that we don't have?" I ask Winnie.

She smiles. I can see the exhaustion in her eyes, but it's second to the happiness that's shining in those green depths. "I have no idea." She laughs.

"We should have done this at our place," I tell her. "Less work packing it all to get it home."

"That's why they invited me, and well... for the cake. They knew they needed muscles for all this loot."

"Muscles. I don't see any muscles," Gabby quips.

"I can show you," Chase whispers, no doubt so our parents won't overhear.

"I'd hate for you to hurt yourself," she counters.

"Aww, are you volunteering to be my nurse?" Chase gives her a wolfish grin. "Because I've had this fantasy—" He throws his head back and laughs when Gabby smacks him on the arm.

"Thank you all for this," Winnie tells our mothers and her sister.

"It's our pleasure. Go through everything and let us know what you still need," her mom tells her.

"Oh, and me too. Janet, we should plan a day to go shopping to pick up the rest of what they need," my mom suggests. I can already see her wheels turning, planning a shopping trip.

"Guys, we can get whatever else it is we might need. I'm not sure there is anything else," I tell them.

"Oh, Harrison." Janet laughs. "That's not going to stop us from buying more gifts. This is our first grandbaby, after all."

I look over at Gabby, who's watching Chase with a small pink bear in his hands. "Gabby, we'll save all of this for you as she grows out of it," I tease her. "That way you have a head start."

"Hold up." She holds her hands out in front of her. "There are no babies in my future. I'd need a decent man for that to happen," she grumbles.

Chase turns to look at her. I've suspected for a while, but I finally see it. The fire in his eyes when he looks at her. It's more than just getting under her skin. If I were a betting man, I'd say my best friend has it bad for my sister-in-law. He opens his mouth to speak, but then shakes his head, turning his attention back to the bear in his hands.

"We'll still save it," Winnie tells her. "Our next one might be a girl."

"Next one?" her dad asks.

She shrugs. "We want more."

By the look on our parents' faces, you would think they just won the lottery. "Really, let us get this all unpacked and inventoried," I say, only half joking. The floor is littered with gifts and items I've never even heard of. I'm grateful for our friends and family, but I doubt we're going to need anything else.

"She's going to need lots of clothes. Those little buggers grow so fast, and she'll be lucky to wear half of what you got."

"Seriously?" I ask my mom.

She nods. "Janet's right. Babies grow so fast, and some people don't think about seasons when they're shopping. Like this." She pulls out a thick pink sleeper. "It says six months. It will be the middle of summer. She likely will never wear this."

"I've got a lot to learn," I say, not really caring that I'm showing my weakness. We're with family after all.

"All right. Let's start loading the truck. Between mine and yours, we should be able to get this in one trip." Chase stands and starts grabbing boxes.

"I can put some of the smaller bags and clothes in my car." Gabby stands too, grabs a handful of gift bags, and follows Chase out the door.

"There's something there." Janet smiles, her eyes glued to where Gabby and Chase just disappeared.

"Mom," Winnie warns her. "Let it be."

"So I'm right?" She claps her hands.

"Honey," Dwayne says gently. "We need to stay out of it. We said we would let the girls make their own choices," he reminds her.

"Pfft," Mom chimes in. "They just need a little push is all. That boy is like a second son to me, I know him."

"Sarah." Dad laughs. "No."

I watch as my mom looks over at Janet, and some kind of secret mom language passes between them. I should warn Chase, but then again, I'd rather watch this play out.

Winnie squeezes my hand, grabbing my attention. She's grinning from ear to ear. "They have no idea what's about to go down." She laughs.

"Should we tell them?" I ask, not really wanting to.

"Nope."

"I love you." Leaning in, I kiss the corner of her mouth. "I love you too, Sophia," I say to her belly before kissing it too.

I hear a chorus of "aww" and look up to find everyone watching me. I just shrug and pull my wife closer. I'll never shy away with showing them how much I love them. Reluctantly, I release my hold on her and help our dads, Chase, and Gabby load everything up in three vehicles. It takes all three of them to haul it all. An hour and a half later, our living room is cluttered with lots of pink, and I couldn't be happier. In four short weeks, I get to meet my daughter. I hope she looks just like her mama.

CHAPTER 18

Winnie

"What more could go wrong?" I say aloud to no one, instantly feeling guilty for putting that out in the universe.

A lot could go wrong. That's been proven over the last few weeks.

Each week—hell, each day—*something* has, in fact, gone wrong. First, my car wouldn't start. Turns out, my battery cables came (mysteriously) unhooked. My online order for a few last-minute Christmas gifts for Harrison was randomly canceled, ensuring they didn't arrive for the holiday. And this morning at two, we were awoken by a call from the security company for the gyms. Two of the four alarms were going off, and the moment Harrison gave them his code to deactivate them, they informed him his number wasn't correct.

I wanted to go with him, but he refused, not knowing what he was getting into and how long he'd be. The problem is that I'm now wide awake, just after four, with no sign of falling back asleep in my future. I'm pacing our living room, alternating between watching the clock and my phone. He was given explicit instructions to text me when he knew what was going on. I shot him a text message about ten minutes ago, but he hasn't responded. I'm about ready to call Chase, since I'm certain Harrison would have called him the moment he got in his truck to head to the gym.

This is most definitely not the way I wanted to spend the final day before the New Year. I'm a week away from my due date and starting to get miserable. Not that I'm sharing that titbit of info with the overbearing alpha in the house. My stomach tightens with Braxton Hicks contractions all day long, but today, they're worse. The walking seems to help, but that only makes my feet swell even more. I'm drinking so much water that I could practically live in the bathroom, and that's not to mention the times I pee by getting kicked in the bladder. Yes, it's happened. Twice.

All in all, I'm ready for this baby to get here. I'm tired, cranky, and don't even want to think about having sex. I'm anxious to get this thing *out* of my body, not put something *in* it. Harrison seems to understand, though I can tell by the way his erection presses against my leg that he's suffering a little with my newly implemented no-sex policy. He hides it well, though, never once complaining. He's amazing like that.

Just after five in the morning, the door between the garage and kitchen opens. I practically run (okay, waddle) to where he enters, throwing his keys down on the table and running his hand through his hair.

"What happened?" I ask, startling him with my sudden presence.

"Shit, Winnie, you scared the crap out of me. I thought you'd be sleeping," he says in the darkened kitchen.

I go straight to his arms. "I couldn't sleep," I confess, nestling into his chest.

"You've been up this whole time?" he asks, rubbing my back as he holds me close.

"Yeah. After you left, there was just no way I was going back to sleep. How did it go at the gym?"

Harrison sighs deeply. He takes my face in his hands and places his lips against mine. The kiss is sweet, sensual, and just what we both need. "It was a mess. The security company is still trying to figure out why the alarms went off. Our members have 24-7 access to the gym with their membership cards to gain access, but no one had used their cards at either location during that time. Yet, somehow the panic was tripped at Dalton and Fair Lakes."

"That's weird, right? I mean, how does the panic get tripped at two locations?"

"At the same time?" he asks, wrapping his arm around my shoulder and guiding me into the living room. "Someone hacked the system."

"Seriously?" I ask, stopping and making eye contact. I can see the worry in his eyes and the fatigue in the lines around them.

"Yeah. It's the only thing we can come up with, especially after my access code was changed. Even Chase's was changed. We had to reset the system in order to gain control on our end," he states, taking a seat on the couch and pulling me down with him. I'm sitting on his lap and can't help but instantly wonder if I'm about to squish him. "Stop it, baby. You're fine."

Leave it to Harrison to know exactly what I'm thinking without saying a word.

"Why don't you come to bed and try to get a little sleep," I tell him, cuddling into his arms and shoulder. Now that he's here, the exhaustion is setting in.

"Can't," he mumbles, running his nose along my neck and inhaling deeply. "I have an early client, and then I'm meeting with Chase to go over security on all four buildings. We want to make sure this breach never happens again."

"You can't catch any sleep?"

"My client will be there at six. I have just enough time to shower and grab a bite to eat," he whispers against my skin. "I want you to try to go back to sleep."

"I'm not sure I can," I tell him, even though I'm more than tired. My mind is racing a billion miles a minute. With everything that has been going on at the gym, the opening of the fourth location earlier this month, him firing Gina, and the baby coming in a week or so, I just can't settle my brain. It's working overtime, and I think that's a big part of the reason I haven't been feeling well lately.

"Promise me you'll try."

I run my fingers through his hair and lock my eyes on his. "I promise."

"Good," he agrees, picking me up in his arms and carrying me to our bedroom.

"What are you doing, you lunatic!" I holler, hanging on for dear life.

"I'm carrying the woman I love to bed so she can rest." As he sets me down in the middle of the unmade blankets, he places a lingering kiss on my forehead.

"Don't forget the appointment," I mumble, as my eyes start to droop.

"I'll be there. I love you," he whispers.

"Love you too," I reply, letting the sudden exhaustion consume me.

I'm in the waiting room for one of my final appointments, but do you know what I don't see? My husband. Err... ex-husband. Anyway, you know that guy who was supposed to meet me here? Yeah, he's not here.

And I'm irritated as hell.

Bad.

Angry, actually.

It's gotta be these out-of-control hormones, but I'm on the verge of yelling and kicking and crying, all at the same time.

"Gwen." I hear my name called from the hallway that leads to the patient rooms. Great, it's Nurse McFlirts-A-Lot, the flirty nurse turned regular at All Fit. I can feel the flush sweep up my cheeks, and I just pray I have enough control over my tongue.

"Let's get you weighed in," she suggests, pointing to the horrible machine that's going to tell me I've eaten too many things in the non-salad variety.

I step up on the scale, pleasantly surprised to see only a half-pound weight gain since last week's appointment. I'll call that progress. I head off to the bathroom to complete the next phase of the appointment, knowing full well the result will show a trace of sugars. They all have since my diagnosis. The key has been the stupid exercise plan my sadistic husband put me on, coupled with a healthier diet. I do admit I've felt good these last few months, but personally, I'm ready to be able to eat peanut M&M's and Dairy Queen Blizzards again.

The nurse places the blood pressure cuff on my arm and starts to squeeze. She slowly lets it out, her eyes on the little ticker. "Uh-oh," she mumbles.

"What?"

"Why don't you go ahead and lie back for a few minutes. Relax," she says calmly, making me anything but.

"Why?"

"Well, your blood pressure is a little high."

"How high?"

"One sixty over one hundred," she says, placing her index and middle finger on my pulse point on my wrist. "Relax."

Right.

No one in the history of pregnant women has ever relaxed just because someone told them to. Ever.

Nurse Flirty waits a few minutes and takes my blood pressure a second time. The results must not be what she wanted because of the face she makes. She quickly writes down a few notes in my chart, hands me a gown to change into, and makes a quick exit, informing me the doctor would be in shortly.

Shortly is actually only a couple of minutes.

"Gwen?" Dr. Taylor asks as she enters the room. "How are you feeling?"

"Fine," I tell her, slightly annoyed she'd ask such a dumb question. I mean, can't she tell how I'm doing? I'm thirty-nine weeks pregnant, have gained five hundred and ten pounds, and my husband slash ex-husband slash fiancé isn't here. Why would I be anything other than fine?

She takes a seat. "Well, your blood pressure's a tad on the high side."

"I've been having those Braxton Hicks contractions all day," I inform her, placing my hands on my abdomen.

"That's a good sign, if not a little on the annoying side," she says with a smile.

"No kidding. I get up fourteen times a night to pee, so sleeping isn't going so great at the moment."

She gives me a knowing grin. "They say that's God's way of preparing you for the sleepless nights you're about to endure when the baby arrives, but I say that's just cruel and unusual punishment. At least let the moms-to-be sleep the few weeks they have left before the baby comes. But the good news is you're in the home stretch. We'll measure your abdomen and check her heartbeat. Have you been feeling her kick ten times by noon?"

"Are you kidding me? She's practicing for her career as a professional soccer player in there," I reply with a laugh.

Dr. Taylor joins in my laughter. "Well, that's a good sign." She does her thing, taking the appropriate measurements, and uses the Doppler to listen to Sophia's heartbeat. "This is one of the last times you'll hear it with this device. Soon, you'll have her in your arms," she says as she helps me clean up the gel. I watch as she grabs the blood pressure cuff once more and places it around my arm. She pulls out her stethoscope and squeezes the bulb, paying close attention to the reading. "Well, it's down a little, but it still concerns me. If you start to feel lightheaded or not right, I want you to go to labor and delivery. Where's Harrison?"

"Oh... he... well, something came up." Tears burn my eyes, but I blink them away, refusing to let them fall now. I'm terrified that if they start, I won't be able to stop them.

She nods. "Well, I want you to have him drive you to the hospital if you don't feel right. High blood pressure at this point in your pregnancy isn't a good sign, especially with gestational diabetes. It could be a sign of gestational hypertension or preeclampsia. I want to be proactive, all right? I'd like you to stop by tomorrow morning and have your blood pressure checked by one of the nurses."

"Okay," I reply, my heart hammering in my chest.

"I'm going to check and see if you're dilating yet," she informs me, pulling out the stirrups and helping me get comfortable. Comfortable. Sure. My doctor has her hand up my crotch.

"You're starting to dilate. I'd say a comfortable two centimeters and thirty percent effaced," she says with a smile as she removes her fingers and pulls off the gloves. "You're progressing quite well. I just want to keep monitoring that blood pressure."

What else could possibly go wrong?

After checking out, I make my way to the parking lot to my car. It's the last day of the year and the snow is starting to fall. I've never really minded snow, but now that I'm waddling through the parking lot, trying to be careful, well, the snow is just a nuisance. As soon as I get inside my vehicle, I crank up the heat and feel the first tear fall.

He's never missed an appointment.

He's been late once or twice, but he always made it. What the hell happened? Angrily swiping away my tears, I check my phone once more to see if I missed a call or message. There's nothing on my screen. A part of me wants to drive to the gym and let him have it, but a bigger part just wants a hug. And maybe some rocky road ice cream.

So that's what I do.

I stop at the grocery store, buy a tub of ice cream, and head to my sister's house. When I pull into her driveway, I check my phone again to see if Harrison has sent me anything, but there's nothing. Turning off the ringer, I throw my phone into my purse and grab the ice cream.

Before I even approach the door, she has it open. "What are you doing here? Wait, is that ice cream?"

I push past her as I state, "I just left the doctor. Yes, it's ice cream. Help me eat it."

Her eyes follow me as I grab two spoons from the kitchen—and not those regular sized spoons either. No, I grab the large, barely-fit-in-your-mouth spoons. "Uhh, Gwenny? I didn't think you were supposed to eat ice cream," she says hesitantly.

I scoop a huge bite of rocky road ice cream and reply, "I'm not. But Harrison missed our appointment and it was either eat ice cream or cut off his balls with a wooden spoon."

"Ouch," she says, coming over to the counter and grabbing the other spoon. "Sounds painful. Why'd he miss?"

"I don't know," I reply, shoveling more cold goodness in my mouth. "He didn't show. I watched him put it in his calendar after last week's appointment. He marked the entire three o'clock hour off so that he didn't miss, but whatever."

"Uh-huh, whatever. Obviously, you're a little peeved."

"A little." I shrug.

"How'd the appointment go?" she asks, taking a much smaller bite of ice cream.

I plop down on the stool and use my spoon to draw a flower into the ice cream. "Not good. My blood pressure was high, but that's probably because I was upset about Harrison missing the appointment. We got a call at two this morning about the alarms going off, and then he had trouble with his security code. They had to reset the whole system."

"They've had a lot of trouble these last few weeks," Gabby adds, setting her spoon down. "You'd think someone was trying to sabotage them."

I glance at her, my heart pounding like a snare drum. "What did you say?"

"What?"

"What did you say?"

"I don't know. I was just thinking out loud."

"You said it sounded like someone was sabotaging them." Just saying the words aloud has my mind racing.

Gabby stands up straight. "Do you think someone is?"

"I don't know," I tell her honestly. "It's just that a lot of weird things have been happening. First with my car, then with the building. Plus, some of the orders were changed, like the new towels for Porter arrived in orange and green instead of white, as ordered."

"Who would mess with that?" she asks, giving me her full attention.

"No clue. I mean, Harrison and Chase are the only ones who order and have access to all of that stuff, right?"

"Well, besides Gina," Gabby adds.

"But she's been gone for three weeks," I note, remembering how upset Harrison was when he found out Gina told me she overheard him saying I was getting fat in my pregnancy. That moment had been the straw that broke the camel's back, and he'd called Chase to fire her immediately. With everything he's been dealing with, he hasn't had time to hire a new assistant yet.

"And didn't these weird things start happening about three weeks ago?" Gabby asks.

I glance her way, and don't need to use words to confirm her suspicions. My stomach tightens painfully, with much more intensity than earlier.

"Wow, what was that? Are you okay?" she asks, coming around to my side of the counter.

"Fine, just those stupid Braxton Hicks contractions," I reply, taking a few deep breaths.

"You sure? That seemed pretty intense."

"Yeah, I'm sure."

"What can I get you?" my sister asks.

"Maybe a glass of water."

She guides me to her living room. "Come on, go sit down on the couch. I'll grab you some water. You probably put your daughter in a sugar coma, since you haven't had ice cream in months." Gabby hustles off to the kitchen to get water. "Where's your phone?" she hollers from the other room.

"In my purse. Why?"

"I'm going to call Harrison," she says, returning with the glass.

"No, don't do that," I demand, taking a slow sip of water. "I'm fine. He's obviously very busy, otherwise, he would have been at my appointment."

She gives me a look that lets me know she doesn't exactly agree with me, but she relents. "You can stay here and relax, but if you're still contracting in an hour, I'm calling him."

"Fine," I grumble.

"In fact, I'll shoot him a text and let him know you're here," she says, grabbing her own phone. I watch as she types out her message and taps Send. "There. At least he'll know where you are."

We spend the next hour visiting, chatting about everything from work to the gym. Chase is still training Gabby, but I'm not sure how much longer that'll continue. She says all he does is push her buttons so that she's all sorts of pissed off by the time she leaves. Gabby can give as good as she gets, most times, but with Chase, I don't know. He pushes her to her limit, both in the gym and out of it, considering she threatens to maim him on a regular basis.

"Do you remember that time we met Harrison and Chase at Twist of Lime right after my twenty-first birthday?" Gabby asks as we reminisce about life before full-time jobs and bills. You know, when trying to figure out what to wear to the bar on a Saturday night was your biggest decision?

"No," I tell her, trying to ignore the tightness in my stomach. This one's just as intense as the contraction I felt almost an hour ago, but I try to hide it.

"You and I went to the cinema to see that new Ryan Reynolds movie. By the time it was over, you had a message from Harrison to meet him uptown. We went, and they were shooting pool with... wait," Gabby says, jumping up from the chair. "Gina!"

"What?" I ask, getting up from the couch.

"Gina was there! Don't you remember? She was hitting on Harrison hard when we walked in. He was being polite, but trying to get her off him?"

For some reason, that night comes back to me easily. I recall walking into the bar and spotting my boyfriend across the room. He was watching Chase shoot, barely paying any attention to the young girl beside him, except for the occasional polite nod and smile. And when I say she was beside him, I mean, hanging on his arm and rubbing herself against his side. I could tell he was uneasy by his body language, but the moment our eyes met across the bar confirmed it. He was practically begging me to rescue him without so much as saying a word.

"I went up there just as she was asking him to give her a ride home," I recall.

Gabby snorts. "Oh, she was wanting a *ride* all right, and maybe in the back seat. She was so disappointed when we arrived, especially when he laid the kiss of all kisses on your lips."

Now *that* I remember. That kiss was a prelude to some amazingly dirty things later that night. "Didn't she go home with Chase?"

Her jaw tics as she stares at me. "Yeah, she did. It all makes sense now, but when I saw her the next day, she said the guy she was trying to take home fell through, so she took his best friend instead." I swear my sister gets pissed as realization sets in—that her friend slept with Chase.

"Why wouldn't Chase remember her?" I wonder aloud.

Again, Gabby snorts in disbelief. "Are you kidding? That man sleeps with anything with a vagina. No way would he remember all of them, especially someone from seven years ago, during a night of drinking."

My stomach clenches tightly, and this time, I'm unable to mask my discomfort. "Shit," I groan, doubling over in pain.

"Gwen?" Gabby rushes to me and helps me sit on the couch. "I'm calling Harrison," she adds, reaching for her phone.

"No, wait." Deep breath, in and out. "I think you need to take me to the hospital."

Everything happens quickly after that. My sister grabs my purse and my hand and leads me toward the passenger seat of my car. I keep my hands protectively around my stomach as she tears out of the driveway. "Gabby, slow down. You're going to get pulled over."

"You're in labor, Gwenny. I don't think I can do slow," she replies, practically taking the corner on two wheels.

The moment we hit Main Street, traffic seems to slow down. It seems busier than usual, even more so than a Friday night, just after six o'clock. "What the heck?" I wonder out loud.

"There must be an accident," Gabby says. "We'll turn off up here."

"It's okay. I haven't had any contractions in a few minutes. Maybe they're false ones again," I reason, wondering if I'm jumping the gun by going to the hospital. I'm not due for another week, so maybe these are just intense Braxton Hicks contractions, preparing me for what's to come soon. I'm just about to tell her to turn around when I see smoke. "Something's on fire."

Gabby looks ahead. "God, I think it's up by the gym."

My heart starts to pound a bruising beat in my chest and my breathing is labored. Fear starts to creep up my neck, setting my nerves on edge. The gym takes up most of the block. There's a bank and travel agency to the north, but that's it. In my heart, I know. I know what I'm about to find isn't going to be good. "Get us up there, Gabby," I whisper, panic setting in as I think about something happening to Harrison.

"They're rerouting traffic. We're going to have to go on foot," she says, turning off into a parking lot about a block away from the gym. "Let's go," she adds, the moment she stops haphazardly in a spot.

I'm out of my car much quicker than I would have anticipated. With my hand in hers, we practically run toward the gym. Two fire trucks are positioned in the street with their hoses running into the building my husband purchased and built into his livelihood. It's dark, but the streetlights give just enough glow that I can see the damage inside.

"Hold it right there," a fireman says, holding up his hands to keep us from proceeding any closer. "You have to back up behind the barricade."

I just start to open my mouth when I see a familiar face. "Chase!" I yell, pulling the attention of our friend.

He runs over to where we stand, panic and relief mixing on his dirty face. "Jesus, Gwen, where in the fuck have you been?" he asks, pulling me into a tight hug.

"What? Where's Harrison?" I glance over his shoulder, but don't spot him anywhere.

"He went looking for you! You haven't been answering your phone and he's freaking out."

"Oh, shit. My phone's on vibrate in my purse," I confess, instantly regretting the immature move of shutting off the ringer when I was mad. "He missed our appointment. I was upset," I add, feeling horrible.

"He's been going crazy," Chase informs.

"I texted him and told him where she was," Gabby adds.

"His phone broke. Everything's gone to complete shit this afternoon," he says, rubbing the back of his neck and glancing at the building.

Gabby steps up to Chase and throws her arms around his neck. If he's startled by her sudden show of affection, he doesn't show it. "What happened?" she asks as she pulls away.

"Everything," he groans. "The phones went down first. They say someone cut our line and it'd take a few hours to get it back up and running. Then the computers. I'm pretty sure it was a virus. I had just checked Harrison's schedule right before it happened because one of his clients needed to reschedule. It said your appointment was at four," he says, but I interrupt.

"My appointment was at three. I watched him put that in his calendar."

"We know that now. He went to the appointment but was told you were already done and gone. He tried to call you, but his cell phone wasn't working. He came back here, confused as hell as to how the mix-up happened. I was on the phone with IT for our software program when the fire alarm went off."

"Christ," Gabby declares.

"We were able to get everyone out, but it was difficult. The place was pretty busy already and one of the yoga classes had just started."

"I can't believe this," I whisper, watching as the firefighters start to pull out of the building.

"We're pretty lucky," Chase says. "They say it started in the girls' locker room. Towels and an accelerant."

"Arson?" This from Gabby.

"Looks that way." He sighs.

"We need to find Harrison." I glance around, trying to figure out where he'd be. Clearly if he's out looking for me, he's going to check all the obvious places first. Our place, my parents, even Gabby's.

"We can't call him. His phone is still jacked up," Chase says, just as a contraction takes hold. I lean over slightly, grabbing my stomach and trying to breathe deeply through the pain.

"Gwen?" Gabby steps up beside me. "Shit, we have to get you to a hospital."

"Harrison?" I ask, gasping through the most intense contraction I've had yet.

"I'll find him," Chase declares, taking me in his arm and starting to guide me toward his truck. "Mine's closer. Take it and get her to the hospital," Chase adds, pulling his keys from his pocket and handing them to my sister.

"Her car is in the lot by the hardware store," Gabby replies, racing toward Chase's big truck.

When we reach it, another contraction takes hold, this one refusing to let up. I moan loudly, fighting through the pain. It's so intense that it's hard to breathe, let alone think. Chase has the door open and is getting ready to help me up when I feel it. Wetness runs down my leg as I make eye contact with my husband's best friend. The fear in his eyes sends me into a full-blown panic.

"Gabby, my water broke!"

CHAPTER 19

Harrison

My heart races, the heavy rhythm beating like a bass drum against my chest. This day was already fucked up, but to make it worse, I missed our appointment. Someone is fucking with us, to the point someone changed the time on my calendar. I've never missed an appointment, and guilt and sadness weigh heavily on me for not being there. Now I don't know where she is. I've tried calling her, with no luck. No one has seen her.

Fear takes hold as I press the accelerator a little farther to the floor. Maybe she's at home, sleeping. She's a week away from her due date, and I worry constantly. What if something happened? What if she's hurt, what if...? I shake my head and press the accelerator even harder. I won't be able to ease this fear until I find her.

With my tires squealing, I pull into our driveway. I hit the button for the garage door. Her car's not there. I still rush into the house, calling out for her with no reply. I search every room and come up empty-handed. "Fuck!" I reach for the house phone that I told her years ago we didn't need. She argued it might come in handy one day. Today is that day. My cell phone is jacked. The screen is locked or some shit. I can't get it to unlock. I can't answer or make calls, send texts. All I can do is stare at the now worthless piece of shit. Just another pile of shit on this fucked-up day.

Quickly, I dial her number, and it again goes straight to voice mail. "Damn it, Winnie, where the hell are you?" I say, crashing the phone down on the receiver. Stalking to the garage, I slam the door, and race to my truck. I barely remember to hit the button to close the garage doors. Not that it matters. Someone could rob us blind, but I don't give a damn. All that matters is finding my wife.

I'm aware that I'm a maniac, and that chances are she's fine, but there's been too much shit happening the last few weeks. The list is ever growing, and now I can't find her. I know she was at her appointment, but that's it. Turning my truck toward Gabby's house, I'm cussing myself for not trying to call her when I had the chance. I also should have called our parents, but hindsight and all that. I'm not turning back, losing ground. I need to find her. I need to see with my own eyes that she and our baby are okay.

Please, God, let them be okay.

I make it to Gabby's in record time, and there are no signs of either of them. The truck is barely in park before the door is flying open and I'm jogging to the front door, pounding. "Gabby!" I yell, trying to peer through the windows.

Nothing.

Silence greets me.

"Damn it!" I race back to my truck and fly out of her driveway, heading toward her parents' place. Worry and fear grip at my chest. Where could she be? She's miserable at this stage of her pregnancy, even though she tries to hide it, I can see how tired and uncomfortable she's been. She has to be at her parents or mine. Those are my last two options. I can't imagine her wanting to do anything but prop her feet up. Where else would she go? Maybe she went to the gym? That's possible. We could be circling around each other. It's a cluster fuck over there right now, but I'll drive by and see if I can spot her car. Luckily, it's not much of a detour to get to her parents' place.

I have to find her.

My eyes scan the sides of the road, looking for her car all while praying I don't find her broken down or worse. I grip the wheel tighter, so tight my knuckles are white, but I don't let go. Instead, I press harder on the accelerator, pushing the limits of the law, and my truck. I don't give a fuck. I'm not stopping for anyone but my wife. Not until I find her. My heart hammers in my chest as my fear of something happening to her grows. I try to tamp it down, but the anxiety is tangible, and it's taken root.

About a block away from the gym, I see a car coming toward me that looks like hers. I slow as it passes and I know it's hers, but she's not driving, Chase is. His hand is out the window flagging me down. I slam on the brakes and do a U-turn. I couldn't give a fuck that I'm breaking the law. Chase is pulled off on the side of the road, and already walking toward my truck when I pull in behind him.

"Where is she?" I ask, not bothering to get out of my truck. I can clearly see she's not in the car with him.

"Gabby took her to the hospital. Her water broke," he says.

I put the truck in reverse and begin to back up. "Meet me there!" I yell out the window. Shifting the truck into drive, I pull out onto the road. I don't bother to look if there are any cars coming. Thankfully there aren't. It's reckless, I know, but I have to get to her. I refuse to miss my baby girl being born, and my wife needs me. They both do.

I'm dazed as I drive to the hospital. The fear of not knowing where she was or if she was okay is replaced by the fear of the unknown. I know women have been having babies for centuries, but with her gestational diabetes, I worry. She's also a week early. Something Dr. Taylor told us could happen, but I worry about Sophia. Is she okay? A million fears and concerns race through my mind. When I finally reach the hospital, I take the first spot I can find. After yanking the keys from the ignition, I run as fast as my legs will carry me to the main entrance.

"Sir," an older lady greets me at the front desk. "Can I help you?" she offers politely.

"My wife," I pant. "Her water broke. She's here." I manage to find my words.

"Of course, how exciting," she says. Her calmness is like a balm to my fear, and I suck in a deep breath. "What's your wife's name?"

"Gwendolyn Drake," I say on exhale.

"She's in the maternity ward." She continues to tell me the room number.

"Thank you," I rush to say, and jog off toward the elevators. I hit the button for the fifth floor and watch as the elevator seems to climb at a snail's pace. At the fourth floor, I move close to the door, and as soon as they slide open on the fifth, I'm rushing out and down the hall. Her room is at the end of the hall, the door is closed, but that does nothing to hide her screams. I push open the door and take in the scene before me.

Gabby is by her side, holding her hand and her leg, while there is a nurse on the other side. Dr. Taylor is between her legs that are in stirrups. I've read that this takes hours, but as I process what I'm seeing, I realize the books aren't always right.

"Harrison," Winnie cries, and I rush to her. The nurse steps out of the way as I move in close and press my lips to hers.

"I'm sorry, baby. Everything was so messed up," I rush to explain.

"Dad," the nurse says, placing her hand on my arm. "We're going to need you to hold her hand and her leg. She's going to need help. It's almost time to push again."

I nod, my eyes finding Dr. Taylor's. "You're just in time, Harrison. You ready to meet your baby girl?"

Emotion clogs my throat as I nod. It's impossible for me to speak. I almost missed this. Turning my attention back to my wife, I bend and press my lips to her forehead. "I-I love you," I croak out.

She smiles. "I'm glad you're here. I didn't want to do this with-o-out y-ou," she pants as Dr. Taylor tells her to push.

"You're doing great," Gabby says soothingly.

Winnie's grip on my hand is tight as she bears down with all her might. The contraction passes, and she slumps back against the bed. Again, I bend down to kiss her. Needing that contact, that connection that flows between us. This time, I linger, resting my forehead against hers. "Thank you," I whisper softly. There is no time to reply as another contraction comes and she's being told to push.

"Grab her leg, Dad," the nurse instructs.

Looking over at Gabby, I copy what she's doing. Holding Winnie's hand tightly in mine, I pull back on her leg, assisting her with the other.

"There you go, Gwen. Keep pushing. You're almost there."

Everything seems to happen at once as time stands still. Winnie exhales in relief as the cries of our baby girl fill the room. "It's a girl," Dr. Taylor announces.

Winnie flops back against the pillows, and her smile is radiant. "You hear that, Winnie? You did it, baby. You did it," I say, kissing her lips.

When I pull back, her palm rests against my cheek. "You're crying," she says through her own tears.

"It's not every day the woman I love makes me a father," I tell her, not bothering to wipe my tears. I know there are more to be shed.

"Harrison." Dr. Taylor pulls my attention away from my wife. "You want to cut the cord?"

I look down at Winnie, and she nods. With shaking hands, I make my way to the end of the bed. Dr. Taylor is holding my daughter. The nurse hands me a pair of scissors and explains to me what I need to do. My hands are shaking so badly, I have to use both of them to operate the scissors. As soon as my job is complete, the nurse takes my daughter. I don't take my eyes off them as they clean her up and call out some kind of score. My head is too jumbled to understand. I watch as they place her on a scale and she cries, not liking that one bit. I want to step in, but I hold still. One nurse stretches her out while the other calls out her length. I watch as they prick the heel of her tiny feet making her cry. I knew this was going to happen, Dr.

Taylor warned us that they would need to check her sugar right away. However, that doesn't make it any easy to watch them draw blood from her tiny foot. Once they're done, they then wrap her up in a blanket, place a hat on her head, and walk her to Winnie. Gabby steps back, tears streaming down her face.

"Here you go, Mommy. Her levels are good. We'll need to test her again after she eats." The nurse smiles as she hands Sophia, our *daughter,* to Winnie.

Our daughter.

Holy shit!

I'm a father.

"She's so tiny," Winnie says, unwrapping her and counting all ten fingers and toes. "Hey, angel, I'm your mommy," she says as Sophia's tiny hand wraps around her finger.

"Thank you, Winnie," I kiss the top of her head and then turn my attention to my daughter. She's so damn tiny, and the most beautiful baby I've ever seen.

"Seven pounds, eight ounces, and nineteen inches long," the nurse tells us. "She passed her Apgar scores with flying colors," she adds. "We need to feed her."

I watch as the nurse shows Winnie how to help our baby girl latch onto her breasts. Baby girl is a champ, at least that's what the nurse tells us and she begins to eat. The sight of my wife breast-feeding our newborn daughter is not something I was prepared for. I feel hot tears prick my eyes, but I blink them away. These two ladies, they are my entire world. I stare at them in wonder, until Sophia's little belly is full. The nurse takes her to again test her sugar, then brings her back to Winnie.

Winnie looks up at me, our daughter belly full, and sleeping in her arms, and I can only imagine that the wonder on her face is the same that's reflected to her on mine. "She's beautiful." I lean down and kiss the top of Sophia's tiny head, before kissing my wife on her lips. "Just like her momma."

"You want to hold her?" she asks.

I nod. I'm scared to death I'm going to break her. She's so damn tiny, but at the same time, I've been waiting months to hold her in my arms. My baby girl. My palms are sweaty, and my hands are shaking. If Winnie notices, she doesn't mention it. She lifts her arms, and I scoop mine underneath, taking Sophia from her. "Hey, baby girl," I choke out. "I'm your daddy."

I lift her head to place another soft kiss there. Never in a million years did I think I could love anyone the way I love Winnie. This tiny little pink bundle, who has her little fist wrapped around my pinky, also has my heart in the palm of her hands, just like her momma. "You're beautiful," I whisper to her. "Not dating until you're thirty," I say, causing everyone in the room to crack up laughing. Lifting my head, I see Winnie smiling, her eyes shimmering with tears. "I told you this already," I remind her.

"That you did," she agrees.

"Congratulations, you guys," Gabby says, wiping her eyes.

"Hey, Soph," I say to my daughter. "You ready to meet your Aunt Gabby?" I stand tall, and carefully pass her over the bed to Gabby.

"Hey, sweet girl. I'm your Aunt Gabby," she introduces herself. "You have a beautiful name for a beautiful little girl," she murmurs. "What's her middle name? Have you all decided?" she asks, not taking her eyes off my daughter.

Winnie looks up at me, and I nod. We talked about it a few days ago. It was my suggestion, and she loved it. "We have," I tell her.

"Well, are you going to tell me?" She finally looks up.

"I mean, do you really want to know?" I tease.

"Your Daddy and your Uncle Chase, they like to tease me. I'm glad you're a girl. We need more women to drown them out," she tells my sleeping daughter. "Gwenny?"

Winnie chuckles through her smile. "Her name is Sophia Gabrielle Drake."

I watch Gabby as she processes what Winnie just said. "What?" she asks, her voice almost inaudible.

"We'd like for you to be her godmother. If something were to ever happen to us, we want to know she's loved and well cared for."

"Of course she is," Gabby says, and bites down on her bottom lip.

The nursing team have finished up and tell us they'll be back in a few so that Winnie can feed Sophia. Funny, I didn't even really register that they were still in the room with us. As they filter out, there's a knock at the door.

"Can I come in?" Chase asks.

"No," Gabby says, as Winnie and I both say yes.

"Hey," he says softly, stopping to stand next to Gabby. "You did good, Gwen." He smiles.

"Hello?" I say, as if I'm offended.

"Come on, Drake, you and I both know that beauty comes from your wife," he jokes.

"You want to hold her?" Winnie asks him.

"She's pretty small. Maybe I should wait."

"Sit down," Gabby instructs. For the first time ever, I watch as he does what she tells him without giving her any lip. Once he's seated, Gabby transfers Sophia to his arms. "Make sure you're supporting her head." Gabby stands beside him, her hand on his shoulder, watching with a grin tilting her lips.

"Hey, Soph, I'm your Uncle Chase. Daddy and I already talked about it and no dating until you're thirty," he tells her. Gabby smacks his shoulder playfully, and it doesn't faze him.

"Hey, Chase," Winnie says to get his attention.

I watch as he struggles to pull his gaze from my daughter to address my wife. "Yeah?"

"I've been meaning to ask you something."

"Shoot," he says, eyes questioning.

Winnie looks up at me and I nod. "We were hoping you'll be her godfather."

I watch my best friend as he swallows hard. He opens his mouth to speak but closes it and swallows again. "What?" he asks quietly.

"If something were to happen to us, we want to know she's loved and well taken care of. That means you," I tell him. "And you," I say, nodding at Gabby.

Chase looks up at Gabby, and something I can't explain passes between them. "I don't know what to say, man. This is— I'm honored."

"Say yes," Winnie prompts.

"Yes." He lifts my daughter and bends his head to whisper in her ear. We can't hear what he says, but from the look on Gabby's face, the emotional side of my best friend, the one he tries so hard to hide, is showing. Gabby's eyes well with tears.

"All right, Momma. Time to eat," a nurse says, barging into the room.

"We're going to give you some time," Gabby says.

Chase stands and carefully passes Sophia to Winnie, who's sitting up in bed. I know she's exhausted. We've both been up since two this morning, but it never shows. She's all smiles as she takes our baby girl into her arms.

Once Gabby and Chase leave, I take the chair next to the bed, and watch as the nurse instructs my wife on breastfeeding. "Don't get discouraged," she tells her. "Sometimes it takes a few tries for them to latch on."

I take in every word, my eyes memorizing every move. The nurse helps Winnie pull down her gown and guide Sophia to her breast. "Look at that," the nurse coos. "She's a natural."

"How do I know if she's getting enough?"

"That's trickier." She goes on to tell us about wet diapers, poopy diapers, if she's gaining weight, and that Winnie's breasts will feel less full. "I'll leave you to it. Press the button if you need anything." With a final reminder to burp her often, she leaves us alone.

Sitting in this hospital room watching my wife breastfeed our newborn baby daughter does something to me. "You've never looked more beautiful," I say, moving my chair as close as I can get it. One hand cradles Winnie's cheek while the other rests on Sophia.

"I'm a mess. You can be real with me, Harrison."

"I've never said truer words. We made this tiny human. This little miracle, and to watch you nurture her... it's a vision that in all my life I'll never forget. I'll never forget a single moment of this day."

"We did it." She smiles.

"You did it, baby. You did all the work, and I'm so damn proud of you. I'm honored you've chosen me for this gift."

"Gift?"

"This life with you. The fact that I get to call you my wife. I get to live each day with you by my side, and this little one. You gave me another present. I never thought the gift of your love could be topped. It's a close race." I grin at her.

"I agree with you that she's a miracle, in more ways than one. I agree in the sense that she was created out of the love that we share. Also, she brought you back to me. It might have taken us a while, and we've had some bumps in the road, but we're finally on steady ground. We have this little angel to thank for that."

"I'd like to think it would have happened. I was coming for you. However, Soph here had other plans. I wasn't acting fast enough." I chuckle softly. I watch as she removes our daughter from her breast and brings her to her shoulder to burp her. It takes a few minutes, but a sound I never expected from my sweet angel echoes in the small room, making us both laugh. Winnie tries to get her to latch on again, but she's snoozing away and wants no part of it.

"She said we should nap when she does." I stand and take Sophia from her, settling back in the chair.

"You have to be exhausted too," she says over a yawn.

"Yeah, but I'm too keyed-up to sleep. Get some rest, baby. We'll be here when you wake up."

She nods. "I love you, Harrison Drake."

"I love you too, and you too, baby girl," I tell our daughter. She's sleeping—oblivious—but that's okay. She's had a big day just like her momma. I watch as Winnie slowly closes her eyes as exhaustion claims her. "Your momma, she's a special person," I tell my daughter. "There aren't enough words to describe how much I love you. Don't ever settle, Sophia. When you're allowed to date at thirty, make sure the man you gift your heart to will cherish it always." I feel sleep taking hold so I place Sophia in her bed, not willing to risk falling asleep with her in my arms.

A soft cry pulls me from sleep. My eyes pop open, and I see Winnie watching as Gabby changes Sophia's diaper. "Hey," I say, my voice gruff.

"Feel better?" Winnie asks.

"Yeah, what time is it?"

"Late, after midnight."

"I'm sorry I dozed off."

"We all did. It's time to feed her again."

"Is there anything I can do?" I ask, standing to stretch.

"Nope." My wife grins.

The door opens, and Chase pops his head in. "Is it safe?" he asks.

I look at Winnie, and she tosses a soft pink blanket over our daughter and nods. "Yeah," I tell him.

He enters carrying a bag from Taco Bell. "Not many options this late at night." He begins setting everything on the small table in the corner. He turns to face us, and that's when he realizes that Winnie is feeding Sophia. "I can go," he says, his cheeks turning red.

"Aww, are you embarrassed?" Gabby coos.

"No, but this is… private."

"You're family," Winnie counters. "Besides, it's not like you can see anything."

"Yeah." He swallows hard and looks over at me. In a couple of strides, he's standing next to me, where I'm leaning against the windowsill. "How do you do it?" he asks, just low enough for me to hear.

"Do what?"

"That's hot," he says, pointing to Winnie and Soph.

"Fucker, she's feeding our daughter." I don't take my eyes off them. Memorizing yet another moment.

"I know. I get it. I'm also a man. I know," he says, wagging his eyebrows.

I don't deny it. He's right. He doesn't need me to tell him he is.

"So what happened at the gym?" Winnie asks. "We've all been here. What's going on?"

"It's out of our hands," Chase explains. "The fire marshal is performing an investigation. No one is allowed in until it's complete. It's a waiting game."

"Do you have any ideas?" she asks.

"Not one," I tell her. "However, it's obvious this is all connected somehow."

She looks up at Gabby, and something passes between them. "Guys, I have a theory," Gabby says, turning to look at Chase and me. "You might want to sit for this," she warns.

We both remain standing.

"Do either of you remember my twenty-first birthday?" she asks.

"Yeah," Chase says. "You wore those tight-as-hell leather pants, and that sparkly tank top, no bra." He goes on to describe her hair and shoes.

Gabby looks surprised. "Y-Yeah. Um, so that night, do you remember there was a girl hanging all over you, Harrison?" I can tell by the way that she's looking at me, she's being cautious.

I think back to that night all those years ago. "Yeah, she was annoying as hell. I was never so glad to see you," I tell my wife.

"That girl was Gina," Winnie tells me.

"What?" Chase and I say at the same time.

"Are you sure?" I ask, even though I know it's possible. I barely spared her a glance that night.

"Surely we would have remembered that?" Chase says, almost as if he's thinking out loud.

"Apparently, not." This from Gabby as she never takes her eyes off Chase. "Do you forget all the women you sleep with?" Gabby asks, her face pinched as if it pains her.

"What are you talking about? I never slept with her."

"That night she told me that the guy she wanted to go home with fell through, so she went home with his best friend."

"It wasn't me," Chase says through clenched teeth.

"Right," Gabby scoffs. "No point in denying it, Chase."

"I'm telling you, Gabrielle, it wasn't me." He turns to look at me. "Ethan was with us that night."

"That's right. He just accepted that new job and was moving away," I say as the memory comes back to me.

"It wasn't you?" Gabby says, her voice sounding strange.

"No, Gabs, it wasn't me. I remember distinctly. I had my eye on a girl way out of reach. I couldn't see past her to notice anyone else." His eyes lock on hers.

"It fits," Winnie says, peeking under the cover at Sophia. "She's snoozing, and I need to burp her."

"Let me." In a couple of long strides, I'm at her side. Grabbing the extra blanket, I place it over my shoulder, like I saw Winnie do earlier. Gabby helps her hold up the blanket while I lift my sleeping daughter into my arms. I go back to the window, and take my spot beside Chase, rubbing my little girl's back. The conversation goes on as we continue to put the pieces together. Sophia burps and Chase laughs loudly, causing her to startle.

"I'm sorry, sweetie," he says, reaching over and lightly running his finger over her cheek. "I didn't expect that from such a little thing," he says gently.

"So what do we do?" Winnie asks.

"I'll make a call. Tell them what we know. Otherwise, we do nothing."

"What do you mean, nothing?" she asks incredulously. "She's torturing us, messing with your business. She started a fire, Harrison."

"I know. But all that matters is that we're all okay. No one was hurt. We have a new baby girl to take home and get settled. We'll let the authorities handle it. Right now we have no concrete proof that this is happening. We'll tell them what we remember, what we think and let them work it out." I'm furious at myself for letting her stay employed by All Fit as long as I did, and at her for everything she's done. However, I refuse to let it ruin the miracle that is my little girl.

"Who are you?" Gabby asks.

"I'm a father," I tell her. "I'm a husband, and a brother-in-law, a friend, a son. I'm lots of things, but most of all, I'm deliriously happy. If it was Gina, which I believe it was, they'll get her."

"And if they don't?" Winnie questions.

"Then we'll figure it out when that happens."

"He's right," Chase agrees. "We can't take matters into our own hands. I mean, what are we going to do? Tie her up in the basement? We'll tell them what we know, and it all leads back to her. We're all confident of that. They'll more than likely need to talk to all four of us, to give our side of the story."

"Count me in," Gabby says.

"Not alone," he tells her.

"It's not the mob." She laughs.

"I'll go with you, Gabby."

"He's right, you know. Just to be on the safe side. Until she's caught, we don't know what she has planned next or where she might be lurking." I hate the thought of Gina out there after my family. I'm not letting her ruin this day, though, Sophia's birthday. Inside, I'm raging mad, and I won't stop until she pays for what she's done.

"You should stay with us," Winnie tells her.

"No. No way. You have a new baby, and you all need to settle in and get a routine. You don't need a house guest."

"You can stay with me." Chase doesn't even hesitate.

"Absolutely not," Gabby says, but there is no heat behind her words.

"Then I'll stay with you."

"Have you lost your mind? I'll be fine," she tells him. There's a slight tremor in her voice. One that tells me she's worried.

"Gabby," Chase says sternly. "Please." His voice is quieter now, almost pleading.

If I hadn't been watching with my own eyes, I never would have believed it. I see Gabby's shoulders fall, and her features soften. "We'll figure it out." It's not a complete agreement, but it's close enough. Chase must think so too. He nods his acceptance and that's that.

Chase pulls his phone out of his pocket, and it reminds me I need to call our parents. "Our parents," I say to Winnie. "Gabby called them both. They'll be here first thing in the morning."

"Detective Benson, Chase Callahan, I have some information that might help with your case." We remain quiet as we listen to Chase give him the details and our suspicion of Gina. From that night all those years ago, to her being fired and the events that have happened since. "Thank you, sir. We'll be waiting to hear from you." Chase ends the call and looks at me. "He's on it. I guess there's video footage from the back of the gym. Apparently, there's a camera she didn't know about or forgot about."

"She didn't know about it. When Winnie started working out there, I realized the back hall wasn't well monitored; there was a blind spot. And not willing to risk her safety, I had them come and install another camera. It was a Sunday. Gina wasn't there," I explain.

"Your alpha male tendencies finally come in handy." He grins. "Who knew you being a caveman when it comes to Gwen would work out in our favor," he jokes. My best friend never misses an opportunity to give me shit. "Time to eat," he says, going back to the table full of tacos and passing them out.

"Then we need to go, let you three get some sleep," Gabby says.

"We have a newborn. There won't be much sleep in our future," I tell her.

"Still. We should get out of your hair. Until later today that is." Winnie opens her mouth to argue, but Gabby holds up her hands to stop her. "Nope. Chase and I will check on the gym, and we'll be back to check on you."

"Chase, please look out for my sister," Winnie asks.

"I've got her," Chase says. There is conviction in his voice, something I've heard from him on very few occasions in our life. I have no doubt he's not going to be letting my sister-in-law out of his sight.

After we say our goodbyes, the nurse comes in and checks on my girls, asking if we want her to take Sophia to the nursery. We both say no, making her laugh. She reminds us to call if we need anything or change our minds, then walks quietly out the door.

"Alone at last," I say, rubbing Sophia's back.

"It's been an adventure." Winnie beams.

"Definitely. You did good, Winnie. You did real good."

"You had a hand in that too." She smiles. "Why don't you put her in her bed, then climb in here with me. We need to sleep while she does."

Doing as she says, I lower Sophia so Mommy can give her a kiss, then place her in her bed. I wheel the bed as close to us as we can get it before kicking off my shoes, and lying down beside my wife. Winnie snuggles up to me and I breathe her in. This is what life is about. The moments, no matter how big or small. Not your career, or how much money you have in the bank. None of that compares to snuggling up with your wife, while your newborn daughter sleeps peacefully beside you.

"It's not over," I whisper, kissing her temple.

"What's not?" she asks sleepily.

"Our story. It's not over. It's just beginning." She hums her agreement as we both drift off to sleep.

CHAPTER 20

Winnie

"So King Harrison had some major groundwork to make up to win Queen Gwendolyn's heart back." I hear the deep timbers of his voice through the baby monitor beside my bed.

I woke up fifteen minutes ago when Sophia started to cry, but Harrison just kissed me on the forehead and told me he had her. The clock reads just after two, a common wake-up time for our daughter, but even though I'm seriously lacking sleep, I've been unable to drift back off.

Instead, I lie here and listen to the sound of a doting father caring for his daughter. At only ten days old, she already adores him. Her eyes light up when she hears his voice and often search for him. When she's tucked safely in his arms, she sleeps soundly and peacefully. It always makes me smile because, well, I know that feeling.

Sliding out of bed, I tiptoe across the hall and stand silently in the doorway. Harrison has her swaddled in a pink blanket and is giving her a bottle of breastmilk. The breastfeeding thing just didn't work out for me, even though I tried, but she just wouldn't latch on. I decided to pump for now, which is nice too for Harrison. He gets to help feed her, something he couldn't do those first few days when I was attempting to get her to latch on.

He gently rocks in the chair and keeps his eyes focused on her as he tells her a story. "King Harrison was determined, though. He knew in his heart his queen was the only woman for him, and it became more clear when he found out about Princess Sophia."

He smiles down at the baby in his arms. "The king was an idiot, you see, like most men. Of course, Princess Sophia isn't going to date until she's thirty, so that's nothing we need to worry about right now. This story is about the stupid king who let his queen get away. He was a total jackass, my little love," he tells her.

A giggle slips from my mouth.

"Ahhh, Princess Sophia, I believe we're not alone. No worries, though. It's only the beautiful queen, and she could definitely vouch for how senseless the king was," he says, his eyes dancing with laughter as I enter the room.

"I think the queen and the king were both a little dense," I reply, stepping up beside the rocking chair. I reach down and run my index finger over her soft cheek, mesmerized by her tiny little features. Her mouth suckles hard on the bottle and her gray eyes watch every move her dad makes.

"Well, this is my bedtime story, and I say the king was the dumbass. Oh, shit. I probably shouldn't say dumbass," he stops, turning wide eyes at me. "Fuck, I said shit."

I can't help but laugh. With my arm around his shoulder, I snuggle against his head and watch our daughter eat. Her eyes start to droop and her sucking begins to slow. Her little belly is finally full, and she's ready for a few more hours of sleep.

"Anyway, the day the princess was born was one of the happiest days of the king's life. He couldn't imagine his life any better than it was right then, in that moment. Except, maybe, if the queen officially wore a ring on her finger so that everything in the kingdom was complete," he says. His words barely register. It isn't until he opens our daughter's tiny little hand that I see the diamond nestled inside.

A gasp spills from my lips as my eyes dart from his to the ring. He's moving, gingerly getting up and pulling the bottle from our now-sleeping daughter's lips. Harrison positions her on his shoulder as he drops to one knee. "Winnie, you are the love of my life. For a while, I was lost. Without you, I was nothing, just an empty shell. But now, with you and our daughter, I'm complete. Everything has fallen into place, and even though you've already agreed, I wanted to make it official. I'll spend the rest of my life proving to you that I was worth the risk. Will you marry me?"

Through tear-filled eyes, I gaze down at the only man I've loved. It's not the first time we've been in this exact position, though there wasn't a baby in the picture the first time. But as I recall his first proposal, when we were so young and naïve about the world, I know that *this* proposal is the one I'll forever remember. He's holding our tiny daughter against his bare shoulder, gazing up at me with so much hope and love that it steals the very air I breathe. I know that our story isn't your typical fairy tale. It wasn't easy, and, at times, it wasn't pretty. But it was ours.

Our story.

Our love.

So there's only one answer I can give him. One answer that speaks from the depths of my soul. "Yes."

The smile that spreads across his handsome face is my favorite. It radiates happiness and love, and as he slips the ring onto my finger, I can't help but pray my smile is the exact same.

"I know I've already asked a thousand times, and you've agreed, but Sophia and I were talking a few nights ago and she told me a ring would make it official," he says, grinning widely up at me as he wraps his big hands around my shaky ones.

I can't help but giggle. "Oh, she did, did she?"

"She did," he confirms. "She's very wise, just like her mom."

Gently, he stands up, holding Sophia tightly in his arms. The image is enough to send my hormones into overdrive. It hasn't even been two weeks, but I'm already craving him like a drunk longs for a nip of whiskey. I'm not sure I'll survive these next few weeks.

"Stop looking at me like that," he demands, lightly patting our daughter's back in an attempt to get a burp.

"Like what?" I ask coyly.

"Like you want to strip naked and screw me senseless," he whispers. Even in the dimly lit room, I can see the desire in his eyes.

"Oh, that's exactly what I was thinking," I reply, running my hands up his bare, muscular forearms.

"Sorry, Queen, but you're out of luck. The doctor says six weeks."

"What do doctors know anyway?" I tease—though, not really teasing.

"A lot more than gymrats, so I'm going to heed her advice."

Sliding my hands up his arms and around his shoulders, I say, "Well, you know there are... *other* things we can do, right?"

"Keep talking."

Just then, a small belch is released from our daughter, making us both smile. I lean forward and place a soft kiss on her forehead, rubbing her back as I go. Harrison slowly walks toward the crib, kisses Sophia in the same spot I just kissed, and gingerly sets her down in the middle. The bed is huge in comparison to her tiny body. We watch as she settles into position and falls fast asleep.

Together, we backtrack to the doorway, our attention still on the crib against the wall. We step out into the hallway and his arms wrap around my lower back. "Now, what was this about *other* things we can do?" he asks, kissing that magical spot behind my ear.

"I'd rather just show you."

"He's late," Gabby says for the tenth time as she glances out the window. She's holding her niece in her arms, while Chase stands close, stealing glances when he thinks no one is looking.

"He'll be here. He wouldn't have asked us to all meet him if he wasn't going to show," Harrison states, setting a bottle of water on the end table beside where I sit.

The detective in charge of the All Fit fire called this morning and asked for a few minutes. He wouldn't tell us anything over the phone, but considering he also called Chase and Gabby, we're hoping for good news.

Chase and Gabby arrived together. He's still crashing on her couch, where he's been stationed since the night of the fire. He insists it's to protect her from whatever threat could be looming, but honestly, I'm not so sure anymore. She refuses to even look at him, and when we were alone in the kitchen, she wouldn't elaborate on their roommating status.

After a few tense minutes, a car finally pulls into the driveway. Detective Benson slides out of the driver's seat and makes his way to the front door. Before Harrison can get there, Chase has the door open and is greeting the older man.

"Thank you for seeing me on a Sunday afternoon," the detective states, shaking everyone's hand as he enters.

"We're hoping this call was because you've figured out who set the fire," Harrison says, taking a seat beside me on the couch, while Gabby and Chase sit together with Sophia on the loveseat, and Detective Benson takes the recliner.

"We have, actually, and I wanted you to hear it from me," he says, pulling a series of photos from a folder and handing them to Harrison.

The first one is an image of Gina entering the gym with a bag, the date and time stamped on the corner. Even though her head is down, there's no disguising her tight tank top and the boobs she can barely conceal beneath it. The second image is of her going into the ladies' locker room, again with her head down to avoid the cameras. The third photo is a clear image of her face, taken as she sneaks down the back hallway and toward the back door.

"This was taken by the camera I had installed without her knowledge," Harrison informs, pointing to the picture of his former assistant.

"Correct. Clearly, she wasn't aware of that camera or else she would have kept her head down as she left," the detective answers.

"Where's the bag she walked in with?" I ask before passing the photos over to Chase and Gabby.

"She left it behind in the locker room. It was nearly destroyed in the fire, but the fire marshal was able to determine that it was the point of origin for the blaze. It contained the accelerant she used. We believe she set the bag in the towel bin, and using a gasoline-soaked rag, set it all ablaze. She had enough accelerant in the bag that the fire spread quickly. Fortunately, your sprinkler system was top notch and helped keep it from getting out of control before the fire department arrived."

Sophia begins to fuss a little, and before either Harrison or I can get up from the couch, Chase sets the photos down on the coffee table and takes his goddaughter. He props her on his shoulder like a pro and lightly rubs her back, without even breaking stride. Gabby is completely shocked by how natural he seems, considering the man was scared shitless of holding her only a handful of days ago. "I thought the cameras were offline," he says quietly, cooing softly at the baby against his chest.

"They were, but our computer crimes division is the best. Our guy was able to retrieve feed from your off-site server, even though your cameras were wiped after the fire. Gina was good, but we were better. She tried to cover her tracks well. We were able to use her IP address to follow her tracks. We learned that Gina also logged in multiple times a day into your computer system and made several adjustments to your calendars and orders, and were able to trace that she was the one who tripped your security systems a few weeks ago."

"Finally," Harrison says with a loud exhale. "I feel like we knew it was her these last eleven days, but having you confirm it is like a weight being lifted."

"She was arrested?" Gabby asks, a sad look on her face. After all, she considered Gina a friend the last ten or so years.

"She was brought in last night. She denied everything, of course, but the DA is moving forward with charges. We have solid evidence. She won't get off on this," he says, placing the photos back in the folder. "There's a good chance this will go to trial, if she keeps screaming innocence. If that happens, you'll all be on the list of witnesses."

"We'll do whatever we have to do to bring her to justice," Harrison informs the man across from him.

Detective Benson just nods. "Well, I've taken enough of your time on this Sunday afternoon," he says as he stands up. "And congratulations on the baby. She's a beauty," he adds, a warm smile on his wrinkled face.

Harrison glances at me. "She's her mother." Even though that's not really the case. Sophia is the spitting image of her daddy, with my nose.

Everyone stands up, and the guys walk the detective to the door. I don't hear what they're saying, but I'm sure it's in appreciation of solving the case. After he's gone, I snuggle into Harrison's side, happy to know that the Gina mess is behind us. It's still hard to believe one petite woman caused all this drama.

"So, we're officially ready to reopen tomorrow morning," Chase says.

Harrison gives him a nod. "We are. Everything is set," he confirms.

They hired a cleaning company to come in and scrub everything down. Fortunately, the flooring is painted and sealed concrete, so there was only minimal water damage from the hoses, and that was contained mostly to the locker room. The rest of the building was covered in a bit of soot, but that washed up nicely after an extensive deep clean. They hired a local IT firm to rework their security and computer systems, ensuring no one would be getting back in anytime soon. All in all, it wasn't nearly as bad as it could have been.

"There's just one problem left," Chase says, adjusting Sophia into the crook of his arm.

"What's that?" Harrison asks, pulling me tighter into his side.

"We still don't have an office assistant," his friend reminds him.

"Actually." Gabby interrupts, stepping around Chase. "I was thinking... what if I was your assistant?" My sister seems nervous and watches Harrison's expression closely, her own eyes giving away how nervous she is.

"You?" he asks, slightly confused.

"I thought you liked your job at World Travel," I say, not really sure why she's suddenly looking for a career change. It's not that I don't think Gabby could handle the job, and frankly, she'd be phenomenal as Harrison's assistant, but she's never once complained about her current position as a travel agent. She's been there for years, ever since she graduated college.

My sister averts her eyes. "I do— *did*, I mean. They made cuts this week. I was laid off," she adds with a shrug of her shoulders.

"What?" I gasp, shocked that my sister is suddenly without a job. She's one of four travel agents in the small family-owned company.

"Why didn't you tell me?" Chase asks, his eyes breathing fire at my sister.

Again, she shrugs. "It just happened Friday afternoon," she says quietly. "Anyway, I know my degree is in hospitality, but I'm a detail-oriented person. I'm timely and I'd never set the gym on fire intentionally," she adds with a smile.

Harrison watches her for a few long seconds. "You're serious?"

She nods. "I mean, unless you don't think you can handle me whipping your ass into shape every day in the office."

He offers her a warm smile. "I think I can handle you." He looks over her shoulder at his friend and manager. "What do you think? Can you deal with Gabby telling you what to do on a daily basis?"

Chase gives him a pointed look. "And that would be different than now how?"

Gabby just shrugs. "It's true. The man's a mess."

I can't help but chuckle at their easy banter. Oh, there's definitely something going on there. It's been brewing for some time, but I'm not sure if either of them are ready to finally admit it. I guess only time will tell, especially if they're going to be working together almost daily.

"Okay. You start Monday. Eight o'clock sharp."

Gabby beams with excitement. "I'll be there!"

Harrison turns to face me, keeping his arms wrapped around my waist. "I'm going to regret hiring your sister, aren't I?" he whispers, swiping his lips across my forehead.

"Oh, definitely. You have no idea what you're in for." I giggle, knowing full well my sister is going to run that ship like a seasoned drill sergeant. He exhales and hugs me to his chest.

"Uh, guys?" Chase says, pulling our attention his way. "I'm pretty sure my beautiful goddaughter just shit all over me."

Gabby gently moves his arm and peeks between him and the baby. "Oh my God!" She bursts into fits of laughter.

"Fix this," he demands to my sister.

"No can do," she says, taking a step to the side. "Uncle Chase is going to clean you up now, Princess. You be nice to him," Gabby says aloud to her sleeping niece. Before she pulls away, she also whispers, "Make sure you pee on him too." Then she kisses her forehead and heads toward the door.

"Where are you going?" I ask.

"Gina's in jail, which means I'm not in danger anymore. I'm going home to move Chase's crap out onto the front porch. Then I'm opening a bottle of wine and watching *American Horror Story* on Netflix."

"Dammit, woman!" Chase loudly whispers behind my sister so he doesn't wake the baby. "You're lucky I'm covered in baby shit right now or..."

"Or what? You'd stress eat ice cream and cover your face with a pillow because you're being forced to watch scary movies and can't sleep? Don't worry, Chase. Your secret is safe with me, little chicken."

Gabby grins, a blinding smile on her face as she heads outside and gets in her car.

Chase sighs.

"You don't like scary movies?" I ask when the silence is too much.

"Of course I do. I'm a man," Chase argues.

"He hates them," Harrison interjects with a smile.

"Fuck off."

"Come on, Chase. Let's get you and the princess cleaned up. Then Harrison can take you home since your ride left you high and dry," I add, smiling at the tic of his jaw. Oh, Chase isn't happy to be left behind.

We watch as our friend heads up to Sophia's bedroom, already having a word with our daughter about her explosive diaper issue. "Wait," Harrison says, stopping me. He returns his arms to my waist and pulls me in close. I can already feel his erection pressing against my stomach.

"Why, Mr. Drake, you seem mighty happy to see me," I tease, running my lips along the edge of his jaw.

"Oh, I'm always happy to see you, baby. I was just thinking maybe we can do more of that *other* stuff you showed me early this morning," he says, waggling his eyebrows suggestively.

"I do like the *other* stuff," I tell him, my lips finding the corner of his mouth.

"My cock really liked it too." Finally, his lips land on mine in a fierce kiss. "I love you, Winnie."

"I love you too."

His lips are urgent and hungry as he trails his hands down my sides and around to my backside, giving it a gentle squeeze.

"Uh, guys? Still covered in baby shit up here!" Chase hollers down the stairs, making us both laugh.

I start to pull away to rescue our friend when Harrison grabs me again. "He can wait another minute," he whispers before taking my lips once more in a fierce, hungry kiss that leaves me breathless and yearning for more.

"Not funny!" Chase yells, causing us both to break out into fits of laughter once more.

"Come on, my love. Let's go rescue our friend from the poopy princess."

Together, we head upstairs, hand in hand. I never thought this was how our story would go, but I wouldn't have it any other way. I have a beautiful daughter and a redo with my husband slash ex-husband slash fiancé. Something tells me this time around will be different. This time around, we'll get it right.

Because our story isn't over.

It's only beginning.

EPILOGUE

Harrison

I remember the first time I did this, waited at the end of the aisle for the love of my life to appear. This time though, things are different. For one, we're in our backyard. We have less than twenty people in attendance, and in my arms is my baby girl. She's four months old today, and she's wearing a little pink lace dress with a matching pink band around her head. This time, I know the pain that comes with losing the love of your life. I know the joy of rekindling that love. There is, however, one thing that remains the same. My love for Winnie. No matter if we were together or apart, my heart was hers. Now, in front of our family, our closest friends, and our daughter, I get to vow to love her until I take my last breath.

"You ready?" Chase asks, standing behind me.

"Is that a real question?" I ask him.

He laughs and reaches for Sophia. "Come to Uncle Chase," he coos. I have to say my best friend is quite enamored with my daughter. Then again, we all are.

"Get your own," I tell him, just as the music starts, and I see Gabby appear on the back porch. Chase turns his head, and his hands fall to his sides. "You're drooling." I chuckle under my breath. He doesn't respond. I don't even think he hears me as his eyes follow my sister-in-law down the aisle. She and her sister look a lot alike, but no one compares to my Winnie.

Gabby stops next to me and places a kiss on Sophia's cheek before taking her spot across from me. Her eyes flash to Chase, and I don't have to look over my shoulder at him to know he's watching her. Instead, I turn my attention to the back door.

Watching.

Waiting.

"Damn," I mutter when I see her. She's wearing a short white dress, covered in lace. It's not a traditional wedding gown, but she looks phenomenal in it. She's been at the gym a lot, working on "losing the baby weight." To me, she was perfect, but she insisted she needed to feel ready. I didn't push her, no matter how badly I wanted to. I tried to tell her there was no need because as soon as she let me, I'd be knocking her up again. However, I could tell it was important to her, so in turn, it was important to me. With Gabby working at the gym, she helped out with Sophia, when she could wrangle her away from Chase. My wife and I worked out together. It was a couple of weeks ago when she told me she was ready. Since it's close friends and family, here we are. I called our mothers, and it was a done deal. Nothing elaborate. Just me and my wife becoming legal in the eyes of the law.

"Look at Mommy, Soph," I say to my daughter. I don't bother to lower my voice. As far as I'm concerned, this is just going through the motions. She's always been my wife. "She's beautiful," I tell our daughter as Winnie stops to stand in front of me. Like her sister, she leans over and kisses our daughter on the cheek. "What about me?" I ask her.

She smiles, her green eyes shimmering in the sunlight. Standing on her tiptoes, she places her lips on my cheek. Well, she intended to, but I turn my head in time and capture her lips with mine.

"Guys." Gabby laughs. "We're not there yet."

"We've always been there," I tell her. Everyone laughs. It's nothing new for me to show my wife what she means to me. Why should today be any different? We've taken a twisted road to get here. Why should the path go back to being straight and narrow?

"I have strict instructions from the groom to make this fast." The minister chuckles, as does everyone else. He goes through the traditional vows, then asks for the rings.

Turning, I hand Sophia to Chase, and pull our rings out of my jeans pocket. I hand mine to Winnie, and we take turns repeating our vows and sliding the rings onto our fingers. They're new—both of them. We're saving our originals for Sophia.

"By the power vested in me—"

I don't hear the rest. I slide my hand behind her neck and pull her into a kiss. One that promises today, tomorrow, and forever. "I love you, Mrs. Drake," I say, pulling back and resting my forehead against hers.

"I love you, Mr. Drake."

Sophia squeals and we pull apart to look at her. She's bouncing in Chase's arms. Her little arms flying around. She has no idea what today means, or how important it was for us to have her here with us. "Is thirteen months apart far enough?" I ask Winnie.

She smiles up at me. "Let's get her out of diapers, then we'll talk."

"How long is that?"

"Two and a half years or so, some longer."

"We can afford diapers," I tell her. Two and a half years... that's too damn long.

"We'll play it by ear," she says, kissing the bottom of my chin.

"I can be very convincing."

"Mmm." Winnie wraps her arms around my waist. "You'll have to show me. You know I'm a hard sell," she says, resting her head against my chest.

"Challenge accepted," I murmur, kissing the top of her head.

Winnie

The moment I see him standing at the end of the aisle, holding our daughter, I feel like the world tilts on its axis. Sure, he holds Sophia all the time, but today... wearing dark jeans that hug his powerful legs and an untucked, crisp white button-down shirt? Yeah, I feel the ground shift beneath my feet.

He's mine.

Forever.

And the look on his face as I slowly make my way toward him lets me know exactly how happy he is that today is finally happening. Pure radiating love. That's what I see when our eyes connect. That's what I feel as I start the short walk in his direction.

"By the power vested in me—" the pastor says, but the rest of his words fade away. Harrison's lips are on mine, claiming me as his own. Today, tomorrow, and forever.

"I love you, Mrs. Drake," he whispers, resting his forehead against mine.

"I love you, Mr. Drake."

My arms are wrapped around his neck. He places one more chaste kiss on my lips as our family and friends cheer us on. It's the pastor's chuckles that finally have us pulling apart, though Harrison only releases me long enough to take our daughter from his best man. As soon as she's in his arms, he wraps one around my waist and pulls me into his side. We've always fit like puzzle pieces, and standing here now, in front of our family and friends, just solidifies it.

We are one.

Husband and wife.

Father and mother.

And yes, maybe someday soon we'll add another little one to our family, but I'm not ready yet. I want to enjoy our time with Sophia before we divide our attention amongst more. Even though I long for a big family, I want to take our time and do it right.

Do it right.

I actually giggle aloud at the thought.

"What's so funny?" Harrison asks, glancing down at me.

"I was just thinking how we didn't do any of this in the right order," I tell him with a smile.

He huffs. "When have I ever done anything based on society's standards?" he asks, the corner of his lips turning upward.

"Very true," I reply, leaning my head against his chest.

His hold on me tightens as he whispers, "Thank you for marrying me again and making my life so full."

Glancing up, I give him a warm smile. "Thank you for coming home with me after the divorce and doing me against the wall."

Now it's his turn to bark out a laugh. "I don't think you're supposed to refer to *doing it* with a pastor standing two feet away," he teases, his eyes dancing with mischief.

I shrug. "When have I ever done anything based on society's standards?" I mirror.

"Touché, Mrs. Drake, touché. Now, what do you say we enjoy some dinner and dancing with our family and friends? Then, this little princess is off to a sleepover with her Aunt Gabby, which means I get to take you inside and do you against the wall. Again. As husband and wife."

"I love the way you think," I tell him as I reach over and hold our daughter's hand. She instantly tries to put my finger in her mouth.

"And I love you," he adds, just before swiping his lips across mine once more.

I thread my hands into his hair, careful not to squish Sophia, who's grabbing hold of my hair and trying to eat it. As our guests mingle in the yard and snap photos with their cell phones, I can't help but smile. Everything in life has led to this.

This moment.
This man.
Our future.
This is our love story.
It's not perfect, but it's ours.
Forever.

The End ... for now.

THANK YOU

Thank you for taking the time to read, It's Not Over.

Chase and Gabby's story is next. Be sure to sign-up for our newsletters to receive new release alerts.

Lacey Black
    www.laceyblackbooks.com/newsletter

Kaylee Ryan
    www.kayleeryan.com/newsletter

Contact Lacey

Facebook: http://bit.ly/2JBssXd
    Reader Group: http://bit.ly/2NWrRU7
    Goodreads: http://bit.ly/2Y4Zzuw
    BookBub: http://bit.ly/2JJhYnl
    Website: http://www.laceyblackbooks.com/

Contact Kaylee
   Facebook: http://bit.ly/2C5DgdF
   Reader Group: http://bit.ly/2ooyWDx
   Goodreads: http://bit.ly/2HodJvx
   BookBub: http://bit.ly/2KulVvH
   Website: http://www.kayleeryan.com/

MORE FROM LACEY BLACK

Bound Together Series:
Submerged | Profited | Entwined

Rivers Edge Series*:*
Trust Me | Fight Me | Expect Me
Protect Me | Boss me | Trust Us

Summer Sisters Series*:*
My Kinda Kisses | My Kinda Night | My Kinda Song My Kinda Mess |
My Kinda Player | My Kinda Forever
My Kinda Wedding

Rockland Falls Series:
Love and Pancakes | Love and Lingerie

Standalone Titles:
Music Notes | Ex's and Ho, Ho, Ho's

Co-written with Kaylee Ryan:
It's Not Over

MORE FROM KAYLEE RYAN

With You Series:
Anywhere with You | More with You | Everything with You

Soul Serenade Series:
Emphatic | Assured
Definite | Insistent

Southern Heart Series:
Southern Pleasure | Southern Desire
Southern Attraction | Southern Devotion

Unexpected Arrivals Series:
Unexpected Reality |Unexpected Fight

Standalone Titles:
Tempting Tatum | Unwrapping Tatum | LevitateJust Say When | I Just Want You | Reminding Avery Hey, Whiskey | When Sparks Collide

Pull You Through | Beyond the Bases
Remedy | The Difference
Trust the Push

Co-written with Lacey Black:
It's Not Over

ACKNOWLEDGMENTS

From Lacey:

Kaylee – Thank you for taking this plunge with me! I can't imagine co-writing with anyone else. From the first time we started tossing around this idea, to the final format, this entire experience has been amazing and one I'll treasure for a lifetime. I definitely can't wait to see what's next! Thank you for trusting me; I've made a forever friend!

From Kaylee:

Lacey – We've talked about this for years, and I can't tell you how excited I am that we took the plunge. Every step of this process has been fun and exciting. I wasn't sure how I would like co-writing and I'm happy to say, it's been an experience of a lifetime. Thank you for that. Not only do I have a new writing partner, but a friend for life. I can't imagine doing this with anyone else. I look forward to what the future holds.

To our Beta readers: Sandra Shipman, Joanne Thompson, Stacy Hahn, Franci Neil, Lauren Fields, and Jamie Bourgeois. You ladies are the glue that helps hold us together. Thank you for taking the time from your lives, your families to read our words. We will be forever grateful.

There are so many people to thank. We apologize if we've missed anyone. Here goes: Hot Tree Editing (Becky Johnson), Perfect Pear Creative Covers (Sommer Stein), Sara Eirew, Alex and Karina Biovin, Kimberly Anne, Tempting Illustrations (Gel Yatz), and the entire crew at Give Me Books. It truly takes a team and we're glad that you're a part of ours.

Bloggers: Thank you for doing what you do. We know that you take time from your lives and your families to promote our work and we appreciate that more than you will ever know. Thank you for taking a part in the release of It's Not Over.

Readers: Thank you for taking a chance on us. We are truly thankful to each of you.

With Love,
    Kaylee & Lacey

Made in the USA
Monee, IL
16 October 2025